Most Fortunate Son

Eric Luck

PublishAmerica
Baltimore

At the specific preference of the author, PublishAmerica allowed this work to remain exactly as the author intended, verbatim, without editorial input.

This is a work of fiction. Names, characters, places and incidents either are the product of the author's imagination or are used fictitiously. Any resemblance to actual persons, living or dead, business establishments, events or locales is entirely coincidental.

ISBN: 1-4241-0538-2
PUBLISHED BY PUBLISHAMERICA, LLLP
www.publishamerica.com
Baltimore

Printed in the United States of America

Dedicated to Cheri and Evan

The greatest joy in my life is when I make either of you smile.
If I get you both, it is heaven.

Acknowledgments

Writing is not quite the solitary sport I had envisioned.

Thanks to David D. Wilson, W.W.I veteran of the U. S. Navy and his wife, Lura; to William A. Luck, W.W.I veteran of the U. S. Army and his wife, Pearl; to B. J. Luck, Korean conflict veteran of the U. S. Navy and his wife, Pat. My memories of you are clear and good and with me every day. I could not be more proud of my heritage or more thankful for important lessons learned from honorable and loving people.

Thanks to my friends and family who may now think that I am not exactly living life, but just gathering material. None of you are in this story. Okay, some part of each of you is in this story. You can pick which part came from you. It is only the good parts.

Thanks to the many Bodie Kohlers in my life for inspiring words, meaningful thoughts, conversation, help and information. Each of you has made me a smarter and better human being. I could still stand significant improvement in all areas.

Particular thanks to: Cathryn Berryman, Dr. Cecil, D.O. Churchill, Eddy Claycomb, Rayelynn Dady, Big Dave, even though you don't read fiction, C.M. Dunn, C.S. Dunn, Robin Forte', Peter Gaudet, Bruce Gray, John and Kelly Hamilton, Meg and Bruce Henderson, Paul Horton, Del Hunt, R.J., Ken Kirkland, Cheri Luck, Evan Luck, W. K. Luck, Art Pasmas, Carlos Pierce, Charles and Eva Roeder, Captain Rusty, William Taggert and Charles Tekstar.

Thanks to those many individuals I have met and spoken with and those I have not, who honorably served our country in the Vietnam War. You have more of our pride than you might have thought. You deserve honor and peace and our unwavering thanks.

1. Ogres

A winter rainstorm was pummeling Ft. Worth, Texas, Sunday night, January 30. Lola and I had fallen asleep to the rain drumming the wood shingle roof of our little house. Our twelve year old daughter, Lily, had come in sometime later and crawled in bed with us, probably mere minutes after thunder began shaking the earth. Not that I noticed.

I was flying without the assistance of any visible help when an empty, wispy white face shaded by a black hood and flowing black cape rose up in front of me. One giant, ominously clawed hand was wrapped around my wife, Lola, and the other held Lily. Each of them was fighting to free themselves from the unidentified evil. As I started flying toward this insidious creature, the phone rang.

No, it was really ringing.

I only dropped the receiver once before mumbling, "Jerry, uh, Wilson."

"Jerry Wilson? This is Angela Delano, Ft. Worth Police Department. Jerry? You there?"

"Mmm, Angela? Really? Who?"

"Jerry, would you please come downstairs? I'm outside at your front door right now."

I could tell it was still dark outside.

"Oh. Yeah. Sure. Is everything OK? Uh. Be right there." I was barely coherent. Why do I always pretend to be awake whenever taking a phone call in the middle of the night as if the caller can't tell I'm asleep? I hung up and pulled on sweat pants as I headed for the stairs. I already had on a T-shirt and boxers, thank goodness. The clock by the bed showed 4:18 a.m. It was sort of Monday morning.

Lola sat up and asked quietly, "Jerry, you alright?"

"Yeah, hon. Go back to sleep." Next to her, Lily did not stir.

At the front door I checked the peephole. Maybe I was still dreaming. Nope. There was Angela and two big, young, Caucasian brutes in uniform. I opened the deadlock, turned the knob and pulled the door open. The rain had stopped, but it was cold and wet outside.

"Come on in Detective. Everything alright?" All three stepped into the entry. Through my grogginess every noise seemed magnified, all loud thumps and wet whomps.

"No. It is not, Jerry. Do you have a client by the name of Joanne Duchtin?" asked Angela.

"Uh, yeah. Why?" I replied. Lola had pulled on a robe and come down behind me.

"She turned up dead tonight. Murdered," said Angela. All three watched me expectantly as she said the words. Lola gasped out loud behind me.

"Man. What happened? How was she killed?" I was stunned, but only by the hour. It didn't surprise me one bit that Joanne had been murdered. Joanne Duchtin lived a very fast life in the nouveau riches circles of Ft. Worth with her slimy-built-like-a-fire-hydrant and look like a thieving-used-car-salesman husband, Warren. My feet were cold. Lola's grip tightened on my shoulder.

"Tell us where you were from noon yesterday to now, Jerry," said Angela. Lola released her grip and moved around to where she could see my face.

"What is it, four in the morning? Get serious Angela. I've got no reason to kill Joanne. She was current on her bills."

Not amused by my normal smart-ass approach, all three police officers said nothing, held my stare and waited. I could tell this was not patient waiting.

"Okay, fine." Now, I was starting to get hacked off. "Noon? All three of us were still at church at University Christian. We all left

8

together at nearly 1:00 p.m. after cleaning up the Activities Center with two other families. This simply amounted to stacking the folding chairs and running the vacuum. We went to Luby's Cafeteria for Sunday dinner arriving there about 1:20 p.m. I had the LuAnn Platter, don't remember what Lola had, Lily ate macaroni and cheese and red Jell-O. We went straight from Luby's to this castle of a mansion that you currently harass me in at 2:00 p.m. We all changed clothes and I cleaned the gutters in front per Lola's instructions. She said it might rain and that I had been promising to clean them for six weeks. I swear it hadn't been more than four weeks. Cold weather makes me not want to clean gutters. So, be sure to add that to any other charges you've got brewing. I watched the Phoenix Open on TV from 3:30 p.m. until 4:45 p.m. I was rooting for big fat Phil Mickelson—kindred spirit—my brotha in weightiness. Bet I didn't miss more than an hour of the tournament by being asleep. Lily sat with me for a few minutes and watched too. Said I drove her away by snoring. I deny that."

I paused for the little laugh, but this audience just waited silently for me to go on.

"Lily and I drove to soccer practice at about 10 minutes 'til 5:00 p.m. I know this because I missed the end of the Phoenix Open to get to soccer practice. Big fat Phil won, by the way. We had soccer practice with all 13 of my 12 year old girls, the Pink Ponies, present and accounted for at 5:00 p.m. We have a big game tomorrow afternoon. We practiced until 6:58 p.m. because another team had the field at 7:00 p.m. Allison's mom was late picking her up. Lily and I waited with her until 7:10 or 7:15 p.m. when her ride finally came. I called Lola on the cell phone. Then Lily and I met her over at Chili's, must have been 7:30 p.m. by then. I had a Bleu Cheese Chipotle Burger. Lola had a Caribbean salad, well, most of it. I finished it. Lily polished off most of her chicken quesadillas. I did have a little of hers as well. All three of us were blimped out. Don't let these very slimming sweats fool you, I'm a smidgen overweight."

Stonefaces. My best 4:00 a.m. stuff ever. Unfortunately, this was about as good as my material ever got and I was gettin' nothin'.

"Lola and Lily went home from there together in Lola's car. I stopped by Bodie's before coming home. Got there at 8:40 p.m. or so. Spent twenty or twenty five minutes with Bodie. He seemed good and I left for home. It took ten minutes to get home from there, so it was about 9:15 p.m. I kissed my girls for a few minutes because Lily had showered by then and was clean. I giggled with them because I was still stinky from practice and dressed in a pink polo shirt under my sweatshirt. They thought I was nuts to wear my official Pink Ponies coaching shirt to just practice when a sweatshirt and a jacket covered it, 'cause nobody could see it anyway. They both love it when I'm a fashion idiot. That's pretty much all the time. How come you guys aren't writing this down? At least take some notes, huh?"

None of the three even twitched.

Maybe I *was* still dreaming.

"Okay. Before showering, I helped to tackle sixth grade Government homework, very successfully I might add, until at least 10:20 p.m. I know that because I was frustrated to have missed the weather—again. I always miss the weather. Tonight's Government lessons did not cover the current police state of Ft. Worth, Texas. That's probably a 7th grade class all to itself. Then I showered—with Lola."

Lola rolled her eyes and blushed, looking away from the officers.

"We watched Ebert and Roeper review movies, or sorta did. Lola woke me twice and said I was snoring. Denied it then and still deny it."

Now Lola smiled.

"Made love with my wife after she woke me up the second time. As you can readily see, I am irresistible."

Lola was no longer smiling.

"It must have thundered during the night because Lily came into our bed and that's the only time she ever comes in anymore. I didn't hear Lily or the thunder or anything else. Fifteen minutes ago I was dreaming of a big, giant ugly ogre bothering my family and the next thing I know, you've got these two Chewbacas in my entry, so I guess dreams really can come true."

Now I stared at Angela, boring a hole right through her head with my best laser eyes.

It was extra-double quiet. Nobody said anything.

Wait for it. Wait.

"Sorry, Jerry. Just doing our job," said Angela.

There's my opening.

"Really, Angela? Were you thinking, 'Hey, this guy is a huge flight risk so let's roust him and his family at 4:00 a.m.? Hurry before any flights to Costa Rica leave D.F.W. or before he hops on his private jet. We are sure he's been hiding his plane from his family and from us because—that's our job?'"

I gave her little quote marks in the air with both hands. I had worked myself into a nice tizzy now. Angela looked at the floor. I got her on the ropes. Now finish her off.

"Come on, Angela. It's not like you don't know me. What's the damn deal?"

Angela gave me nothing, as usual.

"Have you talked to her runt of a husband, Warren?" I demanded. "That bastard would sleep with a dipsy-dumpster if it had big boobs."

"We will," said Angela.

"Oh, but I was your leading suspect? You guys better paste it together! Her husband needed her dead to pursue the new, even hotter girlfriend than the last hot girlfriend. Now, get out of here so my family can finish sleeping." I actually made a shooing motion at them. "Please be careful on the drawbridge on your way out."

One of the uniformed storm troopers sneered at me. He was just mad I had compared him to an ugly ogre. Hey, if the shoe fits.

"I'll need to talk to you later this morning, Jerry. Call me before 10:00 a.m. at work," said Angela. She had remained completely even-tempered through all my smart-ass-ness, but she always does.

2. Angela

At 9:30 a.m. on Monday I walked into the Police Station where I used to work until Lola got pregnant about thirteen years ago. I asked to see Detective Delano. She was in a meeting so I had to wait. Great.

Detective Angela Delano Ng is an Italian-American girl from New Jersey who married David Ng, a Chinese guy. Their marriage must weather all the stereotypes and family difficulties you might imagine for such a situation. That last name, "Ng," is supposedly the American version of "Smith" in China. In other words, it is a pretty common last name over there.

Angela is as white as you can be and still be one-quarter Italian. Neither of their families liked anything about this marriage idea. Angela and David have been married a little less than three years and don't have children yet. Both are 32 years old. I can guess that the children issue isn't too far below the simmering surface of Angela and David's lives.

David Ng did his undergraduate work at Texas A & M in Biology with a minor in Criminal Justice. Biology was to please his traditional Chinese mother, although she would have preferred medicine, specifically. The Criminal Justice minor, he did for himself. That was probably an enormously defiant decision. What a rebel. His minor doesn't show on the diploma that his mother has framed and hung in her dining room. So she doesn't have to tell anyone about it. Since he never made any grade but an "A" in any American school, there is plenty for his mother to talk about besides his "minor" interests.

When David Ng talks, most people from America cannot understand more than one word out of ten that he speaks. Maybe that's a little exaggeration, but not by much. His Chinese sounds like Chinese and his English sounds like Chinese. He came to America as a young adult with his family. David is an assistant professor of Biology at West Texas Baptist University. He works for my friend, Dr. Bodie Kohler. Seems like Dr. Kohler and David's wife, Angela are just about the only Americans who can understand David Ng without having to hear him say it again very slowly. But David is a smart guy and a hard worker.

After a couple of years of marriage and what I presume to be thoughtful reflection, Angela finally took her husband's last name, but only added to her own. No hyphen. Anyone semi-observant can see that it was a painful decision. It probably felt to her like she had lost her own family or her identity to a foreign language and an unfamiliar foreign country, all without ever leaving home.

She is trying to make her way in a man's world of law enforcement with what she must view as a lost identity. Her business card reads "Angela Delano Ng." I have only heard her tell people she is "Angela Delano," even while handing them her card. Most people probably think that Ng stands for something impressive, like "Nuclear geoscientist" or "Noteworthy grade," because she doesn't mention it.

Angela shares her difficulties with her husband. Her husband confides in his boss and friend, Dr. Bodie Kohler. Eventually, with encouragement from David, Angela finally talked directly to Bodie about one of her cases because of his scientific knowledge. The resulting relationship developed into something solid over the last few years. It is founded on similar interests and their mutual emotional attachment to her husband. Despite knowing that Bodie and I are close friends and often work together, Angela has begun to call on Bodie more often. She seeks from Bodie exactly what I want from him; advice, counsel and his emotional stability. She wants to draw strength from his total lack of resentment for her having married a Chinese guy, unlike her own family. I suspect she has begun to think of Bodie as family. I know David does. I do too, but neither Angela nor I think of each other as family. Well, maybe we think of each other as arguing family.

As you might imagine, the Ft. Worth Police Department is barely sprinkled with: a) women, b) young attractive women, c) Italians, d) New Jersey-ites, or e) any combination of a, b, c and/or d married to a Chinese guy. It's quite a life she's carved out for herself. Angela is an attractive brunette with way penetrating brown eyes and a good deal of veneered self confidence and by my accounting, a pretty good detective. In my estimation, her troubles are seldom, if ever, apparent to those who work with her. She is feisty, but calm. It's a great combo, feisty-calm. I married a girl with feisty-calm, so I know it when I see it.

Angela likes me okay, I guess. Because of my close relationship with Bodie, she probably suspects I know more about her than I really do. She is naturally guarded around me because of that and because of the ex-cop thing. Sometimes she and Bodie and I will talk over cases, sometimes even her cases. But Angela and I usually keep the conversations close to the subject and as emotionally safe from each other as possible.

This time it was not usual.

"Thanks for coming in, Jerry," said Angela as she came down the hall and waved me in her direction.

"Hey, no problem, I was up early anyway," I said, purposely scowling as we walked toward her cubicle.

We both sat down. "Tell me about Warren Duchtin," said Angela.

"I'll tell you what I know. I hope you already have all this stuff, though," I said with some snotty tone. I was still fried about this morning.

"Warren Duchtin is about my age, fifty-ish. He owns a company that sells a product called *Perma-Press Plaques*. It sounds like a laundry product to me but apparently it's a pressing process so that people can have their diplomas, photos or important papers framed onto a piece of hardwood. Some kind of giant press smashes the paper onto the wood and seals it in a clear finish polymer so you can hang it on the wall. Sounds okay, but who would figure it's possible to make a living selling such crap? Warren's outward appearance indicates it must be a very good living."

Angela shrugged at my comments but said nothing.

"Warren's new silver Mercedes sedan is usually parked outside his two story office building that houses his operation at the south end of downtown. The car is so new the temporary tag was still on the back two days ago. His thirty year old wife of six years has, well, *had* a strong belief that Warren was spending time and earnings entertaining a certain six-foot tall, estimated 25 year old blonde woman. She's got absolutely no ass and legs that go all the way to the ground. There's enough artificial enhancement above the waist that even the least alert male in Ft. Worth would spin his head like the devil-possessed little girl in the *Exorcist* movie to catch a look. By all reports, no portion of such legs ever approaches the state of 'covered'. As if those legs are not long enough, they are accessorized by spike heels, maybe 24/7. These are the kind of slip-in heels the kids call 'fuck-me pumps'."

This cussing rudeness, which I normally do not participate in, accomplished my mission because Angela winced. But she still said nothing. I celebrated her pained reaction silently.

"Hard not to notice such a couple if they are, in fact, a couple. Needless to say the alleged escorting of such a female was recently noticed by a friendly acquaintance of the very angry Mrs. Duchtin. The hot-in-more-ways-than-one Mrs. Duchtin is, uh, sorry, *was* no slouch in the looks department herself and has hired, uh, had hired us to document Warren's time-spending with photos or other appropriate evidence. I believe Mrs. Duchtin aims to own her a *Perma-Press Plaque* company."

Now Angela nodded.

I continued, "I have taken twenty lovely photos of this colorful new couple together, in a public place on one occasion. There was no outward expression of affection toward each other yet. They were just sitting at the Water Gardens on a warm winter afternoon last week. She did have some flowers with her, but I did not see her receive them and he didn't bring them with him. It was a unique and exciting show to see this female creature move from a standing position to a seated one on the granite steps of the Water Gardens. I can currently only prove that she and Mr. Duchtin know each other. Previous reports of a significant lack of leg drapery with accompanying heels are extremely accurate. Adding to such weirdness is the fact that there is no water in the Water Gardens right now. It's all under repair. We have no idea why they were sitting there. It was not crowded as I guess there are not many people anxious to look at dried up Water Gardens. Hey, it was a nice day. Any more illicit activity is probably being conducted in the relative darkness of night. I had hoped so. Sometimes I love this job."

Angela finally spoke, "What was your arrangement with Joanne Duchtin?"

"Anger with her husband was driving her. Joanne didn't even blink at my $350 a day plus expenses and half that for my associate, the honorable Dr. Bodie Kohler, whenever I deem his accompaniment necessary. She advanced me $2,500, about a week's worth of effort. Since I believe all the money for this case came from Warren anyway, I think she would have gladly paid twice that for my help."

No response, so I tried a question of my own, "How did Joanne die?"

"She was beaten severely. We think she was also shot in the face, maybe after the beating. Hard to tell. Body's in tough shape. We're waiting on autopsy results. Found the body in a ravine north of Lake Worth, but she wasn't out there on a fishing trip. Warren reported her missing. We ID'd it with dentals." Angela was finally giving something up. "So, you got no proof yet of an affair with this blonde?"

"Nope. Just what I told you about," I replied.

"I need copies of those pictures as soon as possible," Angela said firmly.

"I'll get you some prints, or would you rather get 'em email."

"Email is fine. Send me jpeg files if you can. Thanks," said Angela.

I tried another; "My biggest question is how you knew Joanne was my client?"

As usual, Angela answered with one of her own, "Had you given any of those twenty photos to Joanne yet?"

"Yeah, I emailed them to her four days ago because that's what she told me to do," I answered, realizing what I was saying as I said it. "Damn! Either Warren looked at her email or Joanne confronted him with the pictures even after I told her that we'd get more."

"Warren told us Joanne had hired you. That leads me to think bad thoughts about Warren," said Angela.

We both pondered the obvious.

"Your name and number were written on a date last week in Joanne's calendar at her house. I saw it there last night. I have no doubt Warren saw it too," said Angela.

"So, does that mean we're friends again?" I asked.

"Get me those photos and don't leave town, Jerry. I may have some more questions for you," Angela said without pause, but she was only a little lordly about it.

"No problem. I'll just postpone my holiday in Italy I've been planning for months. Waxahachie is nice this time of year. Can I run down there?"

I had done enough damage. I stared at her a little longer just on principle.

She ignored that too.

3. Pink Ponies

"LET'S GO PO-NIES!" Clap. Clap. Clap-Clap-Clap. "LET'S GO PO-NIES!" Clap. Clap. Clap-Clap-Clap.

The Pink Ponies passed the soccer ball down the sideline towards another attack on their opponents' goal and tried to look not-annoyed by their parents' rhythmic cheer. Even though they are used to it, it is annoying to them all.

They are twelve. Everything is annoying.

From my experience, twelve year old girls are incapable of not looking annoyed with their parents at any time. Ever. Surely such emotion mastery will occur in the thirteenth year of life. Hey, I can hope. I was totally focused on the task at hand, yelling for my own daughter, "Fill the space, Lily! Fill the space! Way to go!"

Each of my players' families is headed into those emotional and change filled Junior High years at warp speed. I fully expect Lily to go over to the dark side any day—inevitable for all teenagers from what Lola and I hear. Many parents are as expectant as I am, but we are all seldom well prepared. Here's a little hint of our near future. The Pink Ponies is their team name left over from when the girls were in recreational leagues during elementary school. The girls have made it clear that it is time to change the name of their club. Under their careful consideration are—Amazon Warriors, Tomb Raiders, Hun Women, Bloody Mud Mamas and any other aggressive title with which they might irritate adults. Each player has specific adults in mind for such irritation. The dark side sometimes rears its head in a clear foreshadow for parents of twelve year olds everywhere. Parents generally choose not to recognize the signs. In a shocking development, the most active of the team parents prefer to keep Pink Ponies or maybe go with Purple Hippos, or how about Sparkly Rainbows?

These are eye rolling choices all, to the girls.

The main difference is that the girls seldom think about it and the involved parents can think of nothing else. The girls know and obviously enjoy this fact. The only hope for compromise might be to align ourselves with one of the large existing soccer clubs in the Ft. Worth/Dallas metroplex, whose names are already clearly defined, like Inter, Texans, Rockets, Comets, Lightning, or Sting. All have benign names and expensive fees. I could not care less about the team name. I love these kids and the sport and especially all the accompanying chaos.

"Ladies! We put a slobberknockin' on 'em today, didn't we?" I said to them after the game. Pre-teen cheers went all around surrounded by smiling parents and impatient siblings ready to go elsewhere immediately. "Well done! Practice tomorrow night at Forest Park at 5:00 p.m. See you there."

The problem with joining one of the big soccer clubs is that there would then be one club, our club, which you couldn't pound to an embarrassing pulp. It's fun to beat those big, snotty clubs. Mostly, it's fun to see their affluent parents look so defeated when some, harrumph, Pink Ponies beat the H-E-double hockey sticks out of their precious dumplings. The girls would never appreciate this subtlety, but that's okay.

I'm more cheerleader than technically proficient coach, but we win a lot more than not, a lot more. Listen, I'm sporting the athletic ability and foot speed of a gardenia bush but I've shown up for three years in my bright pink coach's shirt. *'Jerry? He's that old, fat-guy with a receding hairline in a pink shirt and size XL black soccer shorts running up and down the sideline and yelling at our daughters.'* How much worse could it be? I'll show up even if the girls choose *Womanchester United*, as one of them suggested.

My wife, Lola, says to just let them be. I think she's right. Lola is usually right. It is one of the big reasons why I married her. Another reason for marrying her is that Lola also says that I am not old, fat or balding. Uh, that's sweet but I have a mirror. I can live with her obviously failing eyesight.

I married later than many people do. I was well into my thirties. Hey, I was busy. And I hadn't found Lola yet. That was fifteen years ago. It doesn't take a professional to analyze that as being an important contribution towards my focus on my family. Once I came in for a landing, there was never a doubt that this was right for me. I adore Lola and as for Lily, well, there are no words. Those feelings are strong. People who think they want to fall in love are in search of what I have whether they know it or not. Despite my acute sense of order, I will admit as quietly as possible that I absolutely thrive on the chaos ever present in my life.

I am a soccer coach for the Pink Ponies in Ft. Worth, Texas, sometimes. I am a private investigator in Ft. Worth, Texas, sometimes. Sometimes I am even a tax accountant. No, I'm not kidding.

Fortunately for me tax season only lasts for a few months each year. So, part of the year I help people with deductions, Schedule "D" and I.R.S. filing deadlines. I also try to get them to understand the fact that our Congress has now imposed the Alternative Minimum Tax (A.M.T.) on nearly everyone in their eternal search for more income for themselves. Originally intended as a method to force high-income individuals to pay their fair share, the wimpy legislature has now allowed A.M.T. to be applied to people at nearly every income level. Then both parties point to the other side of the aisle for blame. Whether you are a Republican or Democrat or otherwise… Hey, if you are an American you should be ashamed of this legislatively self-issued license to rob regular people. Is anybody still awake? Yeah, I know.

I already had my college degree in Accounting and my C.P.A. by the time I became a police officer. Accounting isn't as much fun as police work. Sorry. Tax work is governed by strict rules, is tedious, structured and pressured but orderly. Investigations are almost without any rules by nature, are varied, random, pressured and so disorderly that every case is different in how you should approach it.

Even using the same approach, every case turns out differently. Investigations can last all year or might not happen at all. But I make time for tax season in between chasing cheating husbands into topless joints and hunting bail-jumping murderers in Mexico.

Having quit the force a few years after marrying Lola, I'd like to say for the record that there are few, if any bail-jumping murderers anywhere in my life. It is the possibility of the occasional, random appearance of any such nefarious character to which my wife most vehemently objects. I have a gun, just not with me all the time. It's a Smith & Wesson .38 revolver left over from my days on the job. I'm licensed to carry it and Lola knows, but doesn't want to think about it. As Lola correctly points out, it is no longer *my* life. It is *our* life. Lola and I decided that our life together might be better if I didn't carry a gun or wear a uniform for bad guys to take target practice. We did not quite foresee that tax accounting would be quite so—tiresome.

If you let it, it will suck the life force right out of you.

So the only thing in common with my two professions is the pressure. Investigations pay more when you can get the work and if you can repel your wife's concerns, albeit legitimate concerns. Tax work is way, way steadier. You can count on it. You can also count on it to not be fun.

For me, tax accounting lasts four months each year depending on how many clients I send to other practitioners. The type of clients I have are unconcerned by tax matters during the remaining eight months of each and every year. That is just the way I like them to be. As a matter of fact, the only tax matters my clients are *ever* concerned with are, "How much money will I get back?" and "How soon?" I don't do taxes for rich guys. If I were to seek more affluent clients who might be concerned with tax laws all year long, it would force me to be a full-time tax accountant. I would rather die in the desert tied to a stake in the middle of a bonfire.

Bodie says stuff like, "Tax work is a sure thing and it happens every year. So do funerals and they are way more interestin' than tax work."

My closest friend, Professor Bodie Kohler—I should say Dr. Bodie Kohler—is a rare man of honor whom I have known for twenty years. He's been pretty crusty for all twenty years I've known him, but worse over the last few. Three years ago he lost his wife Patsy to a heart attack. She was only sixty-five years old. It should not have been her time. That event was not in the plan the Kohlers had envisioned for this stage of life.

I guess it never is. Pat was Bodie's life once the kids grew up. They had ridden life's roller coaster together since they were teenagers. Neither would have ever hoped to ride it alone. When that light went out, it was really, really dark for awhile for Bodie—lost in a cave dark; drunken stupor in a shuttered-up country house dark.

Bodie has people in his life that look up to him. He has people who love him. I am one of them. Lola is too.

Dr. Kohler has no interest in tax work, but my investigations really bring out the best in him. I think he gets to live out some buried fantasy through me whenever I've got a case going. This stuff is like a cheap detective novel for him every time. I guess I'm his entertainment, but I know he cares about my family and me. He should be allowed a little entertainment. I'm willing and able.

Bodie often goes with me on stakeouts. He helps me with other stuff too, but I am painfully sensitive to putting him in any kind of danger. Lola would wish that I had somebody looking after me with identical concerns.

Last year I was working on an insurance fraud case. This extended family and their pals were driving around various cities and towns in North Texas causing traffic accidents with junk cars that were fairly recent models and filing false claims. They filed claims for medical conditions that did not exist, for work on their cars that never took place and lost wages from jobs that none of them were capable of being hired for in the first place. As happens with most cases like this, they spent all funds on drugs as fast as they made it. But this outfit was pretty smart. They didn't actually consume their product. Their business was simply diversified. The insurance fraud company fed profits to the drug selling business, which then funneled those profits into the insurance fraud company, the auto stealing/stripping company and the video poker company. Every company laundered every other company's profits. It was a conglomerate. Smart crooks are scary. Fortunately, there are few of that type.

It wasn't long into the investigation before everybody I needed to talk to knew me and knew that my questions might to lead to them being arrested. This rendered me crippled to do the job. Bodie and I concocted a script for him to follow. He became Dr. Benjamin Casey. Yeah, I know. Like the old TV show, but it was a really old show. Not that many people remember. Zero young people remember it. Listen, if it's not somewhat entertaining, Bodie's not interested in participating. He remembers that *Ben Casey Show*. He actually demanded to be referred to as Colonel Sanders for awhile, so Dr. Benjamin Casey seemed like an excellent choice at the time.

That white hair, goatee and slow-speaking Southern charm is so disarming to good guys and bad guys alike. I think we could have called him Dr. Marcus Welby or Dr. Barnaby Jones and gotten away with it. Actually, despite Bodie's request, we have never introduced him to anyone as Dr. Casey since that insurance case last year. But we might need Dr. Benjiman Casey again someday. There is no doubt that the possibility of Bodie using the name Colonel Sanders will arise again. That possibility will unquestionably originate with Bodie.

Bodie is capable of turning off the crustiness of his everyday-self at will. But there is a certain "want to" factor involved there. He would deny this, but his pointed fact-finding with that whole group culminated in him getting answers that resulted in the arrest, prosecution and conviction of six bad guys. Six! And they were the main bad guys, the big fish. As he astutely pointed out to me after the trials, Bodie won't even be alive when that bunch finally gets out of prison. It was enormously satisfying for Bodie and was sheer fun for me.

Bodie has an older, experienced eye on cases and the varied analyses required. I can get overly focused, too task-oriented and miss the big picture. Bodie sees the whole thing, the whole time. Remember that guy on the old *Ed Sullivan Show* who would spin the plates on the broomsticks? He would keep putting up more and more plates to spin, the whole time having to go back and add extra spin to the ones that had been spinning the longest, always just before they ran out of gas and crashed to the floor. Bodie could do that. I swear he could spin dozens of them at once. I could spin one, maybe two and they would spin really well. Add more than that and I start looking for a cool, dark place to curl up in a ball and take a nap.

4. Happiness Graph

"Ah need to pee," said Bodie from inside my car at a volume so I could hear him from where I stood outside. Sometime during his forties Bodie started feeling like he had to pee all the time. I'm talking all the time. By the time he reached fifty five, Dr. Bodie Kohler really did have to pee all the time. Now, he's seventy-four years old. So the whole time I've known Bodie, all twenty years, he's needed to pee.

"Jerrah!" Bodie shouted out the cracked car window into the cold winter darkness for something, anything to happen. "Let's go! This fella's goin' to work all night. We've been here so long ah bet even Gert's got to pee."

I turned toward the car. In the back seat the gentle, black-furred Gert raised her head and lifted one eyebrow at mention of her name. Just as quickly, Gert laid her head back down. She was used to such exchanges between the two of us. The dog clearly was just happy to be along on this stakeout and had no interest in a potentially cheating husband that her guys were watching. At ten years old, she just wanted to be in on "it," whatever "it" was, and to nap near her guys. I climbed into my five year old Taurus and started the engine, really to just get the heater started.

"We might get faster results on this guy if we tried to get him on tax evasion like Al Capone," I said. "Not because he's smart like Al. Just because we've had some pitiful luck catching him this week and tax season is coming up." Bodie and I already decided together that Joanne's death wasn't going to stop us from finding out what we could, even with nobody paying the bills.

Bodie started in again, in his rich and slowly spoken North Carolina bred accent, which sounds really lovely almost regardless of what words are spoken. "Jerrah, you always say that cell phones, faxes, computahs and digital cameras have changed the detective business forevah, but here we sit like fools in the dark as if none of those magnificent items had ever been invented at all. Ah suppose any of those little miracles makes a decent papah-weight."

Bodie has no clue how funny he really can be.

"You can take a digital picture of your subject if somethin' happens, but you still have to wait for a happenin'. What ah see is that you still have to sit in the freezin-ass car and wait for a happenin' to happen. Would you like to speak to that, Jerrah?"

Now, this is a common question from Bodie that he usually throws out to his students during class. Sometimes this question from him is rhetorical and my sense was that this was one of those times. I kept quiet. It was the right choice.

He continued without missing a beat, "Mah teeth are floatin' and looks like this height challenged gentleman is goin' to keep his poker in his pants for another night. So, ¿Donde' esta el cuarto de baño? ¿Sabe, muchacho?"

No response from me but a smile. Even in Spanish or more like Spanglish, that accent is really pleasant. Bodie finished, "Let's roll, Mistah Jerrah."

With only a little reservation, I slipped the trusty Taurus into "D" and headed for Bodie's home.

Professor Bodie Kohler is the department Chair of Biology at West Texas Baptist University located on the outskirts of Ft. Worth, Texas. W.T.B is the redheaded stepchild college of Ft. Worth, always the also-ran to Texas Christian University. Teaching his students and his granddaughter Marisa are the focus of his life now. If he retired, it might be all right with Bodie, but not to W.T.B and not to his students. Maybe not with Bodie either, because Marisa Kohler is a freshman nursing student at West Texas Baptist whom Bodie adores with absolute, intense abandon. As for adoring Marisa's father and Bodie's younger son, Clayton Kohler? Not so much.

Clayton Kohler can think of all sorts of things for his father to do with his money except whatever Bodie wants to do with it. Bodie pretty much doesn't want to do anything with it except buy dog treats for Gertie. Clayton is a fifty year old disappointment of a son who once had enormous potential as a mathematician, a scientist or a teacher, if only he had put forth a little effort toward any of those ends. Not all assistant managers of housewares at the Safeway are disappointments. Clayton is that because his father demanded more of him and Clayton did not respond. Well, he responded, just not in a good way.

Bodie's significant talent for subtle sarcasm does not allow much relationship improvement with his younger son. Fortunately, when Clayton's mother, Patsy, was alive, only Clayton's potential showed. There always seemed to be hope for Clayton when Patsy was alive. Since she died, the disappointment has belched a putrid smell. It's not quite clear if the same thing would have happened if Patsy had not died so young, but it's pretty clear.

Clayton is Bodie's younger son because James was older. James Kohler was born nearly five years before Clayton in 1950. This was the Kohler household's historically happiest period from what Bodie tells me, or tells Gert loudly enough so I can hear. The only time it got better was three years later when daughter Laura was born. That was the absolute best of Kohler family times. A little over a year after Laura, in early 1955, Clayton was born into the idyllic scene and the Kohler family happiness graph had peaked. When the three children of Bodie and Patsy Kohler were young, learning to walk and learning to talk, some combination of *The Donna Reed Show*, *Father Knows Best* and *Leave it to Beaver* presented a reasonably accurate picture of life as they knew it.

It did not play out like any television script.

James died in 1968 at age eighteen in a marshy, lonely, violent jungle in Vietnam when Clayton was thirteen years old and Laura was eleven.

Bodie is now closing in on seventy five years old. He walks with a limp but stubbornly resists use of a cane, which would clearly ease his everyday efforts. In the last five years, Bodie has been barraged with a continuous onslaught of perennial health problems. None are serious and none are trivial. Any could lead to a health spiral that could present him with the end of his life in a very short time. Bodie knows this as well as his loved ones. The professor has no interest in holding such prospects back by eating healthy and exercising. It isn't that he doesn't care. In my opinion he prefers to ignore such a possibility because other parts of life are infinitely more interesting.

Cigars are his most consistent companion since Patsy is gone. In one sense, they took her place because Patsy would not allow them during their life together. As a result, his voice has taken on a richer, raspier quality. It's a voice still strong, just different.

Bodie's hearing problems are a different matter. Without his hearing aids he is crippled. It's that simple. He almost always has them but still finds them annoying. Sometimes the batteries start to whine. I can hear the whine but he doesn't seem to hear it. Sometimes he will fail to respond to something I have said and I start thinking he doesn't have those hearing aids in so I ask. I've never caught him without them, so that just confirms that he often has no interest in whatever I'm saying.

On his short list of friends are his ten year old black Labrador, Gert, the professor's assistant David Ng, David's wife, Angela, and me. The one person in Bodie's life who is void of disappointment is his granddaughter, Marisa Kohler. An excellent student throughout high school, terrific athlete in soccer and cross country, smart, witty, beautiful and busy living up to her potential and her father's combined. She is studying nursing which she has wanted to do since she was eleven and her own mother died of breast cancer. That was seven years ago. After serving as primary caretaker to her flawed father, Clayton, for the last several years, the difficulties of studying nursing at a university seem way easy.

It was a huge break for Bodie when his granddaughter came to W.T.B for college. Having grown up in Ft. Worth, I believe that Marisa preferred to go to college out of town. But she knows how much her father and grandfather rely on her. Maybe that's a shame for Marisa but I see her with her grandfather a lot. It is a very good thing for Bodie and Marisa as well. Marisa checks in with her grandfather three or four times a week at school. It has brought Bodie back among the living to have Marisa so included in his life. With Marisa at W.T.B, there is no doubt that Bodie will be there at least as long as she is in undergraduate school there, if his health holds up. She makes everyday stuff worthy of anticipation for him. His life has lacked anticipation since loosing Patsy. Teaching Biology is still exciting to him. Well, it's more exciting than sitting in my stupid car even with Gert and me to entertain him.

If you think the dog isn't one of us, consider that when Gert, Bodie and I are together Bodie will talk to Gert instead of me. He speaks right out loud as if there is complete understanding. They have to just let me hear them because I'm there too. I guess it's more within Bodie's comfort zone especially if there are emotions being expressed. At least that's what Lola tells me.

As we drive home, Bodie often offers up some gentle musings out loud while looking out the window.

"Gert, ah can't decide if ah see too many movies or not quite enough of them. Probably not enough since we lost Patsy. That snack-pack deal that all the theaters offah is a communist plot. Oh sure, you can get the small drink, but the lahge is only twenty five cents more. Gertie, how can you pass that up?"

Gert cocked her head to one side at the unmistakable tone change and sound of her name from her favorite guy, anticipating dog fun. Hearing her own name from Bodie *is* dog fun for Gert.

"Bodie? Just don't get the drink when you go in," I said, speaking for Gert, too. You can always count on me to oversimplify the troubles of others. I guess it's not so surprising when my good friends would rather talk to dogs than to me.

Ignoring me, Bodie continued to speak to the passenger window and to Gert. I suppose that's because Gert never minimizes anything. "Pat always liked to get popcorn, but that gallon of liquid refreshment is mah main enemy. She always helped drink that stupid bucket of soda, but you know Gert, it got harder and harder to make it all the way through a 100 minute film without havin' to pee. Sure, ah could utilize some self-control and not drink it at all, if I could just find some self-control. When Patsy died it seemed she took all mah self-control with her."

Bodie says such things without any outward sadness at all. It's just an observation—a statement of fact.

"So, ah'll pee right before the movie starts and hope. That's it. Sittin' in the car for hours on end waitin' for somethin' to happen is about the same, ah suppose. Waitin' is waitin'. Patience is not mah strength and nevah has been. What is my strength, you ask Jerrah?" He didn't look my way at all. "Well, as we both know ah don't have one, except maybe Marisa."

None of this little talk with Gertie, even the brief acknowledgment of my presence in the car with them, required a response from Gert or me for that matter. I smiled anyway.

"You know what ah've been wonderin', Jerrah?" This time he looked right at me with a thoughtful, penetrating look. "Ah've been wonderin' for quite some time now how exactly James really lived and died in Vietnam."

I hadn't heard Bodie mention James in years.

Bodie continued, "The Marines nevah did tell us very much in 1968. They just told us that he was gone and had died in battle in service of his country."

This time there was a very tired sadness in Bodie's look and his raspy voice. The old man seemed to age right there in the front seat of the Taurus. The power evaporated from him as he said the words. "Oh, we got him back and had the funeral and everything, but now you know as much about how and why he died as ah do. It was war. We were tryin' to kill them and they were tryin' to kill us. Patsy always wished she knew more, but it was an easy thing to keep from pursuin'. It was so long ago and everything. Ah've just been wishin' now that ah had found out somethin' for her."

I weighed a response as I drove on.

I said, "Bodie, he's been gone a long time." Immediately I knew what an absurd and unhelpful retort this had been.

Bodie turned back to the window and said, "Ah really need to pee."

I didn't know what to think or say. I'm like that a lot.

Dropped off at their house, Bodie and Gert will undoubtedly fire up the microwave for a late supper with *Dateline* or the local news as their only dinner guest. Bodie will talk to Gert about Patsy until the microwave dings, as has been his unavoidable nightly ritual for three years now. Or maybe he'll talk about James. Bodie will make his way along the well-worn path to the bathroom again. He won't notice how worn out that carpet has become. Too many other things in life are way more worthy of Bodie's attention than worn carpet. Gert will fall into full-relaxed mode as pleased as always just to be talked to.

As we pulled up to his little white, shingle-sided house not far from the T.C.U. campus, I said, "Bodie? I've got soccer practice with the girls tomorrow afternoon. I'll need to chase this guy again tomorrow night if you're interested. I would love to have you go with me."

Bodie opened the door, got out in his slow, calculated way and opened the back door to let Gert out. He leaned back into the front passenger door of the Taurus. "Hell yes ah'm going with you. We'll catch that cheatin' turd tomorrow without a doubt. His poor wife."

Bodie shut the Taurus passenger door gently, as is his manner. Gert was already seeking dog bladder relief in the front yard as Bodie limped up to his front door looking to do the same thing, but inside. It is 10:15 p.m. and I missed the news and weather again. Once Bodie and Gert were inside I headed home to my girls.

5. Whipped

Lily was nearly asleep but she smiled at me when I kissed her good night. Her gorgeous face was lit only by the light of her computer screen saver, which was a series of pictures of Britney Simpson or Jessica Timberlake or maybe Justin Spears in concert. Turns out it is Britney Spears and I know this only because there is a caption on the screen which reads, "Britney Spears in Concert." Otherwise I might have thought Lily got her screen saver from *Playboy Magazine*. Britney needs to put some clothes on. Where is her dad, anyway?

Everything I know about Britney Spears, Justin Timberlake and computers was taught to me by my daughter. I swear, if she were really interested and allowed herself the time away from Instant Messaging and video games to write the program, she and her pals could figure out how to transmit margaritas over the Internet. I live with my fears.

Looking at her sleeping, I caught the same rush of goose bumps I get every time she smiles at something I have done. That is less often at twelve than it was at eleven. Those smiles seem to come in my direction half as often as when she was five, which makes them about ten times more important to me. In her groggy state of half-sleep, all parental defense shields are down and she can be my little girl for a minute. That is really, really good.

31

Lily is becoming a wonderful person and it is fun to watch, even the tougher, more emotional parts. Girls are different than boys. Girls are complicated. As I leave her room, I notice clothing scattered about that, even in the dark, is—interesting. I have chaperoned a few after school get-togethers up at her school. These seem to be way, way more important to the moms than to the kids. That means that stopping them from occurring is akin to solving unrest in the Middle East. But if they are going to happen then I'm going to be there. A common trait among both girls and boys at this age is one burning desire. That is to wear clothing that an adult would not even wear to a cheesy resort luau even if liquored-up while getting dressed for it.

As I do my best to pick up her room in the dark, I am confident that any differences between the sexes are not as influenced by environment as some ladies might have you think. Bodie has told me that his sons came out of the womb making grenade explosion noises with their mouths. Maybe that's a slight exaggeration but the conviction of his belief shows. If so, there is no way that was taught or learned. Patsy even agreed with him on this but she never believed it until she had her own children. It is in the genetic makeup. We don't have any control over it. It is just part of the deal. From what I can tell, boys are fun. I kissed my daughter again, but sleep has taken any more smiles away from me for now. Girls are fun too. This I know for a fact.

I summarized my night's events for Lola while we changed for bed, adding more detail when I got to the only interesting part. That means the part about Bodie speaking of James. Lola knows that story as well as me. Despite being nine years younger than I am, she's way smarter so I like talking to her about it. Hey, I'm no chimp in the smarts department. I like looking at her too so it works out all around for me. From the outside of our marriage I am confident male observers would label me "whipped." So be it. All I know is that it is really fun to be good friends with the woman I love. Whip that.

"Why didn't you ask Bodie more about James, Jerry? That's what he wanted—your help. God, you never ask the right questions or enough questions. Pretend you're a detective, why don't you?" Lola said.

Ouch.

This is a woman capable of wielding the word "jackass" with full and utter confidence and, occasionally, a little too much enthusiasm. Not only do I know this, I like it. I like it a lot.

I stood by the bed with only T-shirt, boxers and my brown socks left to remove before bed. I was quite a vision, I'm sure. I had my defense ready and fired it off, "Hey! We were in a huge hurry. Huge! Bodie was only talking so much because he had to pee, really bad! So did Gert. So,—I—was concentrating—on—driving."

She's turned me into a trail-off talker.

It was really weak and a futile response. I realized it as soon as I uttered the word "pee."

Lola just chuckled a happy taunt from a prone position on our bed. She lay on her left side on top of the covers facing me with her lovely head held up by her bent, naked left arm, elbow cushioned into the pillow. The shoulder strap on her nightgown had slid down her left shoulder because her left side was down on the bed. Gravity would allow nothing to hold it up. Sometimes gravity is awesome. The front of her neck tightened as she chortled at me. The curve at the top of her right breast glistened at me with a taunt of its own.

"Good one," she said smartly, staring at me with a flirty, victorious grin on that beautiful, flawless face. Her long, dark curly hair shined. Her eyes are a deep green even with only a small lamp on in our bedroom. They sparkled with energy and total pleasure at having caught me yet again being a ridiculous male. The curves of her naked body beneath a silky peach nightgown were completely smooth from the top of her breasts to the middle of a lovely thigh or two. I ached with the happiness of being alone in the room with her.

We both laughed loudly. I hopped onto the bed on my right side facing her. I rolled her onto her back while she was still smiling. She let me kiss her deeply. Lola smelled so fresh. Like soap and vanilla. Totally edible. I slowly and gently smoothed the silky peach fabric onto the surface of her body with my palm. I felt from her breast down her side, up over her hip and as far down her body as my arm would stretch until I could feel taut, tan legs. Tan, even in the bleak of winter. No idea how she does that. I moved the hem of her nightgown up her body, baring those beautiful thighs. Then she whispered to me through a closed-eye smile, "Take those socks off, dear."

Yep. Whipped.

6. Night Shift

The next night after soccer practice it was raining. But Bodie, Gert and I were back in position in the Taurus across the street from Warren Duchtin's office near downtown Ft. Worth. This is a part of near-downtown that is a little seedy. There is no way to be completely comfortable there. Besides, both Bodie and I believed in our hearts that Warren was responsible for Joanne's death so we were appropriately tense.

We were glad it was raining like crazy in this part of town at 9:00 p.m. Maybe it discouraged the riff-raff from milling about. We looked carefully around for any police surveillance of Warren but saw no hint. It is unexplainable why they wouldn't have been watching him after the information I got for them. I had emailed the photos to Angela shortly after our meeting yesterday.

"If this lovely young blonde woman we are lookin' for steps out into this rain, she might just melt," said Bodie. "How was little girl soccah practice?"

"Great. The field was wet, but we worked really hard on passing the ball into an empty space for a player on a run to overtake. They really seem to get how much better it is to pass to the space in front of a run than to try to pass to another player's feet with a defender right on them. Then the girls worked hard on driving the ball deep in the offensive zone towards the corners and then booting it back across the middle for a scoring opportu..."

"Uh, Jerrah?" asked Bodie.

"Yeah?"

"Ah really do not care about soccah. Ah was actually interested in whatevah you and the delightful Miss Lily are doin', you undahstand?" Bodie replied.

"Oh," I paused. "Hey, we had a great time today. The only one having more fun than the Pink Ponies was me."

"Wonduhful," replied Bodie. "Ah just do not know what all that zone stuff means and ah do not really need to know. Oh, there's our boy now," said Bodie.

Warren Duchtin was sprinting through the driving rain from his office door the twenty feet to his big Mercedes. As usual, he sported a wild print, unbuttoned shirt, barrel belly, gold chains and medallions, smarmy mustache, dyed nearly black thinning hair, shortness and general stumpy-ness. Funny that since I now believed that he killed Joanne, his repulsive characteristics were even more cartoon-like and magnified than before.

He got in and drove the giant car slowly out of the parking lot. He headed north towards the Interstate. Warren's physical size made the car look all the bigger. We were parked on the street across from his office anticipating his direction and we were right. In this rain, it was likely he would not be noticing us. Everyone was making their careful way tonight. There were few people out in this weather. It was easy to keep the Mercedes in sight from a good distance. Duchtin headed West on Interstate 30 presumably towards his home in River Oaks. Maybe he was going to the funeral home to grieve his wife. Yeah, right. He could possibly be headed to the Country Club to celebrate his wife's death, but it could be one of several country clubs to which he belonged. If he went to any of these places except the funeral home, it would not be to meet Miss Blondielegs. Those are his regular rounds and it's not likely he would be seen near his normal haunts with her, not yet anyway.

"Might be our lucky night," said the smiling Bodie, "or at least somebody's lucky night."

Gert even looked up at that comment. I chuckled as we watched

Duchtin's Mercedes exit at Hulen Street, well short of his normal exit. Duchtin turned south on Hulen. He and the rest of the sparse traffic were all very wet and driving well under the speed limit. I had to be careful to keep my own speed down or else risk being noticed by accidentally catching up to him.

Duchtin turned left after the railroad yard, behind a strip shopping center and into a neighborhood with blocks and blocks of apartments. Bodie and I knew this area as living space for T.C.U. students who had finally talked their parents into letting them move off campus. This was the acreage where the old Cullen Davis estate once stood. I think his modern-looking house is now a restaurant back there somewhere in the middle of all the newer apartments. Somebody shot Cullen's ex-wife, Priscilla, her T.C.U. basketball player boyfriend and Cullen's daughter one night in the mid-1970s. The boyfriend died but Priscilla survived. I think Cullen was accused but acquitted of the shooting. The point is that many Ft. Worth natives, including me, have since viewed this whole area as a little haunted or at a bare minimum, extra creepy. It's eerie enough following around that slithering spare, Warren Duchtin.

There was a wide selection of apartments to be had in that area. The range was from average-cheap to ridiculously high rent, depending on what you could slide by your parents. Some young working adults were mixed in there too. But, this is not your prime housing area for fifty-ish, shrimpy but well-heeled businessmen.

Duchtin turned into one of the complexes and pulled up to a security shack. I stopped on the street where we could see his car. He did not roll down a window for any discussion but the iron gate opened ever so slowly. Duchtin waited and then drove through the open gate. He must have had an electronic remote opener for the gate. It closed just as slowly after he pulled through. The Mercedes disappeared into the complex. There was plenty of time for me to have followed him in before that slow moving gate closed. But I had hung back cautiously. I wasn't thinking that fast. Why was my first instinct always to follow the stupid rules?

"Looks like one of us is goin' to have to get wet," Bodie said without guilt. The rain poured relentlessly.

I pulled the Taurus up to the guard shack. The slicker coated guard leaned out towards the Taurus only as far as to preserve his own dryness. He made a window-rolling down signal, fist rolling around as if he actually knew what a manual operated window in a car once was like. That meant the guard was definitely over forty. Believe me, 99.9% of the residents in this area are not even aware that car windows were ever anything but electric. "Who are you here to see?" the smiling guard asked innocently.

"I'm looking for a new place to live and wonder where the leasing office might be located," I asked brilliantly. Cold and rainy winter night, 9:15 p.m. and some guy was looking for an apartment? Good call.

"Pull up and park right over there," the guard said pointing about two car lengths to the right of the guard shack, but outside the sealed iron gate, "right next to the big 'Leasing Office' sign," now he was shaking his head slightly as he looked away from me with total disinterest. "There's somebody in there 'til ten o'clock."

Ah, a fellow trail-off talker.

I had clearly dazzled this guy. "Oh, thanks," I said. I parked and turned off the car. Now here's where having an umbrella in the car for those just-in-case times would have really paid off.

Bodie and Gert each turned and looked at me, neither intending to move. "Leave the keys so ah can catch the news on the radio," said Bodie. Bodie wouldn't have gone with me if it had been clear, calm and 78 degrees. We both know his physical limitations. I complied with his request and headed out into the deluge holding my digital camera underneath my favorite tweed sport coat for weather protection. I can confirm that even cheap polyester blended tweed does not shed water very well. It was about fifteen feet to the door and by the time my blazing sprint ended there, it looked like I had done an underwater inspection of the complex's swimming pool. Nice.

Then I caught my first break of the night. The office was unmanned and quiet except for the piped-in elevator music and a little water fountain on the desk gurgling away. That gurgle was accompanied only by the sound dripping water made when it fell off me onto the blue carpet. Next to the L-shaped desk was an open lobby area with a big cushy couch and a couple of expensive looking chairs. I didn't see anyone and didn't hear anyone. I walked quickly and confidently through the office/lobby dripping a water trail behind and then out the glass door on the back wall into the interior of the complex.

Outside was a covered walkway to the first row of buildings. There was covered but open resident parking. I kept going expecting someone to step out and question my presence at any second. My crack investigative instincts told me to proceed anywhere the covered walkway went because otherwise I'd be getting wetter from the monsoon currently unleashed on Ft. Worth. Okay, it really didn't matter because it was not possible for me to be any wetter.

At the end of the covered sidewalk, I could see a series of smaller apartment or town home buildings sitting further back into the complex. There were four or five units to each brick building with open covered parking for each building. These brick buildings were a lot better looking than the rows of regular looking apartment buildings that were closer to the street and the leasing office. These in the back were nice, really nice. Clearly they were on the upper end of any rental scale you'd like to compare. Each building sat at an odd angle to the other buildings and the grounds in between each were spectacular. None of these apartments had a view of anything further away than fifty yards. But I could clearly see that when the landscaping was not underwater, like tonight, it was really double awesome. I was sure that residents were charged big maintenance fees to support it.

I ran the fifty yards across to the first brick building and another covered walk and porch that were attached. Now I looked like a Navy Seal emerging from the sea on an important mission in a tweed wetsuit. Through the rain I could see the silver Mercedes resting unoccupied and comfortable in a covered space beside the second building. Next to it was a bright red Porsche. The Porsche had permanent Texas plates, but it clearly hadn't been off the showroom floor for long. All the parking areas were lit well. I was thankful for that and the covered place where I could stand nearby. At least I was not out in the open. Now I had to hope to get lucky. That is the absolute core truth of what my job actually requires.

The front doors of the four units in my building of focus could be clearly seen from where I was standing. But at some point, someone was going to wonder who I was and what I was doing. *'Hello, 911? I'd like to report a really triple wet guy with a camera under his arm standing in the walkway with his hands in his pockets. He's behind the five foot azalea bushes next to Building 1 which is full of rich residents. Most of those residents are mean, constipated attorneys looking for nervous wet guys to have arrested and file lawsuits against.'*

I was alone with my fears and smelling like a wet Husky dog in high mud-season. The rain pelted continuously. I stayed under the covered protection of the portico, allowing me to preserve my current wet factor at a steady "swamped" level.

I usually set my old but faithful digital camera to *Night Scene Mode*, an automatic setting with which I am quite familiar on this camera. The built-in flash will go off automatically unless you manually shut it down and I did so, or thought I did. The digital zoom on this camera would pull you closer at a factor of eleven times. That is really good for a camera this old.

I need to update my equipment with a new digital S.L.R. so I can buy bigger zoom lenses and interchange them. But my work is not a tennis match where you know when play will continue. With this work you have split seconds of opportunity. Changing a lens is usually not an option because the moment would be gone. Besides, at my income level I sometimes have to make choices like—buy a new digital camera set-up or buy braces for my daughter. So far Lily was coming in first.

For this night job I needed the camera in *Continuous Mode.* When you press the shutter button firmly it will fire off about two and a half frames per second until you release the button. Even if you use this camera as often as I do it is easy to forget that *Continuous Mode* only works if you have the camera set on *Manual Program.* Then you have to set the shutter speed yourself. I did so. Get as many shots as you can, as fast as you can.

You have to know enough to set the aperture settings manually. At night you need the aperture wide open coupled with a slow shutter speed to capture all available light, especially when you are going without the flash. That means if there is quick action in your shot, it will blur because the aperture stays open so wide and so long. I was not expecting any sudden movements by anyone or anything.

Checking my watch continuously did not make anything happen more quickly. As I shifted from one foot to the other in a failed attempt to be warm, I made up possible scenarios of why Duchtin was here. He could be showing *Perma-Press* products to wealthy old ladies who needed to hang the wills of their recently deceased husbands on the wall for all to admire. Maybe he was looking at jewelry samples to buy something nice for his mother. Nah, this guy doesn't have a mother. He might be meeting with a hit man he is hiring to eliminate a soaked, tweed-coated dweeb who had been following him for about a week now—the door to an upstairs unit opened slowly.

I pointed the camera at the opening door about thirty or forty yards away and upstairs from where I watched. I zoomed in on the doorway enough to catch full body shots of anyone who passed through the door. The auto-focus whirred when I activated it. I could read the unit number on the door—2020. With the rain pouring there was no way I could hear anyone up there. Fortunately they couldn't hear the camera or me either. But I could see clearly. The view was only disturbed by the rain between the opening door and me. All I could see so far was the fully clothed back of Duchtin backing out of the town home really slowly and onto its covered balcony/porch. There was no porch light, but there was a light on inside the entry of the town home and enough ambient light in the complex that the pictures should be good.

With digital you don't have your eye pressed against the viewfinder like with a conventional film camera. You have the little one or two inch screen to look at, so I was holding the camera about half an arm's length from my own head. I was watching the little screen and not looking directly at the doorway. Miss Blondielegs stepped up into the doorway and into my full view but remained just inside the entry. She had on the ever present high heels and a sleek, silky looking negligee-type robe in baby blue that barely covered her significant breasts and her money maker. This outfit was allowing those long legs the benefit of a full airing out. She seemed unaware of the actual outside temperature or weather but was focused on Duchtin's round, fat face. In those heels she was way taller than Duchtin. Without those heels she was way taller than Duchtin. She was absolutely traffic-stopping magnificent, in a really tall and slutty sort of way.

Duchtin had not been in there with her very long. With her state of undress I made a mental note to make fun of his sexual stamina at the earliest possibility. Duchtin stepped up into the doorway towards her and slid his left hand inside the front of the semi-open robe. Miss Blondielegs was clearly willing to allow this. She wrapped her arms down around the squatty Duchtin's very fortunate neck. The robe tie fell away gently and her robe opened completely.

The little screen on my camera was just not gonna do it for me.

I had to look up at the balcony unfiltered by the camera.

I pushed the shutter button hard and the shutter clicked continuously at the scene of the open robe and Duchtin's mauling squeeze of her giant bared right breast. My unobstructed view of her body, naked beneath the lucky baby blue robe-ette clearly revealed a dark, well-waxed and groomed landing strip at the top of those amazing legs. Even from forty yards, I can introduce conclusive evidence that she is not a natural blonde.

I am just shocked.

As I broke into a happy grin and began to hope my silent, shaking laugh would not affect the quality of the shots, I realized the flash was intermittently going off as the camera clicked through shot after shot of the scene. The hot flush of distress instantly flowed through me.

Duchtin realized there was a flash at the same instant I did. I was already running through the rain before his wits gathered enough comprehension to run for the stairs and pursue me. I vaguely heard his clomping steps hit the stairs as I got to the covered walkway near the leasing office. Hey, he had to remove himself from her, so that must have been good for a second or two head-start for me. Plus his stumpy little legs won't go that fast. What a fireplug this guy is and what a colossal ass besides.

I pulled the glass office door—locked! Total ungoverned, sweltering hot panic swept every fiber in me. It must be after 10:00 p.m.

I ran to my right toward the iron gate where residents and Duchtin drove through into the complex. It was slowly closing as a car had just left the complex. It was my biggest stroke of luck this night, maybe ever. The guard never even looked up through the pouring rain as I slid through the slow moving gate right before it sealed shut with a loud metallic thud. The headlights of the Mercedes were hitting the gate as I looked back. But the gate had not yet begun to open again as I reached for the Taurus door.

Now, *it* was locked!

I pulled again, but Bodie had to find the automatic door lock switch on his door and hit it for me to get in.

He couldn't make the switch unlock the door because I was pulling the handle continuously in my frantic panic screaming, "Open, Open, OPEN, OPEN!"

It finally opened and I jumped in, started the car with the keys already in the ignition and tore out of the wet parking lot. The guard came all the way out of his shack in response to my spinning tires. The Mercedes sat at the gate waiting for it to open wide enough for Duchtin to escape and hunt me down to the death.

I drove back to Interstate 30 at warp speed and headed back toward downtown. Finally I slowed to about seventy miles per hour, pretty good for underwater driving in my old brown beast. I expected gun shots to explode into the Taurus from a pursuing Mercedes at any time.

I was talking to Bodie and Gert as fast as I could tell them the story, hoping and wishing that the pictures turned out. I drove the Taurus south on Interstate 35 going way too fast. I watched the highway in my mirror more than the highway in my windshield. After exiting onto Berry Street and heading back on my roundabout route toward Bodie's house, I finally slowed down a little realizing the Mercedes was nowhere near us. I reminded myself over and over that Duchtin did not know who had been following him.

On more than one occasion in casual conversations I have heard Marisa conclude a funny story about her teenage love life (which story is always mild enough that no one would be embarrassed to tell it to their grandfather) with one of her favorite sayings, which is, "Men—are icky." The one we watched tonight was certainly that and worse. Now, we had to see if the camera had let me down as much as I feared.

While Bodie and Gert relieved themselves at their respective and proper locations, I sat at Bodie's kitchen table. The battery to the camera was dead. I plugged in the charger which allowed me to run it off household electricity. I hooked the camera to it, flipped on the power button and put the dial setting to *Picture Review*. The last one taken comes up first. It was a very blurry shot of Warren Duchtin looking straight at the camera frozen in time as he had taken his first running step towards the stairs. Miss Blondielegs was in the background in perfect focus leaning forward towards the rapidly exiting Mr. Duchtin. Her mouth was open wide as were her eyes in a look of total shock. Her open robe displayed a full frontal view of her spectacular, nearly naked body. It showed her from the top of her peroxide hair all the way down to the tips of her extremely high heels. In this shot, she was distinctly, uniquely and unmistakably identifiable. Not so the blurred Warren Duchtin.

I pressed the button to go back one frame.

"Oh, baby! Money shot!" I yelled out so Bodie could hear.

In this picture you could see the semi-bared Miss Blondielegs just pulling away from kissing Duchtin with nothing on but a tiny, open front baby blue robe and the smile on her face. His left hand was just leaving her right boob. Mr. Duchtin was already in profile, turning toward the flash and clearly in focus.

In all there were eight photos. Six were awesome. The entire series should have won me a Pulitzer. Except I don't really know why Pulitzers are awarded, but I deserved some kind of award.

"Ah believe, Jerrah, that you surprised this charmin' young woman with your sneaky behavyuh tonight," said Bodie, as he attentively reviewed the explicit pics on the tiny screen of my camera.

"She do a little somethin' for you, Bodie?"

"Do not resort to workin' blue, Jerrah. It is unbecomin'."

Speaking of unbecoming, I'm using one of Bodie's dish towels to dry my wet head off a little. There is a puddle forming on my chair and beneath me at the kitchen table. This is the kind of scene that can only occur if no wife is present. It doesn't have to be my wife. I mean any wife.

I still have adrenaline running fast and hard all through me. Even I notice that my speech is way more fast paced than normal. "Bodie? We need to find out who this girl is. Once we have that info maybe Angela can leverage it into proving Duchtin killed Joanne. Let's talk tomorrow. I'll bet you could do more good on that than I could — getting info on her. Let me think about it. I can figure this out. We can find out who she is. That sleazy Warren Duchtin is toast."

There was a knock at Bodie's front door and we both jumped. Gert barked, but she always did if someone knocked on the door. It's about 10:30 p.m. Had Warren Duchtin found us?

"Papa?"

It was Marisa.

The door opened and in she came. "Papa? Like, are you alright?" Bodie and I had already stood and turned toward the knock. We were both certain we needed to be ready to defend ourselves from the invading Cossacks. My heart was beating right out of my chest. For a moment I could only hear my heartbeat and the sound of water dripping off me onto Bodie's worn carpet.

Bodie moved to hug his granddaughter. Relief filled the room. Even Gert stopped barking and started wagging at the sight of her. "Oh, Papa. I called and called for you tonight. I left, like, three messages, but I just couldn't go to sleep tonight without hearing from you. I knew you were with Jerry last night, but you forgot to tell me that you were, like, going again tonight. I was worried when you never called me back. I had to come and check. How are you? And Jerry!"

Uh oh.

She scolded me; "I'm going to have to have your cell phone number if you are going to like, keep him out so late and so often. I see from your sporty ensemble that, like, swimming laps while fully clothed was on tonight's agenda at some point." She grinned and Bodie laughed.

Hey, I don't like being in trouble at all, but especially with a pretty eighteen year old girl that I care for very much. She was empowered by my obvious and genuine remorse and continued, "As a matter of fact, I want your cell phone number regardless so hand it over."

"I'm okay too. Thanks for worrying," I said, feigning hurt at her lack of concern for me. She smiled a million dollar smile that could light up North Texas. Marisa is very pretty and really good and she loves her family more than life. We can hope that Lily turns out as well. Now, I'm interested to see what Bodie decides Marisa needs to know about tonight's activities.

"Sweet Marisa, Ah am fine. Jerrah and Gert are fine, too. Jerrah will get you his cell numbah and then you too will be fine. Thank you so much for worryin' about me but there is no need. We have been focused on yet anothah of Jerrah's most excellent adventures and yet we remain extremely safe and cautiously careful at all times. As a mattah of fact, Gert and ah sat in the car all evenin' and listened to the radio while Jerrah was off checkin' on his business in this monsoon. The weather was simply not conducive to mah active participation tonight, so Gert and ah were along for a very pleasant ride. How are you doin' darlin' and how is your fathuh doin'?"

Just as I suspected there were no details offered about what kind of ride it had become. I pondered how I would file my own report at home. 'Pleasant?' That's a word that I could maybe use later in a description of tonight's adventures. Lola's focus would not be on Bodie so I had better plot a decent presentation.

Marisa said, "It has been a tough week, Papa. Studies are hard because every professor believes their class is, like, the only one you have, so it's just so demanding. I went for a long run tonight before dinner and felt better until, like, I couldn't reach you." She shot me a fake angry scowl, enjoying this tease a little too much. Then she continued. "Dad is okay. He's just been working and we haven't, like, seen each other much lately. I hope you are cutting back on those nasty cigars. I want you to start taking your cane when you go with Jerry."

"Ah have recently greatly reduced mah interest in those nasty cigahs, darlin'."

Bodie flat out lied and Marisa knew it.

"And that cane is best used as a proper and effective discipline tool for mah most annoyin', noisy young neighbor child, for it is useless as a walkin' aid. But ah promise to be more diligent in the future. Ah love you with all mah heart."

Finally some truth emerged from his little speech.

Marisa didn't buy it even for a second. "See that you do be more diligent, Papa, and I love you too." She knows further admonishing is senseless so she turns to the weakest link in the room; "Jerry?"

I handed her my business card immediately. It had my home phone, cell phone, separate work phone numbers for tax consult or investigations, home address since that is where my office is located. It showed email and all other info about me except maybe my soccer coaching credentials. I would willingly disclose that on the card if there was any room left.

"Call me anytime, Marisa. You know that." I said this just to see her smile again and it paid off. She hugged me without reservation knowing full well that she would then be soaked. She kissed me on the cheek. I was pleased she wasn't really angry with either of us. Then she hugged Bodie, kissed him and held him a little longer than necessary. He glowed from her attention. A moment's pause to rub Gertie behind the ears, then she said, "I'm off to study. Quiz tomorrow. Love you both." As she pulled the door closed, the essence of an early springtime left the room.

Bodie, Gert and I were finally calmed down in his quiet little house thanks to Marisa's diversion of attention. Bodie filled his teapot with tap water. He set it on the gas range and turned a dial. The blue flame leapt up around the sides of the teapot. 'High' is the only setting any male knows about on any appliance. If it can't be cooked on high, it has no usefulness in a male's life.

"How about some tea, Jerrah?" asked Bodie. Lola had warned me that I hadn't been alert enough previously to Bodie's needs and I was proud to have remembered her advice for an entire day.

"Thanks Bodie. That sounds great."

I hate tea.

Bodie had more to say, "You know, Marisa is a great source of joy to me and since she is practically grown, hell, between her and Clayton, she *is* the adult—well—ah just am feelin' bad about viewin' her as anything else but an adult. Ah really should be able to tell her things such as our excitin' agenda this evenin'. But ah am quite confident she would disapprove of our speedy getaway. It would not be unreasonable for her to conclude that we might have been in some degree of danger at any given moment this evenin'. It occurs to me that between the two of us, she and ah, she may well be the adult of that twosome as well. Would you care to speak to that, Jerrah?"

"Sure, that makes all sorts of sense to me, Bodie. I was feeling bad myself just because I was in trouble with her tonight. There's no doubt that she's more grown up than I am. Lola says Lily is more grown up than I am," I replied.

"Jerrah, she's always been that way. You might remember when her mother, Victoria, was so sick. Marisa just took over the whole house. Marisa was only eleven years old. Clayton nevah *had* to take any responsibility because…"

I already knew of most of Bodie's criticisms of his son Clayton. Many times Bodie has stopped in mid sentence when his comment was about to involve Clayton. Like most parents, Bodie is uncomfortable saying bad things about his own son.

Bodie silently got up to fix us some tea and then he started speaking again as he put teabags in the mugs. The water was nowhere close to hot yet. "Ah have some letters for you to read. They were written by James—from Vietnam—in the weeks before his death in 1968. In the letters there are some references to his buddies as well as his superiors.

Puhhaps these names would be helpful in finding some of them. I am hopeful that some of them have survived to present day and might tell us somethin' of interest regardin' James. Puhhaps not. Do you feel they might be helpful?"

"We'll take a look, Bodie. Maybe so, I hope so. And I'll do my best to find out the story for you."

Maybe I'll never know why Bodie has become interested in exploring this subject. After talking with Lola last night, I realized what I do know. If it's important to Bodie, it is important to me.

"When you have read James's letters, we will need to visit further on the mattah as I have learned more over time than is reflected there. The things ah have learned will help us, without a doubt. Jerrah, ah intend to pay you your goin' rate for your efforts. Ah won't hear another thing about it," said Bodie. He reached into the drawer just left of the stove as the tea kettle began to whistle.

We both jumped briefly at the whistle. Neither of us had forgotten about Warren Duchtin.

He pulled out a bundle of five or six tattered envelopes. On top of the pile was a check dated today and made out to me in the amount of $1,500. It was labeled on the subject line with the words 'Advance—James Kohler case'. The envelopes to the letters were old and gently tied around with a yellow ribbon. It was Patsy's touch, without a doubt.

7. Star Spangled Eyes

The next morning, accompanied by coffee and Lola, I read all six letters. I knew I would read them all several more times.

I never knew James. Now I'm sorry not to have gotten to meet him. It hasn't escaped my notice that I am only a few years younger than James would be. We have to learn more. I hope there is more we can learn.

Three of the six letters were addressed to "Mr. and Mrs. Kohler" at their home, the same house where Bodie still lives. Those three were fairly generic letters home from war and generally upbeat. They were filled with thinly veiled statements meant to make everybody feel good about an obviously bad situation.

Dear Mom and Dad, Doing fine...hoping to take a little break for a day or two...making new friends...guys in my unit all get nicknames like Skeeter, Slackjaw, Pinch, RayJ, Navasota, Boomer...guys becoming close, like brothers...a little crazy...food not great, but we're all in it together...Making the best of a tough situation...doing an important job...all of us proud to be doing our duty...

All was phrasing you might expect or at least hope for if you were a parent. It was a more innocent time then and James' writing reflected that in these letters. Among the letters sent to both his parents, the roughest parts were not that bad.

We went two months on patrol without anybody even taking a shot at us. Nothing. Hard to be nervous after a couple of months of calm like this. It's about like being in Ft. Worth, except the rain is different. It's warmer water coming out of the sky. That and nobody speaks any English. Maybe a word or two. At night if we're on patrol, if you're not on guard duty you dig a hole. Put your poncho over it and catch some sleep. When you wake up, whether it's rained or not, you are in a hole full of water anyway just from the condensation off your poncho.

It can be unbelievably boring when nothing happens for weeks at a time. Then we'll have the most thrilling firefight with VC that you can imagine, usually at night. It's amazing, but you never see them. You might see muzzle flashes and that's what we shoot at. We hear them yelling in Vietnamese, but only at a distance and we have no idea what they are saying. That's scary because you just let your mind wander over all the possibilities.

Heart pounding stuff for a Mom or Dad, but mild compared to the three letters addressed only to Bodie at his West Texas Baptist University Post Office Box.

July 5, 1967
Dear Dad,
I'm okay, but it's been rough. Please don't show this to Mom. I need to tell you what is going on around me. Some of it is important, some just me venting. You'll be able to sort it out. Mom doesn't need this. You get it because you served during war. I know you can handle it. If you can, then I can.

The enemy is all round us. I don't mean we are surrounded, I mean they are all mixed in with the other Vietnamese so you don't know who the good guys are and who the bad guys are.

One day we were questioning a young pregnant woman. Says she is not VC. Says her husband is in the South Viet. army and is fighting for freedom. She watches our men walk away down a jungle trail and a booby trap goes off. Four GIs killed, three injured, all seriously. It was chaos. She ran. Maybe she knew about it and didn't tell us. Maybe she set it up. Maybe she was just scared. Enemies and friends look exactly the same, dress the same and act the

49

same. *They all blend into our surroundings. Everyone and everything is suspicious. Just when you start thinking you are stupid to be so nervous, something else blows up.*

We went through a village on a specific mission last month before the sun came up. Rousted everybody out of bed, kicked down doors, dragged them all out. Intel had it a VC stronghold. Some were in bunkers under huts, maybe to hide VC, maybe to protect themselves from the bombing and shelling from both sides. No way to know for sure. We had to view all those bunkers as VC hiding places.

We took enemy fire while we worked. It continued to intensify as the morning went on and we backed up to just outside the edge of the village. Ended up we fought for two days and two nights. Thirty caliber machine guns and mortars opened up on us after dark each night. They were like jackhammers and they went most of the night, off and on. We were all thinking when we first got there; it might be just another village. But we never know when this will be our reception.

No helicopters could come in to move out our wounded. Lots of our guys died that didn't have to. Then the rain came. Nothing to do but lay there and wait. Don't move. Can't move. We could hear our guys dying and crying but we can't do a thing. We will all hear those cries for the rest of our lives.

The fourth day at dawn, we reentered the village. The silence was strange. The enemy had evaporated. They were gone. Only ones left are old men and women of all ages. Children screaming and crying words that we knew meant they were not VC. Probably begging us to spare them. We burned every hut. Destroyed every bunker. I lost a lot of friends in those fields. The result was not good for anyone.

This week we had to go back to that same village. New intel. Got the exact same treatment. Within weeks the VC were back in the same place we had chased them out of. All fortifications were back. Just like we'd never been there at all. How about our guys who died taking that village the first time? What a waste. We blew the whole thing up again. All of us were thinking of the guys we lost before. We all fought with more purpose than before.

The jungle is a scary place. No sunlight reaches the ground in the jungle. It's always dark and always wet. Undergrowth is so thick we have to pull with bare hands just to get through. Some have machetes. Some just follow those who do have them. Bombs and shells hang from trees with trip wires just hoping we go by that way. Sometimes we see them first. Sometimes we don't. We don't know where to step or which one will be our last. Some of the important reasons why we are here doing this job are getting lost in the fear. Everybody just hopes to get to the end of another day so they can cross it off. The

number of days they have left to be here is everybody's focus. Been here 140
days. Have 225 left to go, then I get to come home.
    Cannot wait. Love, James

I am exactly Clayton's age. I was thirteen when these letters were
written. It was a little early for my awareness to be effective in
understanding what was going on in Vietnam. As I got older, I saw all
the Vietnam era movies—*Deer Hunter, Platoon, Coming Home, and Born
on the Fourth of July.* There was bleakness to the tone of those movies
that was clear, but foreign to me because I was never in Vietnam. These
letters captured that same bleak darkness of those movies. This was
painful.

Sept., 1967
Dear Dad,
    *Tough stuff here. I'm doing OK. Many of my buddies are gone now.
Bouncing Betties are the NVA & VC mines and booby traps. These bombs
leap up out of the earth just long enough for you to see them flying in front
of you. Then they explode shattering bodies and lives. I've seen at least a
dozen Betty explosions. All had casualties. Every loss was a friend. None have
gotten me yet. Some shrapnel burns. Close enough.*
    *If we get to a village & have intel on it being VC, we blow every bldg up.
Huts, bunkers, everything. We take all extra rice we see to keep it from getting
to VC. We herd peasants into a corral. They sit there all day crying and staring
at us like we are from some other planet. We take their food; destroy their
villages and way of life regardless of their loyalties because we are scared.
Scared of what we don't know. In any of these villages we don't know or
understand anything we see. If they hated us before, they hate us still. If they
backed us before, not any more. It's a no win deal. Enemy is all around.*
    *When we enter a village we are certain is VC, things are sometimes
different. Last week is a good example. Snipers fired on us first. Then more. We
set up defenses & advanced slowly. By dark, we had heavy casualties. They fired
on us all night. Mortars started an hour before dawn. Our guys are hurt and
yelling in the dark for help, but you can only hear them between shells falling.*
    *Daytime has suffocating heat that is unbelievably humid in the morning
and unbelievably dry by afternoon. So stifling you can't believe it. Texas heat
is nothing. Seems like it always rains—every night. Skeeter and Pinch died this
p.m. Couldn't medivac them out. Too hot—different kind of hot—enemy fire.*

Might've saved Skeeter with a chopper. Pinch, no way. Good men both. By near sunset, Sarge called in napalm and we pulled back. The whole jungle exploded in a fireball. The heat flash from hundreds of yards away was like nothing I can imagine to compare to. Nothing survived, even in bunkers. It numbs you to anything to see that. War's not as scary anymore though, so that's something anyway.

The longer I'm here, the more hesitant I get to make friends. All new guys don't hesitate at all. Then some of them die.

RayJ & me gotta go. Movin' out.

Much love, James

I passed each letter to Lola as I read them. She cried. I knew she would. Hell, I cried. Never having a son doesn't matter. You can feel the pain in these letters regardless.

"Where do you go from here," asked Lola, sniffling through the last of them.

"Bodie says he wants to talk to me after I'm done reading them. Says he has more info than shows here that he learned much later after James died. It could help lead us from here," I replied. "Depending on what Bodie has, I should probably go see if I can find any of these guys James talked about and see what they're willing to say."

James's last letter to only Bodie was dated the same day as his last letter sent to both his parents, but they were very different letters. The more significant was to Bodie only:

December 17, 1967

Dear Dad,

Pretty good week. Everyone's glad for Christmas to come, but sad to be spending it here so emotions are running pretty high in our unit. Supposed to get a new squad commander next month. Sgt. Murph is going home. He may think about it but he doesn't talk about it. Squad is pretty experienced by now. No deaths in several weeks, so all of us have patrols under our belts. Newbies are hard to take the longer I'm here. I guess I was this annoying to the old timers when I got here. Lots of the newbies are arriving scared. That's the hardest part to deal with. They seem to arrive expecting to get shot, knowing they've got to survive a whole year just to get back home. Makes their reactions not quite what we'd hope for in life and death situations.

Guess it was the same for you & newbies in Korea?

RayJ and I still together but we've lost lots of buddies. It's tough to take. Corporal Raymond Andrew Johnson is his real name. From Boston, Mass. He's a big brute of a black man. Says Boston isn't the best place to be a black man, but is a great place if you are a big man. Don't really know what that means, but I always laugh anyway, cause he does. He is a fine man, a good man and that is more important than being black or white. You and Mom taught me well. Not everyone here had parents like you. Lots of guys don't feel the same about blacks or about much of anything. I'll tell you this; I'd give my life for him. And I don't doubt he'd do the same.

You and Mom, Laura and Clayton have a great Christmas and we will try to do the same here. I miss you all and love you. Be thinking of you. Much love, James

After lunch, I went to see Bodie with the letters in hand.

When we started talking about James, it was immediately clear to me that Bodie had thought about all this a lot. I am amazed he had never said anything to me previously. I've known him twenty years. I would call our relationship close, or would have before this. We have talked about James before as well as Clayton and Laura. But how did this story never emerge before now?

I started, "These letters are not exactly *Archie and Jughead* comic books in intensity. My instincts are to chase after the guys he talked about and have a go at them for more info. You said that after I'd read the letters you'd talk to me about other information you have that might help. What do you think?"

"Jerrah," Bodie answered. "Ah believe in order for you to grasp this situation properly, you are goin' to have to know a bit of background to James's story. Some you may know and some you may not. Patsy and ah learned a good bit more about James's portion of the Vietnam war, but not until after he had died.

"As you now have realized from one of the letters, ah served with a multi force unit during the Korean conflict. It was toward the end of festivities over there, but those were still real bullets bein' used. It was a horrific time in mah life. Not much from this period of mah life has been shared with anyone, some with Patsy. Some with mah fellow soldiers as the years have gone by. That nearly covers it. James knew ah had served and that ah had been in Korea. That's about the sum of his knowledge of mah service. Once he was exposed to war himself, he and ah were brothers of sorts and he discovered that. He felt that. That and his lack of understandin' of how special his mother was led his letters directly to me. This was not a big error on his part. He was young."

"Does that mean you showed the letters to Patsy?" I asked.

"Yes. Ah showed them to her right after receivin' each. James was naturally protective of his mother. But she was as entitled as ah was to know what her son was endurin'. We cried togethuh over these letters many, many times. It is the only way it could have been. James nevah got to undahstand this because he was nevah a parent.

"Vietnam was a unique war, Jerrah, not only to my experience, but unique to history."

Bodie will be forever a teacher, I thought.

"Draftees into the service were committed for only one year, so for many drafted soldiers, survival became focus one, as you can see from James's letters. James was ideological about his service in Vietnam when he left home. He was every bit as ideological as ah had been a generation before. But World War II and Korea were different, a different time. Presidents Kennedy and Johnson encouraged Americans to join the crusade in Vietnam to halt the spread of global Communism. James felt like it was his generation's turn to do its duty, just as his fathuh had done before him. James was not alone. Many soldiers felt the same way, even the draftees. The U.S. had never been defeated in any war. These fellas felt like they were John Wayne or Audie Murphy, dashing G.I.s with no fear. They would save this third world country from the ravages of Communism, get their medals and come home and get the girl. Get all the girls because that is how the movies showed it bein' done.

"At that time the American public did not have the patience to ponduh the personal level of these decisions. How these boys decided to go and fight for their country was simply not part of the 'protest' scenario so popular at the time. Such a view would not further their cause. Instead, it made more marketable news to show people shoutin' insults to our returnin' servicemen. When our boys did come home, they often never presented themselves as former soldiers from fear of people's reactions. How our country got into Vietnam is worthy of study, of understandin'. Howevah, ah would prefer you catch up on such studies on your time when ah am not payin' the bill," laughed Bodie.

I laughed too, pleased that he could and would.

Bodie continued, "We now know that by the end of 1967 there were thousands of Communist soldiers amassed near the center of the country where the North was split from the South, for a surprise offensive against us and our allies. Hanoi had given its word that durin' Tet, the lunar New Year; it would observe a cease-fire. They asked us for the same, a truce of sorts and the U.S. had readily agreed, hopeful, but cautious. As we now know, this was a ruse. After makin' their promise of a cease-fire, the North Vietnamese proceeded to attack and invade over one hundred South Vietnamese cities during Tet. These were unprecedented attacks for them. This Tet offensive moved the war from the rice paddies and jungles of the country directly into the cities and towns. It was previously unthinkable and a complete surprise to the South Vietnamese and to the Americans.

"Despite the surprise, in many towns and cities the attacks were well defended. The fightin' was brutal on both sides. One important new development of that time was the broadcastin' of war footage on American television. For the first time the TV networks were sendin' their most important reporters to Vietnam for a first-hand look at developments. The war was in our livin' rooms, really for the first time. This in a country that was very tired of war and tired of losing its young sons.

"One of the first attacks of Tet, and one of the more significant attacks, was the invasion of the U.S. Embassy in Saigon, South Vietnam's capitol. We now know that many had been involved in the plannin' for this attack for many months. But fewer than twenty Vietcong commandos carried out execution of the plan on January 31, 1968. Enterin' the compound in a truck before dawn, within five minutes the V.C. had killed five G.I.s. Of particular significance was the television coverage that was broadcast here in the U.S. We were shown automatic weapons blazin', dead bodies, smoke from fires, dazed American soldiers and Vietnamese civilians. The television captured all the chaos and confusion in frightenin' detail. Millions of Americans saw the highlights of the attack right in their dens. It was quite groundbreakin'. As a parent, ah can tell you that the parents of every soldier stationed in Vietnam were glued to their televisions for any possible glimpse of familiarity, including Patsy and me. It was so very startlin' because it was real.

55

"There were many battlefields in the Tet offensive, as ah have told you. One was an inland town called Khe Sanh. Near the D.M.Z. between North and South Vietnam, Khe Sanh is toward the Laos border. It was a link to the Vietnam coast for the many villages along the Mekong River. There was a Special Forces encampment at Khe Sanh set up mostly to train locals to clean up some of the Communist sanctuary areas in Laos. The Americans believed this area would be a big battleground with the North in short order. Durin' the Tet offensive, much of that buildup of North Vietnamese troops was not far from Khe Sanh. This was on the news here and Patsy and ah always suspected James was in Khe Sanh, but we nevah knew for sure at that time.

"What we learned later was that at that exact moment there were thousands of North Vietnamese soldiers along with many artillery and armored units headed to Khe Sanh and that the American military knew this. General Westmoreland, the American commander, moved thousands more men into Khe Sanh right away. The thrust of the American defense though, was air power. In somethin' they called 'Operation Niagara,' the Americans deluged the North Vietnamese Army with fallin' bombs. At the same time, Westmoreland had his underlings studyin' when and how to best utilize tactical nuclear weapons. Years later, he said he would have used them without hesitation. Westmoreland believed it might have brought the North to their knees as it had the Japanese in W.W.II. We'll never know because when President Johnson found out it was bein' studied, he put the kibosh on the whole idea, afraid the press would find out.

"American B-52s smothered the North's Army with bombs around Khe Sanh. Interviewed after the war, North Vietnamese commanders told reporters that most units took enormous casualties from the bombin' and artillery. The battle of Khe Sanh lasted just over two months. These were agonizin' months for me and for Patsy because, despite havin' no evidence, we believed in our hearts that James was there. The U.S. bombin' stretched over all nine weeks. The pictures on the news were so very frightenin'. They say nearly 100,000 tons of bombs were dropped on them. One hundred thousand tons is simply an unimaginable number. The Communists lost over 10,000 lives. It is just as hard to imagine that number. Fewer than 500 U.S. Marines were killed in action over that same period throughout Vietnam. One of those Marines was Corporal James Patrick Kohler. They told us he was killed in the jungle by a sniper, but his friend, Raymond Johnson confirmed James died in the town of Hue' on the coast. It turns out James was not even in Khe Sanh."

Tears were on Bodie's cheeks. Mine too.

Bodie kept on, but ah do not know how, "Raymond Andrew Johnson, who James refers to often in his letters, is still alive. He is a thrivin', successful businessman in Boston, Massachusetts. He's in insurance or bonds and financial plannin' type of stuff. We met him in 1974. He was going back to college at that time. Before he started, he came to Ft. Worth to see Patsy and me. He is a lovely man and you should speak to him. While he seemed forthcomin' and made an effort to comfort us by giving us information regardin' James, ah will always suspect that he knows more than he was willin' to say. Raymond was wounded in Hue' and evacuated. That was his explanation for his reason for limited knowledge of James's death. We correspond with Christmas cards each year, at a minimum. Ah should have introduced him to you three years ago when he came here for Patsy's funeral, but he wasn't here long, just to pay respects and say hello. A project such as this was the farthest thing from mah feeble mind at the time."

"Bodie? Did you think I didn't notice the only 300 pound black man among a handful of black people and 200 white people at the funeral? I saw him, but had no idea who he was. I asked Laura, but she didn't know either."

"Yes," said Bodie. "Laura had left our nest by the time Raymond came to see us in 1974, so she would not have known him."

"So, Patsy knew everything you knew about James and Vietnam at her death. Bodie, you have no reason to feel guilty about not finding out more before she died," I said.

"Puhhaps not, but as you grow closer to the end of your life, Jerrah, you realize some things you might have done bettah. Ah could have done a bettah job on this when Patsy was alive. But there was such finality about James's death. The details seemed meaningless at the time. It is such a difficulty to live to see your child's death. Ah would not wish it on anyone. Ah might have done a bettah job eventually, if Patsy had lived longer. You nevah know, Jerrah, how long you have in this life. Ah need to do this now while ah have a little time. There's that and my suspicions that there is somethin' else involved here besides an enemy sniper in the jungle. Why did it turn out he died in Hue' when they told us it was by a sniper bullet in the jungle? Raymond dismissed it all as miscommunication at the time." Bodie paused for a moment and then said, "Maybe mah efforts might be bettah spent on mending my relationship with my only livin' son. Ah will give that some proper consideration."

"I'll leave that judgment to you, Bodie. I'm going to see if I can locate Raymond Andrew Johnson of Boston, Massachusetts. It's been thirty years since you and Raymond talked about James and he didn't want to tell you anything more. Maybe time has healed some of his wounds. Lola can help me if that's alright with you." I knew it would be fine.

"Certainly," replied Bodie, "Glad to have Miss Lola help us anytime. Now leave me be, Jerrah. The delightful Miss Marisa is due here this evenin' for dinnah and ah must prepare," which meant Bodie wanted to take a nap. "Adios, muchacho," said señor Bodie.

It was nearly 3:00 p.m. and I headed home charged-up for my mission to find RayJ.

8. Baby Needs New Shoes

"Jerry? Lily and I are going over to *Target* and to *Dillards*. She needs some shoes and I need some stuff for the kitchen. I'm only telling you because my car is up at *Grease Monkey* for an annual inspection so I'm taking your car. Mine should be ready by 6:00 p.m. Could you be my hero and walk down there and pick it up for me? I would be eternally grateful and your slave for life," said Lola.

"Yeah, like that deal hasn't already been struck years ago. Some offer!" I grabbed her and pulled her close. "Sounds like *I'm* already *your* slave. So how's that work again?" I tickled Lola's neck with my lips in just the right spot to elicit a giggle. Then I attacked her neck with a growl purely to make her laugh out loud.

"Would you two knock it off," Lily was just getting home from school and annoyed, as usual, but maybe fake annoyed this time. "Honestly, what kind of example are you setting for your impressionable young child with this repulsive behavior?" I released the lovely, smiling Lola with only one arm and grabbed the grinning Lily too, lifting her thin, young athletic body up in the air so her neck was at my mouth level for smothering neck kisses and she shrieked with glee. The girls both giggled with fake fear at my smothering attacks as I alternated necks.

I finally released them both, but reluctantly. "Ahhhhh, I am not yet satisfied and must have more neck sugar at a later time. Go and make multiple purchases, as is your purpose, m'ladies. I require one chocolate malt to-go from *Johnny's* in payment for the use of my trusty Taurus. Return soon or I shall send my knights after you and you will be imprisoned in the tower for impudence. And I love you both more than chocolate layer cake." They left laughing. My only goal was accomplished.

Left alone in the quiet of our house, in a couple of hours I had found on the Internet under *Certified Financial Planners*, a web site of some type of certification of such people. Business addresses and phone numbers for C.F.P.s all over the country were available. Sure enough, I located Raymond A. Johnson, C.F.P., and President of Keystone Partners in Boston, Massachusetts, and there was all the information I would need to reach him. By the time I had found Raymond's information it was already 5:40 p.m. in Ft. Worth, 6:40 in Boston. I'd have to try him in the morning. By now it was almost time to pick up Lola's car so I trudged off in the dark towards the Grease Monkey, a full ¾ of a mile away. I'd be lucky if my heart didn't burst from the exertion.

I wish I were capable of spending idle brain time thinking about the coming professional baseball season. Pitchers and catchers report to spring training next week. But right now it's too hard to push James Kohler from my mind to make room. If not thinking of James then I thought of that putz, Warren Duchtin. He needed some serious jail time soon. So a nice walk on a winter's evening turned into a giant hike of worry for me. If my attentions were not diverted from the focus of the moment, life could sometimes be one big ulcer-fest for me.

I picked up Lola's car and paid the ransom for it. They always seem to find something to fix on a car, any car, come inspection time. It never costs less than $100 to get your car back. Even on a car as new as Lola's. It was a two year old Volkswagen Jetta and this was the first inspection since the car left the showroom. I drove home frustrated by that, but I had quite a worldwide gripe list going by then. As I pulled up, I could see a Ft. Worth Police squad car was sitting out front of my house. Pulling in the driveway, I saw Angela and one of her young uniformed officers emerge. I could tell by the looks on their faces that they weren't bringing me a plate of brownies and an apology for the other morning. *What a dog pile of a week this has been,* I thought.

"Jerry, can we talk to you for a few minutes inside?" asked Angela.

"Sure, come on in. You know the way. I ought to just get you a key," I replied.

Everybody came in. Angela and the officer headed straight for the couch without me saying anything to them. They sat down, so I sat in the big brown upholstered chair facing them, and I broke the tension, "How about some coffee? I could use some. Feelin' sleepy from waking up so early lately…"

"Jerry. Right about dark tonight, about 5:15 to 5:30 p.m. our friend, Dr. Bodie Kohler, was physically attacked at his house. He is hospitalized in serious condition, not critical, just serious," started Angela shakily.

"Wait!" I stood up, not knowing what else to do. I didn't really know why I wanted her to wait. Mostly I wanted it to not be true. "It's only a few minutes before 7:00 now. Where is he?"

"He is in John Peter Smith Hospital in Intensive Care. He has a broken collarbone, broken pelvis and a concussion. He has lots of bruises and cuts, some more serious than others. They were looking for other broken bones right off. He's lost some blood. He's lost a lot of blood. Somebody messed him up with a purpose," Angela was emotional but she did not cry.

"Duchtin!" I yelled in anger, still standing.

Angela and the officer remained seated and still.

"Maybe," Angela was cold and firmer in her tone now that she had the worst news out in the open. "We're trying to find him now. We were worried we might find you in a similar situation, so we came straight here from Dr. Kohler's house. I just got off the phone with the hospital, so I'm confident of the latest information on Dr. Kohler. We got hold of his son, Clayton and daughter, Laura. They are both on their way to the hospital."

"Marisa?" I stammered.

"We assumed Marisa's dad would call her, but we can do it if you think we should," said Angela.

"I'll go to the hospital. If Clayton hasn't called her, I'll do it. Thanks. Get Duchtin. I know he's behind this. Did Bodie say anything?" I asked.

"No. Not yet. He, uh, wasn't able to talk."

Clearly, she hadn't wanted to tell me that part and I flushed red with anger as she continued, "We have officers at the hospital. Listen, Jerry. We don't know that this could have been a random burglary of his home. While it's logical you would suspect Duchtin, we have to be calculated about this," reasoned Angela.

"So, let me get this straight. You are extra-double unreasonable with the likes of my sorry ass at 4:00 a.m. yesterday, but oh so logical, cautious and calculated about that asshole's rights the same stinkin' week?"

I must have questioned with a little too much enthusiasm. The officer with Angela is not one of the guys from yesterday morning, so he looked like he had a big question mark over his head. He was big and defensive as he stood up at the tone of my question, but he didn't say anything. I had worked myself up now, "Screw calculated! How did you find him?"

"Next door neighbor kid was playing around out front of his own house and saw Bodie's front door was wide open with no sign of anybody. Even the kid thought it was a little unusual for quarter to six on a February evening. After a few minutes watching the door, the kid went in to investigate and found Bodie a bloody mess in the dining room under the table. Bodie was out cold. Kid thought he was dead," said Angela. She was calming back into detective mode now and she remained seated.

"Hah! That thirteen year old from next door? Bodie hates that kid! Says he's a 'noise machine'. Maybe he'll like him more now," I told Angela.

"He should. The kid called 911 and had us there in five minutes. If Bodie was as bad as they are telling me, the kid saved him. Really, the kid must have just missed the maker of this mess by a couple of minutes or so, but he didn't see anything that's going to help. We're checking other neighbors now," said Angela.

"Hard for me to believe Duchtin would do this himself. My guess is that he had it done, but you make his Mercedes outside of Bodie's and I'll...," I cut it off, remembering these were cops. "Duchtin must have seen us at his girlfriend's apartment complex. He could have gotten our names out of Joanne before he killed her I guess. Maybe he got our descriptions out of the guard at his girlfriend's complex. Who knows?

Bodie's white hair and goatee are really distinctive. But Duchtin did this. I just know it. I've got to get Lola and Lily on the phone. I'm going to the hospital," I finished while dialing Lola's cell phone.

"Where's Lola?" asked Angela, concerned about every little thing now.

"Target and Dillards. Lily needed shoes." I can't believe I remembered for three plus hours what Lola told me. Adrenaline must improve one's memory. I got phone mail on Lola's phone—"Lola, call me on my cell. I picked up your car and have to run an errand. It's a little after 7:00 p.m. now. Love you.'"

"Call me if you need me, Jerry, or if you find out something new on Bodie," said Angela as she and the officer headed across my lawn to their car. No reason to answer her. Now I'm pissed at Angela and the rest of the entire world except my own girls. I crawled in Lola's Jetta and headed to the hospital.

Clayton and Laura were standing in the Intensive Care Waiting Room when I walked up. The atmosphere was hand-wringing tense. I suppose that is always the tension level in this waiting room.

"The police filled me in. What's the latest on Bodie?" I asked.

"He's going to have to stabilize before they can do surgery to repair any internal damage," said Laura. "They are fearful that there is some internal bleeding besides the broken pelvis and collarbone. The concussion just complicates—things." Then the flood of tears came for Laura.

Clayton had turned away from me when I walked up, but he turned back and finished for Laura, "They just did some more tests. We can't see him at all until there is more stability in his condition. Not out of the woods by a long shot." I have always gotten along with Clayton better than his own daughter or sister, Laura. But there is a stiff distance between Clayton and everybody else in the world. That seems to be the way he prefers it.

"Laura, how's your family?" I asked quietly. I seldom saw Laura. She's married to Josh Teague, a construction contractor in Azle, a near-Ft. Worth suburb, and they have two kids, both boys and both in high school.

"Fine. Everybody's fine. Thanks, Jerry." Laura had been crying and it was clear she didn't know what to think about next. I hugged her tight.

"Have you called Marisa?" I asked Clayton.

"Well, interesting you should ask. She had cooked dinner for Dad at her dorm. She arrived at his house a few minutes ago to heat it up and eat with him. There are still crime scene officers at his house and they kept her there. She was nearly hysterical. I spoke with her just now. They are bringing her down here."

"Nuts, I should have tried to catch her. Bodie told me she was coming over tonight." I added this to my list of complaints against the world today. I stood with Bodie's two youngest children as nervous as either of them for what might be next.

Marisa joined us at about 8:00 p.m. brought by squad car. After hugs and tears we all sat silently. By 9:00 the doctor had finally come out to tell us there were no changes to Bodie. They still wanted to do surgery, but they didn't believe it was emergency surgery anymore. They felt they could afford to wait until Bodie was more stable, so I guess that's something. None of us were comforted in the least by it though. Laura sat down with Marisa and me when the doctor left. Clayton retreated to the far side of the waiting room, just somewhere other than with us or with anyone else.

"Marisa!" I jumped a little when I thought to ask, "Where's Gert? I completely forgot to ask anyone."

Laura answered for her, "That kid from next door who found Dad took Gertie. He said to be sure to tell Dr. Kohler that Gert will be fine at his house until Dad gets better."

"Oh, man," I said, "Bodie's got some apologizing to do to that kid for all the nasty thoughts he's had about him for the last couple of years." I sat back down and flipped through the only reading material around. It was a *Highlights* magazine, a magazine for kids. Ideally from the content, it must be for eight year old kids or younger. I was mesmerized until I realized I hadn't heard from Lola. I tore myself away from the children's word puzzle to feel my pockets for the cell phone. I immediately saw Detective Angela Delano walking down the hall toward us, looking like she was in dire need to make an immediate arrest for something.

"I see you have no storm trooper accompaniment, Angela," I remarked, no let up in attitude from me. "First time this week I believe. I hope your pals have Duchtin in custody somewhere with a big lock on the barred doors to a torture chamber."

Angela positioned herself into the open chair next to me while I smarted off, only half locating herself on the chair. Clayton stood across the room leaning against the wall, barely interested since he knew Angela wasn't a doctor. Marisa was seated on the other side of me leaning her head on my shoulder while I had flipped through the magazine. Laura was an end table's distance the other side of Marisa.

Both of them looked at Angela, but she didn't speak right away and she didn't really look at any of us.

Then Angela looked at me.

"Lola and Lily have been in a car accident," she said firmly.

My world fogged to a dull roar in my ears and my blurring view of Angela's pale, serious face.

9. Never in New Jersey

Angela and Marisa couldn't keep up with me as I ran from Intensive Care down to the Emergency Room at John Peter Smith Hospital. At the Emergency reception counter, there were four police officers and two paramedics just leaving the officers. As I ran up noisily, they all turned toward me, ready to defend themselves from an unexpected and unknown onslaught.

"Lola or Lily Wilson just brought in?" I shouted at the nurse.

"You can't go in. Let the doctors do their jobs, sir," said the nurse, as she started around the counter to stop me.

I came to a stop beside the desk before they all would have physically restrained me. I could see two sets of triage teams working in separate curtain drawn cubicles, side-by-side. There was no way to tell for sure if the patients were my wife and child. Medical people were in a full scramble around each of them. Then I saw Lily's running shoe sticking out of a cover sheet on one of the gurneys. All I could do was shout, "NO."

My knees collapsed.

I don't know what happened after that.

I woke up what I presume to be a short time later to see Marisa's weeping face. I was lying down and she was standing by me. Looking across my own curtained cubicle I could see the back of Detective Delano. She was talking on her cell phone.

"Lola's alright," said Marisa. "She broke her arm and is bruised, but they don't think her internal injuries are, like, all that bad. Jerry? Can you hear me?" She sobbed between every word.

I could understand her. I just didn't want to.

"Lily?" I asked weakly and very afraid to hear any answer. "Tell me."

"They are taking her to surgery now," said Marisa.

Lily was alive.

"They think it might be her spleen. It's bleeding inside."

Marisa had plenty to cry about. We all did.

Angela had moved out into reception and was talking to uniforms, from what I could see through my clouded eyes. I sat up on my gurney. Marisa hugged me and sobbed. I was numb.

Angela came in with a doctor and introduced him. I wouldn't know him again if he were standing right next to me. Very little was registering with my brain.

"Mr. Wilson? Your wife will be fine. I have reviewed x-rays. She will have to deal with the inconvenience of a broken left arm. She has some cuts where she put her arms up to protect herself in the rollover, but the worst will be the bruising and sore muscles. They will hurt for awhile. We will cast the arm and keep her here a day or two to be sure we caught everything. You can see her whenever you are able. She is still here in Emergency. We're getting her a room now but it will take a little while.

"Your daughter has been taken to surgery. Unfortunately, she will lose her spleen as it was ruptured in the crash. We are very confident her recovery will be complete. Additionally, her left ankle was broken. It doesn't look bad enough to require surgical attention. There are also some broken bones in her face around her right eye that we must repair. Both the general surgeon and the plastic surgeon will probably talk to you in the surgery waiting area after they have finished. Patient liaison will escort you shortly so you will know you are in the right place. Comfort-wise, again, the worst for your daughter will be the pain of bruising and overall soreness. She will be here longer than your wife. Maybe a week, but we believe she will be fine, Mr. Wilson. Let's get her through this surgery then we'll see. She looks young and in great shape. It will make a difference. Hang in there."

The doctor headed off to other emergencies.

That's all I got. Well, that's all I can remember.

Marisa had stopped sobbing out loud but sniffled about fifty beats per minute.

As soon as Angela started talking to me I became more alert. "They had left the shopping center. We have three witnesses. All stopped on the highway after the crash to help and none of them would leave your family. They all made sure to identify themselves to officers at the scene. Ft. Worth is a special place and we have amazing people here. Never in New Jersey would it end up this way. All of them saw the same blue van ram your car from behind on the Loop. No plates were ID'd. They may have had them covered or maybe took them off, but our guys are on it. We'll get them. The Taurus flipped several times, Jerry. The paramedics were crucial for Lily. She'll make it because of them and because of these doctors. Lola and Lily are really lucky."

As usual, I said exactly what I thought to Angela, "I don't feel lucky and they don't look lucky. I've got to see Lola." That is all I thought and all I was capable of thinking. I got down off the gurney. Marisa grabbed me around the waist, no small feat because she's not very big. We headed toward the cubicle where I had seen the doctors working earlier on Lola.

Lola looked like somebody had been beating her with a club.

She looked dead.

The left side of her face was swollen and bruised. Her bottom lip was cut and swollen. Her nose looked like she had been in a prizefight and lost. There was a cut on her forehead that stretched up and on into her hair. Across her shoulder and left collarbone I could see it was purple and yellow where the seatbelt strap had held her in place when the car flipped. The purple continued underneath her hospital gown where I couldn't see. I presumed it went all the way to her waist, but I was thinking the worst about everything about now. Her left arm was elevated on one side of the bed and was bandaged from the elbow down to the hand. It was wrapped in what looked like a splint and an elastic bandage. Her wedding ring diamond sparkled against the pillow and bandages. I was surprised they hadn't taken it off of her. The only parts of her left hand that could be seen were her fingers but they did not seem swollen.

Marisa let me go and I stepped up to touch Lola. There was a big bruise on her right bicep so I put my hand on her right forearm, hoping it wouldn't hurt her. She did not wake up, but I could tell she was breathing.

I was numb at the sight of her. Marisa found a folding chair and brought it to me. I sat next to Lola and watched her sleep—and breathe.

It was awhile before the patient liaison person found us. She made entirely too much noise coming in, but it didn't roust Lola.

"Mr. Wilson? Your daughter is in surgery. If you would like, you can follow me up to the Waiting Room. We will see the doctors as soon as they have finished. By that time, they will have your wife in a room. Perhaps she will be awake by then and you can speak with her."

"How long will Lily's surgery take?" I asked.

"We are not positive, but a minimum of three hours, mostly because of the work to the bones in her face. Her spleen will be first. It could take longer so please don't get upset if they are not out to see you in three hours," said the lady.

"I'll wait with Lola for a couple of hours, thanks," I said quietly to her.

"Alright. Let me explain where the Surgical Waiting room is located so you can get to the right place...."

I sat back down next to Lola. The lady kept talking. I have no idea what she said. I looked at my watch and it was 11:00 p.m. It felt like 4:00 a.m. again. I did remember that I needed to find that waiting room by 1:00 a.m., but that sure didn't seem logical. Nobody should have to find anything at 1:00 a.m.

Lola still had not moved. Marisa was there and that lady seemed to still be talking.

After awhile the blabbermouth lady finally left.

Marisa put her arm around me and we just watched Lola. Finally, Marisa leaned down and told me, "I'm going to go check on Papa. I will catch up to you in the surgical Waiting Room at like 1:00 a.m. Okay, Jerry?"

"Yeah, okay," was all I could muster and she left. It just seemed to me that every room in the hospital was a "waiting" room.

Sometime later, I do not know when, I opened my own eyes and looked over. Lola was smiling at me, well; it was sort-of a smile. It was the best she could do with that lip and those bruises.

"You look great in that gown," I said. "I think we'd better get you one in every color 'cause its doin' somethin' for me. I've just been sitting here fantasizing about the rear view." I smiled at those beautiful green eyes that were welling up with tears.

"Where's Lily?" Lola asked, only it sounded like '*Hair's Illy?*' I knew exactly how she felt.

"She's okay," I said overly dramatically. I was totally unconvincing. "She's in surgery. They have to remove her spleen, but said it would not limit her life in any way, and they have to repair some broken bones in her face. But there is a plastic surgeon there to take care of that. I've got to be up there by 1:00 a.m. Oh, that's only twenty minutes. They are getting you a room. Marisa will meet me up there. Lily will be fine. I just know it."

I was talking too fast, as usual. I thought I had risen to the occasion for a moment. But it didn't keep Lola from crying.

"The blue van hit us twice," said Lola. It sounded like she said, '*Da bue ban hit us tice.*' Her mouth wasn't working too well, but I got it. "Once from the back, then I tried to outrun them. I don't know why they did this to us. They caught up and hit us from Lily's side on the back. It fishtailed and I couldn't control it once they...."

'Fishtailed' sounded like '*hish-hailed*', which made me smile even through my tears.

Lola couldn't hold back her tears either. "They...we flipped over and over. The airbags came out. I don't remember anything else. Just loud sounds when we hit. I was scared. AP 25 something," she said through little sobs.

"What?" I said. It took a second, but I got that too.

Lola calmed a little, "AP 25 something. I only got part of the plate," said Lola, but it sounded more like '*AP 25 humthin. Uh onie goh taht uh da tlate.*' Her lip just wasn't on full power.

She cried harder. When I kissed her upper lip gently my own tears dripped on her.

"I'll call Angela," I said.

And I did. Whipped out the cell phone and came back to life in one motion. I was so angry that adrenaline was the best medicine I could have gotten. Somebody would pay for this with their own blood and sooner than they think.

"Hello, Angela? It's Jerry. Lola woke up."

"How is she? How's Lily?" asked Angela and I instantly knew her interest was not surface. She felt this and it hurt her too.

"Lola's hanging in. Lily's in surgery. Listen, Lola got a partial plate on the blue van—AP two five, in that order. Hang on. Lola? Was it a Texas plate?"

Lola nodded with her head still down on the pillow and winced at the same time. She looked like everything hurt.

"It is a Texas plate. She didn't get any other numbers or letters," I said to the phone. "Angela? Get these guys or I will."

"Yeah, we're on 'em, Jerry." Angela hung up.

I believed her, but I know she believed me as well.

Medical people were in the curtained cubicle with us as I hung up. They were here to take Lola to her room. "Go check on Lily, please Jerry. I'll be fine. Come tell me as soon as you know something," said Lola.

"I will. I'll be in surgical Waiting, but they said it could be 2:00 a. m. or later before anyone would come out. They said not to worry if no one came out by then. It could easily take longer."

I kissed Lola's upper lip again. They wheeled her out as she cried quietly. She was scared. I knew that because I was scared too, for Lily and for us. Then I remembered I had forgotten to tell Lola about Bodie. She had no idea. I also realized that I had no idea where to go. I headed to the nurse's station to ask where Surgery Waiting was located so I could go wait somewhere else.

It was 1:15 a.m. Marisa was already there when I walked in.

"Good," she said. "I was afraid, like, they had come out and you had already left," said Marisa. What's happening with Lola?"

"She woke up. She's upset, but okay. They are taking her to a room now. She got a partial plate on the blue van. Angela is running it now. How's Bodie?" I asked.

"Same. Laura is there, waiting. Like, have you seen Dad? Laura said she thinks he left and he doesn't seem to have his cell phone on," said Marisa.

"No, but I'm not very aware of Clayton right now. He could be lurking nearby and I wouldn't notice," I replied. Marisa knew I didn't mean anything by that. That's just the way her dad is all the time. "No sign of any of Lily's doctors?" I asked.

"Not since I got here at 1:00 a.m.," said Marisa. "I'll wait with you. Laura will call me if she needs me."

We sat to wait. I spotted another *Highlights* magazine on one of the side tables and headed for the word puzzle page, but I was thinking cuss words, a whole string of them.

It was 3:10 a.m. before a nurse came out and said Lily was fine. Surgery went well and the doctor was on his way out. It seemed that another hour went by before we saw him. But I checked. It was seven minutes.

"Lily is doing great," the doctor told us. "Her spleen surgery went well and she tolerated the procedure flawlessly. We were lucky to be able to take the spleen out by laparoscopy, meaning a couple of very small incisions instead of one big one. It will mean a much shorter recovery time for Lily. There was no damage to the pancreas or the stomach or anything else that we could determine. We will watch her closely. She was very stable as the others finished her spleen and I started on the bones around her right eye. The orbital socket was broken, but not shattered. The operation went really well. She will hurt for awhile, but we will try to control the pain with a morphine drip. It is self administered by Lily with a little button, but it is impossible for her to give herself too much. We have found when patients have some pain control of their own, they do much better, even if the actual control they have is relatively negligible. Her ankle did not require surgical repair. It has already been put in a cast. It will be five or six weeks for that cast. At her age, the bones heal fast. It will inhibit the speed of the rest of her recovery for her not to walk around, so we made it a lightweight fiberglass cast so she can at least hobble around and use other muscles. She should sit up tomorrow, even if she doesn't feel good enough for it. There is a drainage tube inserted into her nose which helps drain the stomach area. If she is doing well it will come out tomorrow. The tubes draining the incision might also come out tomorrow. Once her pain is under control we can take out the IV. Next day, we will help her walk to the bathroom. Day three she starts laps to the nurse's station. Add one lap a day for three days. Then it's off to physical therapy daily. It will be hard but it's the best chance she has to return to her regular life as it was before. Without a spleen she might be more susceptible to infection than before, so you and your wife will need to be sensitive to that. Vaccinations and antibiotic treatments vary from patient to patient, but can last up to a year post-op. There is no reason she can't do everything she could do before. After she's out of recovery, we will put her in the same room as her mother, unless you think they should be in separate rooms, Mr. Wilson."

"Nope. They wouldn't hear of that. Her mother wants her nearby now," I said.

"I'll check in on her tomorrow. The nurses are in constant contact with me, so I am nearby even when it doesn't seem so. Check with the nurses if you have questions or problems. Otherwise I will see you tomorrow." Just like that, the doctor left. Four hours of surgery and I get a forty-second update.

"Jerry?" Marisa asked gently.

I sat there stupefied. More than usual, I mean.

"I'm so glad it went well," she said. "It sounds like they will be fine. I'm going back to be with Laura and check on Papa unless you like, need me here for anything."

"Okay. As soon as Lily is in the room with Lola, I'll be over with you. Thanks, Marisa for being here through this. What a night," I said. "What a night."

An hour later, Lily and Lola were sleeping in the same room. There was a uniformed officer down the hall at the nurse's station. It was a nice touch by Angela. We still don't have these guys or know why they attacked my family. I've got a pretty good idea, but we have to be able to prove it. Duchtin hasn't been found yet. I glanced once more at my sleeping girls and then at the officer outside. I gave him a nod of recognition. He did the same to me. It was one of the officers who had been at my house the other morning with Angela and I spoke to him, "I guess you and I are going to be up by 4:00 every morning for awhile." He just smiled.

I headed back to Intensive Care to check on Bodie.

Laura was lying down across three chairs in the waiting room, her eyes closed. Marisa was up and looking out the window. When I saw her, I was envious of her, remembering how easy it had been when I was in college to stay up long hours. Well, not easy, but easy compared to now. I was drag-ass exhausted now. "How's Bodie?" I asked Marisa.

"He is the same. They think they will do surgery at 6:00 a.m. if he is stable but he is not right now. It is exploratory surgery because they aren't sure of internal bleeding. His blood pressure is all over the place. I can't reach Dad. Jerry, I'm, like, worried about him. I know he's weird, but he should be here," said Marisa.

"He's probably napping in a comfortable chair somewhere between here and the hospital cafeteria. Let me rest here for a bit with you. If he hasn't turned up by 6:00, I'll search the hospital for him. We'll find him, Marisa." I hugged her, kissed her head and sat down nearby.

Marisa continued to study the horizon out the window. I fell asleep leaning back in the waiting room chair in about eleven seconds. That's not even my personal best.

10. Brain Swell

It was 8:45 a.m. when I was awakened by my awareness of an increase in human activity in the waiting room. I had a sense of being late for something. I was uncomfortable.

Had I really slept for several hours in this position? Sure felt like it. From a sideways view, being semi-prone on the chairs, I could see Marisa and Laura talking to two doctors. I painfully propped myself up. I tried to shake out the cobwebs while taking stock of exactly where I was and what was happening. I stood to join the conversation as a listener while trying to remember. The tone was grim.

"So, we will just have to wait and see how he does. Okay?" said one of the doctors and they both turned heel and left. Marisa was crying. She turned and walked out too.

"Laura? What happened?" I asked.

"Dad's brain is swollen from the beating."

There was little to no emotion in Laura's voice. She was worn.

"Surgery is off for now. Now they think if there was some internal bleeding, it is way down now. They are formulating a plan, but they have to relieve the pressure or there could be brain damage. There may be brain damage anyway. They just don't know yet. After that news, there is an enormous list of things that are wrong with him. He has to stay in Intensive Care. They are discussing keeping him in an artificially induced coma in hopes that his body will heal some. It's so unfair. It just seems so hopeless."

Laura and I sat down together and just let it be silent around us. With nothing to do or to say it really did seem hopeless.

Finally I told Laura, "I promised Marisa I would go look around the hospital for Clayton, so if she comes back tell her that's where I am. I'll keep my cell phone turned on." I felt like I had taken a whipping as well. Sleeping in a chair is not a good plan at my age.

I handed Laura one of my business cards, "Call me on my cell if you need me, Laura. I'm around here somewhere." She just nodded. She was just really beaten down.

I looked all over that hospital and never found Clayton. I found Marisa outside in the cold sitting in a courtyard crying quietly. There was no comforting her. I just sat next to her and held her. The cold air felt good and made me more awake. She finally calmed down a little. We went back up to sit with Laura. I stayed with them for awhile, but started worrying about Lily and had to go back to my girls.

They were both still sleeping. I just sat and watched, so thankful that they were alive and I could see them and smell them and hug them. Finally I slept too.

I woke up still sitting, well, kind of sitting, in the chair in Lola and Lily's room. I sat straight up with no idea where I was or what I was doing there.

"Dad?" said Lily.

And there she was sitting up. It was more like leaning up in her bed looking pale and thin, and alive. There was Lola who really was sitting up in the other bed. They were both smiling at me. Both were bruised more than I thought they should be. From her forehead down to just below her upper lip, Lily had on what looked like a white hockey goalie mask. It was bizarre. I still didn't know where we all were.

"When you sat straight up you looked just like *Odie* the dog in the *Garfield* cartoons," said my daughter. Both girls giggled like this was hysterical. I smiled but had no idea why they were talking about me or where we were.

"What time is it?" I asked no one in particular.

"6:22 p.m. It's evening, Jerry," said Lola, but it sounded like *'six-tenny-too, it's edening, Harry'*. This added to my confusion.

"Really? What day is it?" I asked.

Both girls giggled some more. Lily pointed at my hair and said something funny about it.

I went over to Lily and hugged her way more gently than I really wanted to.

"How are you, baby?" I asked.

"I feel pretty good, Dad. This afternoon, I walked to the bathroom with help and they took out the catheter and that stupid nose tube. It was the worst!" she said.

I could tell her energy level was pretty low, but that smile did wonders for me.

"How did I miss that?" I said looking at Lola. "They told me that wouldn't happen for another day. Did I sleep that long?" Lola gently shook her head 'no'.

"You were zonked, Dad," said Lily, "and we didn't want to wake you. The doctor said if I got myself to the bathroom they'd take the catheter and that awful tube out. It felt like a big hose was stuffed down my nose into my throat. I wanted it away from me sooo bad, so I did what they said I had to do to get it away from me. And you snore."

She smiled bigger as we always play this game of 'you snore, no, you snore, no, you snore.' I usually finish this with a giant tickle, but I just touched her head today, carefully, and smiled big. "Come here my little hockey goalie," I said as I smoothed her head gently again.

"I need to tell you guys about something that you missed while you were playing demolition derby," I said.

I had dreamed about Bodie and knew that both the girls needed to know what was going on. Bodie and his family are fresh examples to me of how lack of communication can cause lasting damage, even to those you are closest to. Lola and I have always erred on the side of giving Lily too much information rather than too little. We have never viewed her age as an obstacle to talking about stuff in front of her. Watching Clayton and Laura just reaffirmed that Lola and I were on the right track for us. Everybody has to choose how to handle tough situations in their own family. We usually choose to talk about it with all three of us.

I told both of them the story about Bodie getting beaten up in his home right before they were attacked in the car. I told them about the case with Duchtin and my suspicions of him. I left out the goriest details of the beating and of Joanne's murder and of Duchtin's obvious sexual escapades, but it was overall pretty uncensored. Lola already knew most of it. Lily's eyes got really big and teary. It's hard for her to understand how all this could happen. I think Lily has seen one "R" rated movie in her life, so there are some obstacles to full information at twelve years old. No "R" movies but you are living an "R" rated life. Life should be rated "NC-17."

Then I told them about the police officer out front for their protection. Instead of making them feel good and safe, they became fearful before my eyes. Maybe I'm not so smart after all. Lola noticed my reaction to their fear immediately and turned it around quickly. She said she and Lily would talk some more about the whole deal and I should go home and get some rest. She ordered it. I complied. She is the best.

Once home, I walked around my empty little house carrying a heavy load of sadness. My brain knows they are okay, but I longed for Lily to be home playing on her computer. She likes to play songs from her roughly three-zillion song MP3 collection. The music police will have me in prison soon over her downloading habits. If you try to listen to music with Lily, you have to accept that you get to listen to approximately twenty to forty seconds of each song. Then it is quickly on to the next one while issuing an extremely opinionated review of the musical ability and lyrical content of each song. I am pretty sure she and her pals have never listened to an entire song, much less an entire album. My defense in court will be that she never listened to an entire stolen song, so please cut my sentence to cover thirty seconds of each one. I'd still be in prison for a hundred years.

I really missed that she wasn't there.

I was up by 4:00 the next morning because I had slept the entire day before in the chair at the hospital. I spent all day at the hospital going between Intensive Care waiting and my girls' room. Lily is already anxious to get out of there and get going, but she's nowhere near ready. Lola is really happy because she has Lily captive in one room where she knows they are safe and Lily cannot leave her sight. That's perfect for the rest of our lives as far as Lola is concerned.

There had been little change to Bodie. Laura was back in the morning. Marisa spent part of last night at the dorm. I don't think she has even considered going to classes. She looks entrenched in the waiting room. There's been no sign of Clayton. Marisa is hacked-off at him for not being there. Laura could not care less.

I left three messages for Angela. I never heard back from her. It is frustrating, but if she had something she'd probably let me know.

After confirming that Lily and Lola were going to sleep for the night, I said hey to the police officer on duty out front. It's a new guy. Then I went back to check on Bodie. Marisa was in the Intensive Care waiting room where I had left her. She was asleep across some chairs. The nurse told me there was no change to Bodie. Another nurse had told her that Laura had gone home at lunchtime. Hey, she's got boys to take care of. The nurse had not seen Clayton, but she had just come on duty at 6:00 p.m. I didn't want to wake Marisa, so I wrote her a note and headed home for sleep of my own.

I knew I wouldn't sleep well and would be back before the sun was up.

I was right.

The next morning after seeing Lola and Lily, who both looked tired, I went to Intensive Care. Marisa looked angry. Not sad, like she had for a couple of days.

"What's up?" I asked her.

"My dad is filing an application to a court of, like, law to have Papa declared incompetent. He wants to exercise some 'Power of Attorney' on Papa's behalf, like, in order to manage all Papa's financial affairs." Marisa practically spit at me while she told me. She was really angry.

"A little early in the game for that, isn't it?" I asked.

"I'm at a loss. Like, what is he doing?" asked Marisa. "There's still a good chance Papa will come out of this. But Dad sure seems anxious to get busy like, writing some checks with Papa's money. It is disgusting! I finally spoke with him on the phone. He hasn't been here, like, at all to check on Papa. Not even once since that first night. He just says he's been busy trying to take care of stuff. He was calling from his attorney's office and was all assuring me that all this didn't really, like, mean anything. I've met Dad's attorney, Ned Pearl. What a sleaze ball. Dad said he was just, like, making sure that the medical bills get paid on time. It just doesn't feel right at all. It would make Papa so sad to see this. Dad even said he might have to, like, put Papa in an assisted living home. Why is he even thinking that right now?"

"Now wait. This is like, day three since Bodie was attacked," I said. Now she had me saying *like*.

"You want me to call my friend, Harry Zinn?" I asked. "He's an estate attorney. I've known him forever. He might even have done Bodie's will, I'm not sure. I told Bodie about him clear back when Patsy died. Maybe there's a way to put Clayton off for awhile until we see how Bodie responds to treatment. Sure seems early in the deal for anybody to be taking over all his affairs."

"Would you please call him?" asked Marisa. "I just want Dad to hang on for a minute to see what happens. This is just so not right."

Cell phones are awesome. Harry is in my autodial phone book and I called him right then. Turns out Harry re-did Bodie's will three years ago and he would help us. He said he already had something that would help.

I checked with Lola. They are doing okay for now so Marisa and I went straight down to Harry's office to see him.

"Look, Dad gets money from Papa already and has for a long time," said Marisa. "I've seen them argue about it sometimes. Dad's like, *'If it were James, you'd give him the money.'* And Papa is all like, *'James would nevah take it from me even if I offered.'* So I know this has been going on for a long time. Papa even caught Dad taking money from him one time at his house about a year ago. It wasn't pretty. They both were yelling, like, pretty bad."

I love Marisa's imitation of her grandfather. But this was all news to me. I hadn't heard anything about this from Bodie. I had offered to Marisa that I would wait outside, but she said she wanted me to sit in. I'm still not sure I should hear all this. Harry just sat there listening and he sometimes nodded.

Marisa continued, "Dad doesn't make much money and I don't know if he just feels entitled to Papa's money for some reason, but he's had designs on it, like, forever. He spent some time last year trying to get Papa to sign his house over to him outside the will so Dad could have the house and Laura wouldn't be involved. Dad said, *'Laura has a house.'* I don't think Laura knows about that. Papa told him to get lost and get lost real hard. Papa told Dad he was, like, *'a liar and a cheat'*. I was there. It was bad. They haven't spoken much this year. They both pretend everything is okay, but it is so not okay."

Finally, Harry waded in, "Clayton has a *General Power of Attorney* appointing him attorney-in-fact for Bodie. It is an encompassing power and unfortunately, it is very broad in coverage. Bodie had me prepare it as part of re-doing his Last Will after Patsy died. It is certainly revocable by Bodie but it doesn't sound like he's in any condition to do that. The first thing I'm going to do is prepare a written revocation of Clayton's P.O.A. for Bodie to sign. If he comes out of it soon, if we can communicate with him and if he has understanding and desire, he can revoke the P.O.A. Listen, both of you. We also have to prepare for the possibility that Bodie does not recover."

Both Harry and I gave a checking glance to Marisa, but she seemed all business.

Harry went on, "It is clear from our discussion that you do not know this next part, Marisa. On your eighteenth birthday last year, you automatically were empowered with a 'Medical Durable Power of Attorney' signed by Bodie three years ago when we did Clayton's General Power. It is somewhat compelling that Bodie wanted you to have that power when you were fifteen years old. The law won't allow that. So we made it effective on your eighteenth birthday. You already have the power to manage Bodie's specific medical needs if he is incapacitated, by his written request. This exact situation puts your position superior to that of your father regarding any decisions that must be made on Bodie's behalf. I have the original instrument here. I am confident that Bodie simply forgot to tell you about it on your birthday. I believe three years ago Bodie made a joke about Clayton *'being too excited to pull the plug if he were in that situation, but Marisa never would, so let's sign up Marisa for that job'*. I guess he was more serious than I thought."

Marisa said, "But wait. What about Laura? Why didn't Papa make the Medical Power of Attorney with Laura?"

Harry answered, "Bodie talked about that, but said Laura has her family to focus on and that he would talk to Laura about it. He thought it would be fine with her. I remember he said that Laura was a lot like Patsy and it wouldn't ruffle her feathers at all. I only presume that he did that. We didn't talk about it again. For right now, Clayton could not put Bodie into any home without Marisa's permission as medical attorney-in-fact. Clayton can't even take Bodie to the doctor without your approval. I am confident Bodie never told Clayton this either or Clayton would not be pursuing his current course of action. If Bodie is declared incompetent, Marisa is in charge, not Clayton, because of the medical situation. But there could be other serious ramifications if Bodie were declared incompetent. I will get you a copy to present to the hospital when you leave here today. Let me think about whether to spring that on Ned and Clayton or not."

Harry was rolling now, "We also need to prepare a 'Durable Power of Attorney for Securities and Savings Bonds Transactions' since most of Bodie's assets are in three accounts; one at First National Bank, one at Treasury Direct and one at Fidelity Investments, if he hasn't changed any of them. This will allow Marisa to renew maturing bonds within those accounts but not make withdrawals. We need to make sure Clayton is not on any joint accounts with Bodie or it sounds like there is a possibility that money might disappear quickly."

I was dizzy from Harry's summary of the situation and I'm a C.P.A., but Harry had more for Marisa, "We should petition the Court for appointment of a limited conservator for your grandfather for his protection. Maybe a neutral, professional fiduciary to serve in such capacity would be acceptable to you. If Clayton's intent were really to get the medical bills paid, this would be a way to ensure that happens while your grandfather is incapacitated. If Clayton is interested in Bodie's money for his own purposes, Clayton will fight this. You may not like Ned Pearl, but he is a good attorney and a formidable opponent. Any course we take will be some trouble. There is no guarantee we will win unless we get Bodie's help. But I think we will slow Clayton down, regardless. Maybe we'll slow him down long enough for Bodie to recover. "

Marisa did not hesitate for a second, "Cool. Let's do it. We have to do it. What Dad is doing is wrong. Saying it out loud here with you really makes that clear."

She is something. She was ready to sue her own dad because she believes in her heart that he is wrong.

"I will email Bodie's doctors and send you a copy, Marisa, via email," said Harry. "We will need their evaluations for our application for conservatorship.

"Marisa? There are two more things. If it goes to litigation, we will have to get another attorney to represent you. The Court will find that I have a conflict of interest since I also represent Bodie. I will help you with this and it will work out because we will all sit on the same side in court. Secondly, all this will cost some money. I'm guessing $15,000 up to trial. It will be another $25,000 to go to trial if your dad fights you."

Oh, man. Game over. I made a face knowing we had just lost the big tournament.

"Okay," said Marisa.

Somebody scrape me up off the floor.

"Uh, Marisa? Did you say that was okay?" I asked her innocently.

"Well, yeah. I did. I have a little money, Jerry. It's from Mom's life insurance policy. That's the only way I get to go to college. That and the discount I get on tuition at W.T.B because Papa is, like, my grandfather and he works there. I'll quit school and spend it all if I have to. I don't want to and I am certain Papa wouldn't want that, but I asked myself if Papa would do this for me if our spots were like, switched. Didn't take me long to figure that out. What do you think he would do, Jerry?"

She looked at me for a few seconds and with my expression I gave her nothing but, like, my best poker face.

"That's what I think too," said Marisa.

11. The Power of an Attorney

From: Harry Zinn
To: Dr. John Monroe, Dr. S. A. Malwhi
cc: Ms. Marisa Kohler
Subject: Bodie Kohler
Drs. Monroe & Malwhi:

I represent Ms. Marisa Kohler in her role as agent under her Medical Durable Power of Attorney, signed by Dr. Bodie Kohler, a patient currently in your care. We have previously notified you and requested a report/letter on Dr. Kohler. This message will summarize for you the applicable statutes and hopefully help you to understand a little about the Court's needs for your report.

It is clear that the controlling focus of the applicable statutes is on the functionality of the person. Does the person's cognitive or physical condition, or both, compromise his or her capability to function safely and independently in respect to communications or decisions necessary for activities of daily living and self-care? For specific example, the health condition of a person might render them incapable of making medical decisions or balancing a checkbook. Their health condition might render them unsafe or incapable of attempting to bathe alone or go to the bathroom or cook soup on the stove. Diagnosis of a brain injury or a stroke-related dementia *would not necessarily be enough to order a guardianship. If their condition compromises the person's functionality for personal care, then some extent of guardianship might well be appropriate—a guardianship having to do with personal financial and business affairs.*

My suggestion is that a physician writing a report/letter response should bear in mind the considerations I've just described to you in order for the report/letter to be most informative to any court to which it might be submitted.

With respect to Marisa's concerns for the welfare of Dr. Kohler, our efforts will be pointed toward asking the Ft. Worth Probate Court to order a very limited, narrowly tailored conservatorship and/or guardianship designed to protect Dr. Kohler against financial exploitation and against him being placed at undue physical risk. For instance, risk of being coerced because of general frailty. Your familiarity with Dr. Kohler as his physicians will be highly informative in regard to the propriety of any protection.

Specifically regarding the authorization for the release of medical information, Marisa hereby authorizes such a report/letter pursuant to her medical P.O.A. A copy of the P.O.A. has been previously furnished to you. I hope this information is helpful in your preparation of the report/letter being requested. Thank you for your professional consideration.

Harry Zinn

"Wow. Way cool," said Marisa and she handed me a printed copy of the e-mail letter from Harry Zinn to Bodie's doctors. We were back in the Intensive Care waiting area.

"Guess what else, Jerry. Dad tried to go to Papa's bank and cash one of Papa's checks. He brought his written Power of Attorney and the check and said the medical bills had to be paid so they should like cash the check for him. Mr. Zinn had already called the bank and then written them a letter to like, put them on notice that Dad might try to pull something like that. The bank sent Dad packing. They told Mr. Zinn that Dad was like, so extra pissed when they wouldn't cash the check for him. He told them that they'd be hearing from his attorney, Ned Pearl."

"Have you seen Clayton?" I asked Marisa.

"No. He still hasn't been back to the hospital that Laura and I know of," said Marisa. "Oh, I talked to Laura about that Medical Power of Attorney. She did know about it because Papa talked to her, but that was so long ago that Laura had forgotten. It was several years ago just like Harry Zinn said. She told me that she was comfortable as long as Papa and I were comfortable. I asked her for her help with all this. She said she will be here to help no matter what." Marisa was clearly pleased to have Laura as an ally.

Bodie was still in a coma and the doctors thought that was a good thing. The other good thing was that they think the brain swelling had lessened. Just that little hope had renewed Marisa and Laura. With their spirits lifted, Laura started telling a few Clayton stories of her own that Marisa didn't know about. Laura had just started one about Clayton having taken checks that Bodie received in the mail down to the bank to get "cashed for Dad" and then keep the money for himself. My cell phone rang. The caller ID says Ft. Worth Police Department.

"Hello, this is Jerry."

"Jerry, this is Angela Delano. We found Warren Duchtin's Mercedes at D.F.W. Airport in a long-term parking lot. Then we found Duchtin. He's in Denver. He's been there since before the attack on Bodie. He had his attorney call us. We had left messages at his office. He claims he's been visiting Joanne's parents who are both in a nursing home in Denver. Says they have been planning Joanne's funeral. He should be in to talk to us tomorrow. That's all I've got. Thought you'd want to know."

"What about the blue van?" I asked.

"Still checking all blue vans in D.F.W. with AP25 on the plate. There are eight. We've found three that are definitely not the one we want," Angela was giving nothing more.

"Thanks," I said and we both hung up. I went back over to tell Marisa and Laura the latest, such as it was. As we were talking about the blue van, in came Clayton headed straight for Marisa. Steam was practically coming out of his ears.

I stepped toward him as he was coming in towards Marisa a little fast for my taste. He stopped short of me when I put both my hands up, but he never took his angry eyes off his daughter, Marisa.

"What the hell do you think you are doing?" he yelled at her.

Marisa recoiled, wide-eyed at his display of anger. "What are you talking about, Dad? And what the hell do you think *you* are doing?" she dished out a little anger of her own towards him.

Clayton said, "We got this email letter from your attorney today, as if you need an attorney. Of all the gall! This is none of your affair! If you think you can get an attorney for my dad, you better think again. I will take care of Zinn. He's as good as fired. I have Power of Attorney. You need to keep your snotty little nose out of where it doesn't belong," said Clayton, even more worked up.

He threw the paper past me at his daughter. Marisa picked it up off the floor and started reading it out loud for Laura, another family in the waiting room and me. I decided it was a good idea to stay positioned between Clayton and Marisa for this little public display.

Dear Mr. Pearl:

We hereby notify you and your client, Mr. Clayton Kohler of our application for conservatorship for Dr. Bodie Kohler in the Ft. Worth Probate Court. Pursuant to the authority granted to Ms. Marisa Kohler in the Durable Medical Power of Attorney to be sent to you under separate cover, my client has requested a report/letter from Dr. Kohler's attending physicians to be submitted to the Court.

Considering recent events in which Clayton Kohler has attempted to coerce Dr. Bodie Kohler through both physical and emotional abuse, I fully anticipate my client will authorize me to proceed with filing the protective order petition currently being drafted.

Upon receipt of the Medical P.O.A., you will note paragraph 3.C. authorizes the agent (my client) to "establish a new residence or domicile for Dr. Kohler...for the purpose of exercising effectively the powers granted to my agent in this document...."

Certainly my client's power to establish a new residence for Dr. Kohler is a far more aggressive exercise of authority than my client's overruling of your client's decision to put Dr. Kohler in an assisted living center as he recently threatened. Our understanding is that Dr. Kohler's physicians will not recommend moving him from the hospital at this time and we ask you to advise your client to cease all activities toward such end.

It has also come to our attention that Clayton Kohler has recently attempted to cash a check made out to Dr. Bodie Kohler and may have committed similar illegal acts in the past. Please instruct your client to return the check to Dr. Kohler so that he may instruct anyone of his choosing to deposit it into his bank account as is his usual practice.

87

We will keep you advised as we make our way through this current medical situation with Dr. Kohler. Thank you for your consideration.
Harry Zinn

The other family had left in the middle of this delightfully dramatic reading. I made the mistake of grinning as Marisa finished reading the letter out loud.

Clayton was looking at me for the first time today. "What are you smiling at? You can kiss my ass," said Clayton, and he pushed at me, but it was a little girlie push.

"Whoa. You may want to rethink your actions there, partner," I said. I was pretty calm for me. "Not only will you not ever touch Marisa—I mean NEVER!—if you touch me again you'll be needing some significant intensive care of your own." I poked Clayton hard in the chest as I spoke, emphasizing words and I enjoyed doing it. "Are we clear?"

Clayton did not respond.

"Scatter on outa here, Clayton," I finished.

Clayton looked only towards Marisa. "I will hurt you, Marisa. I mean it. That Harry Zinn is fired as Dad's attorney. You'll have your day, but this is *my* business with *my* dad. Do not involve yourself in my business you little bitch! You stay out of it!"

"That's it!" I yelled at Clayton. I grabbed his right hand which had its index finger pointed at Marisa. I twisted hard to Clayton's right which spun him around to face away from Marisa and from me. I had taken down more than a few crooks in my day. All were tougher than this punk. I shoved Clayton's face into the wall with my forearm hard on his neck. He 'oomphed' air out of his lungs as I leaned hard on him for a second. As I backed away just an inch or two, Clayton sprung off the wall. He tried to spin to his right away from the arm pain I was inflicting on him. Clayton tried a feeble, inexperienced swing at my head. Without drawing back my fist—much—I extended a right that landed squarely on Clayton's nose. Even a lightly powered punch square on a nose can leave the recipient seeing stars. Clayton's blood shot out of his nostrils and down his shirt. He grabbed for it to stem the flow. We got to see his stunned look for a split second before he turned and stumbled shakily down the hall away from us. I stayed where I was.

Marisa wouldn't let it sit. She shouted after her father, "I'm just interested in Papa's well being, Dad! How about you? You don't get Papa's money until he's dead and that's not yet!"

If Clayton heard, and I believe it would have been impossible not to hear, he did not respond as he staggered down the hall.

Marisa was shaking but she did not cry. Laura came and put her arm around Marisa. Laura spoke quietly to her so I couldn't hear, but Marisa was nodding so Laura's words must have been helpful. Little, eighteen year old Marisa had stood up to her dad. Laura and I were proud and we told her so. I think she was too troubled to be proud of herself just yet.

They are going to let Lola go home tomorrow. I'm pretty sure she won't go except to change clothes. We're a one-car family now, so I would have to shuttle back and forth from the house to the hospital. She won't leave Lily for very long. Lola was mostly moving around at will, limited only by the arm cast. Her bruises looked rough but the soreness was a little better.

Lily was feeling worse particularly underneath that hockey mask. The mask is held off her face by little pieces of foam around the outside. The foam only touched her face where it would not hurt, in theory. Her incision for the spleen surgery was hurting too. All this together just seems to have sapped her energy. She was not moving around much except when the nurses said she should walk around awhile. She complied every time without complaint. She let me hold her around the shoulders and she held on to my waist on her cast side. We looked like quite a pair taking laps around the nurse's station and back. We were the odd couple in a three legged race. We were up to five laps, twice a day. We did so many because of Lily, not me. If it were me, I'd do one and then stop to watch *Judge Judy*. We don't do quick laps but we finish them all. By the time we got done I was as tired as Lily. My tiredness was emotional and physical. Seeing this all impact on her sapped my energy more than the laps.

Lola and I talked about the situation with Warren Duchtin. I told her that until the police get him boxed in, I was going to have to carry my gun with me. This is the touchiest of subjects between Lola and me. If I think a situation demands it on any case, I have always promised to talk with her about it first and explain my reasons. The deal has always been that unless Lola has reasons that convince me that I am wrong about a given situation, my judgment has to take precedence over her preference. This is one of those times. To my amazement she agreed with me.

"Hopefully, you won't use the stupid gun on Clayton or any of the rest of us good guys," she said. She also made a joke about Barney Fife and for me to keep the only bullet in my shirt pocket at all times. Real funny. I live in such a stroke free environment.

The van attack has had more than just a physical impact on her. But, she asked that I only carry it in the car and not into the hospital. She is probably right. As long as we have police protection here I probably don't need it with me. My preference would be to carry an automatic attack rifle and a grenade belt at all times. Probably won't fly.

The doctor says Bodie seemed to be a little better tonight. We wouldn't know because he just lays there. He is still in a coma. The doctors were cautiously optimistic that surgery will not be necessary at all. All his vital signs were more stable than any time since he arrived at the hospital. Maybe his body was healing itself a little bit like they had hoped.

Marisa and I spoke with Harry Zinn this evening on a speakerphone the hospital let us use. We told him about the confrontation with Clayton. He was reassuring to Marisa. Tomorrow he will be filing Marisa's *Petition for Appointment of Conservation for Request for Protective Order* on behalf of Bodie.

It all sounded so serious. I guess it was serious. He also told me not to punch anybody else involved in the case. That will severely impact my overall effectiveness. Marisa is the one who told him about me punching Clayton. It wouldn't surprise me if that idiot Clayton tried to have me arrested for smacking him. If he did, so be it. Anybody who steals from his elderly parent, threatens his daughter and lies about all of it needs to be punched right in the nose. I'd do it again. If they took me to jail over it, when I got out I'd do it again then too.

Marisa went over to Bodie's house to look around for anything that might help Harry. Bodie gave Marisa the key to his house years ago. I can't imagine why a fourteen year old needed a key to a house that is a fifteen minute drive from where she lives. She wasn't old enough to drive when Bodie originally gave her the key. It just goes to show how much Bodie has always trusted Marisa. I seriously doubt if Bodie ever gave Clayton a key. I went with her, but I was strictly the muscle on this job in case Clayton showed up. I was hoping. He didn't.

Laura and Marisa had hired a cleanup company to come in and clean the blood and mess in the dining room where they had beaten Bodie. It looked extra clean and neat when we were there. It even looks like they shampooed the carpet. It looked really good. I am amazed that there are cleaning companies that specialize in crime scene cleanup. Now how can they make a living at that? There aren't that many violent crimes in Ft. Worth.

Marisa went through all the papers that she could see. It didn't look like she was too interested in digging very hard. We were both a little uncomfortable poking around in Bodie's house with him not there. One of the things she found in a desk drawer was a note from two years ago. It was typewritten with no handwriting on it at all. The note was really wrinkled like it had once been wadded up and thrown away then retrieved and smoothed back out again. It said:

1/4/03
Dad:
This is a reminder that if you choose not to sign the house to me, neither Marisa nor I will be back to see you again. If so, you should just sell the house and move in with Laura and Josh. Remember, my lawyer will know if you do not send the deed and that would be contrary to what you owe me. I am your oldest living biological son.

So weird. It wasn't signed, but who of us that would ever read the note wouldn't know it was from Clayton? It hardly made any sense. "Oldest living biological son?" And who in the world actually uses the word "nor?" I mean, really. Marisa had no idea this note existed and she made no more sense of it than I did. When we called Harry Zinn about it, he said that the note is going into the petition as evidence. Of what? Clayton's nuttiness maximus? They ought to have a hearing on Clayton's competence with this note as the centerpiece. The note doesn't mean squat about Bodie's competence, but when we told Harry about it on the phone, he said it speaks volumes to attempted coercion and undue influence of Clayton toward Bodie. That Clayton is wackier than any of us thought.

While we were over at Bodie's, Marisa and I went next door to check on Gert and to thank the young boy who found Bodie. When we rang the doorbell, Gertie barked at us at the door just like she does at home. He's really a nice kid and his mom was great too. They were genuinely concerned about Bodie and worried about some nut loose in the neighborhood beating people up. I told them the police already had a suspect. They were relieved.

Gert was glad to see us, but she seemed really comfortable with this family. She had already been given a blanket on the floor and clearly thought of it as her spot at this house. I offered to pay kennel rates for them keeping Gert, but they wouldn't hear of it. They said Dr. Kohler would have helped them out if it had been reversed. Bodie won't put up with not paying them. He can fix it later, but at least we don't have to worry about Gert for awhile. What great people.

On the way back, Marisa and I talked about how this petition would happen now.

"Once the petition is filed," said Marisa, "Mr. Zinn says that Ned Pearl and Dad will then file their objections to the petition. He said some of their objections would look fairly legitimate to a judge. The ones that seem ridiculous to us would probably seem that way to a judge too. He warned that we just shouldn't expect the judge to say so. I guess he, like, has to remain objective to do his job. Then we get to object to their objections and so forth until the hearing."

This all seemed worthwhile only when you consider that it's possible Bodie will recover. It was just so hard to believe it's humanly possible to remain objective if you see that Clayton has stolen Bodie's money before and tried to do it again recently. But, I guess you have to consider that, after all, he is the oldest living biological son.

12. A Good Day

It was a good day, Thursday, February 3.

Lola was a bruised but free woman and Bodie woke up.

I was with Lola and Lily at about 10:30 a.m. We were waiting for the nurses to come check Lola out so she could then stay in the same room as only a mom and not as a patient. Marisa came running into the room all breathless, "Jerry! Pa...pa...woke...up!"

I put Marisa in a bear hug and laughed with her while she breathed. Lola slapped her own right thigh with her good hand and laughed. Even Lily the hockey goalie in the other bed was smiling big, but not clapping. That would hurt too much right now.

When Marisa finally caught her breath, she told us the story, "Laura and I were just hanging around the waiting room like usual, but Dad was there sitting like all the way across the room from us. He came in about twenty minutes before the nurse came in. He had big strips of white tape across his nose and cotton stuffed in his nostrils. He, like, hadn't said a word to either one of us. Not a nod, not a wink, nothing. It's the first time he's been up here for Papa since that first night except, like, when he came in wanting to kill me for interfering. That wasn't coming down here for Papa!"

It was fun to see her so animated and smiling again. Lola picked up on it too. Lily's eyes were getting bigger under that mask as the story unfolded.

"So, anyway, the nurse comes in and straight over to me and Laura. Jerry, don't forget that I gave them that Medical Power of Attorney like Mr. Zinn told me. They've been like coming straight over and talking to me and Laura. Well, Dad hasn't been there anyway. So, the nurse Amanda, the one we like the best, came in and faced us with her back to Dad and said really quietly, 'Listen. Dr. Kohler is awake.' So, Dad was, like, leaning toward us trying to hear. I could hear him breathing through the cotton in his nose. Amanda's back was to him so he really couldn't hear her. But when Laura and I heard what Amanda said, I sort of squealed a laugh out and we both stood up and, like, hugged each other. Then Dad got up and came over closer, but not quite all the way to where he was near us. Then Amanda says to us, still kind of quiet, *'We will watch him for another hour and ask him a few questions. He is only answering short ones right now like 'Are you in pain?'* and Papa said *'Mah head hurts some.'* We asked him if he knows where he is and he answered *'hospital'*. Well, Laura and I were, like, jumping up and down every time Amanda said another answer from Papa. Dad kept coming over closer. Then Amanda says they asked him his name and he says *'Dr. Bodie Kohler, ma'am, at yoh suhvice.'* Oh, we were laughing like so hard! Then Amanda says, but she was at regular volume now, so I know Dad heard this, *'In another hour, if he is still this good, one and only one of you will be able to see Dr. Kohler for five minutes each hour and we are very strict on that time because it is Intensive Care.'* Well, Dad heard that part for sure and he stomped out of the Waiting Room and down the hall. We haven't seen him since. We did not know what he could be mad about, but we don't even care. Isn't it wonderful about Papa? I have to go back up. Laura will go in the first hour to see him, if he can have visitors. I will talk to you later."

Springtime is back. It is named "Marisa."

Harry Zinn filed the petition this morning while Bodie was waking up. Marisa and I called him and he was thrilled about Bodie's improvement. He says this is still the right action to take. If Bodie continues to improve to where he can understand what has happened, we can suggest that he revoke Clayton's P.O.A. It will be up to Bodie to decide.

Laura went in to see Bodie in the first hour they would let anyone in. Marisa and Lola and I waited on the edge of our chairs the full five minutes Laura was in there. She came out grinning from ear to ear.

"Well, he's pretty groggy, but not bad," said Laura. "He knew who I was right away. He asked about the boys and Josh. He asked about Gert several times, even after I told him she was fine. He says he doesn't remember being attacked. He asked how many days ago it happened, and he feels bad that Marisa's dinner was ruined that she cooked for him that night. So he remembered something about that night. He wanted to know where Marisa was. I explained the visiting schedule in Intensive Care and he scoffed and cussed at that plan. But he was ready for sleep before the end of five minutes. He dozed off while I was still sitting there. He asked if Clayton was coming in to see him. I told him 'Not right now.' I didn't tell him any of that story nor did I tell him about Lola and Lily's car crash. I just didn't think it was the right time."

"Absolutely right," I said. "There is time for that later."

Laura said, "He didn't have his hearing aids in. Did they bring them down when they brought him in?"

We all just shrugged.

"Well, we better find them and get them down here. I'm just so excited that he needs them again. In about forty five minutes, Marisa, you can go in to see him. But they cautioned me that some hours, Bodie might not wake up during those five minutes, so we shouldn't be too disappointed if we miss him sometimes. They said if that happens, we still have to wait another hour before trying again."

"That's okay," said Marisa. "I don't have anywhere else to be. But even if Dad shows up, he'll just have to wait until I've been in to see him once before he gets to go."

I could tell she meant it.

I thought Laura might leave once she saw Bodie, but she was too excited. She sat with us the rest of the afternoon until dinnertime. Marisa went in to see Bodie an hour later and came out crying. Good crying. "Papa cried too," she said. "I told him I would look after him like I know he would do for me, but I didn't tell him about the things that are happening. It will be better to talk about that later. Laura was right. He asked if Dad was coming in and he said to tell Dad that he is too tired to see him right now. Oh, and he asked about Gert again.

I think he will remember this time that Gertie is okay."

There had been no sign of Clayton and no sign of the cops to arrest me for busting his nose either.

Laura went in once more, but Bodie slept through that five minute visit. She had to go home and get dinner for her boys. She said they would all be down here tomorrow to see Bodie. That would require four hours of waiting to complete four five minute visits. Maybe she will rethink that idea when she calms down a little.

Marisa asked if I wanted to go visit Bodie in her place tonight, but I told her I would wait until tomorrow. Maybe he would keep improving. She insisted that I take a turn, claiming that Bodie would like to see me. Even though she insisted, I think Marisa was a little disappointed I agreed to go in because she didn't want to miss going in herself.

The only thing I wanted to know was about Duchtin. I wanted to see Bodie look at me and tell me he doesn't remember. I wanted him to be a little sharper when I finally went in. But I went anyway. I was kind of nervous when I took my turn.

Bodie's white hair was all over the place. Nearly a week's beard growth around the wooly goatee made him look like Santa Claus was laid-up in the hospital after a week-long bender. It was so noticeable only because Bodie was always so put together in those type areas. 'Presentation,' he might call it. What I could see of his face was mostly purple and red. There was dried blood under his nose, which had tape all across it onto his bruised and chafed cheeks. This beating was not mild even if it had been on a man half Bodie's age.

His entire head was wrapped in bandages and one ear was covered with bandages as well. The bruising on the under side of his forearms were clearly defensive bruises where he had tried to ward off blows. Bodie looked smaller than before. It was some combination of fragility and lost weight.

Opening his eyes, there was no recognition there for a few seconds, just an empty glassy eyed look. He could tell that somebody was there, but didn't recognize it was me. When he finally did, I got the smile of confirmation.

"Jerrah? You look—like hell, boy. You'd best—get it togethuh," he smiled again and winked, knowing full well it would make me laugh. "You need—some sleep. Why, it has done—wondahs for me, wouldn't you say?" His speech was even slower than usual. I didn't think that was possible. His thoughts were fairly clear.

"I'd say you are a mess, you old goat," I replied smiling. My smile dissolved away quickly and I fired question one and two in my mind, "Bodie? Did Duchtin do this? Was he there?" I was talking fast enough for both of us, anxious to hear an answer. I would just have to wait for Bodie to get it out. He looked at me for almost a full minute. Then I remembered that he did not have his hearing aids so maybe he didn't hear me. Guess again.

"Marisa says Gertie is well taken care of so ah am glad of that. Ah wish she was here. Puhhaps we could petition the authority at this hospital to allow an injured man an occasional cigah. Don't you think? Tell mah son that I will have to speak to him much later. Too tired now. Ah suspect ah will have to speak—to the lovely Detective Delano—regardin' your very subject—quite soon, Jerrah, ah imagine—but for now—I am quite weary. If Clayton was coming in to see me, please—tell him ah—am— just too tired."

Bodie closed his eyes. I guess he was going to sleep some more. It was a convenient way for him to avoid answering me. Maybe he was just sleepy. Jeez, he was wordy and roundabout even when he knew the situation didn't call for it. And he was repeating himself a little. I laughed and just shook my head. He was already back asleep. I sat there a few more minutes before leaving. I was glad just to see him alive and somewhat responsive. I hustled out with that attitude to give Marisa and Lola a full report on my short visit.

Lola and I went back to see Lily. The officer was still out front. Lily was sleeping and she had the room to herself. We watched her for a long time. Both of us were happy about it. Finally Lola left and went outside the room. Then she reappeared in Lily's room and whispered to me, "I checked with the officer and I checked with the nurses to make sure they would watch her closely. I told them we would be back early in the morning."

Lola looked at me and smiled. I would crawl through fire for that smile.

She said, "Let's go home."

So we did. We were both happy about that too.

It was a good day.

13. Sports Talk

Next morning, Lola and I were both up early and to the hospital to see Lily. She looked as good as any kid ever looked in a hockey mask. Lola stayed with her and I went to see Marisa in Intensive Care.

When I walked up Marisa said, "Papa is better this morning. The nurse had Papa's hearing aids. Guess they stayed in while they beat him up, because they were taken out in the Emergency Room. He put them in this morning, but he cussed them good first. Detective Delano is in with him now, but they told her she could have, like, five minutes only." Marisa smiled, obviously happy that the police didn't get any better treatment than she did.

"Did Angela call you about Bodie?" I asked Marisa.

Marisa replied, "No. She has been checking with the nurses by phone. They told me. She also says Dad called once today to ask about Papa so maybe there is some hope for Dad. He hasn't been down here though. Oh! I talked to Mr. Zinn. Here. I got a copy of the petition filing. Look at this. It's, like, really mean towards Dad and I'm glad. I just hope it makes Dad stop and think about what he's doing."

Poor Marisa. She hasn't yet realized that her dad knows exactly what he is doing. Clayton doesn't think what he's doing is wrong.

"Mr. Zinn says they will file objections today and deny most of it and not to worry about it," said Marisa. I looked at the Petition, an official looking document. Marisa was right. The mean parts are the best parts:

Petitioner: Marisa Kohler, Granddaughter

#5. A conservator is required because the respondent is unable to manage property and affairs effectively because of an inability to effectively receive or evaluate information or both or to make or communicated decisions, even with the use of appropriate and reasonably available technological assistance. The respondent has property, which will be wasted or dissipated unless proper management is provided.

#8. Limited Conservatorship is requested. The following powers should be granted to the limited conservator: Narrowly tailored and strictly limited power to assure that the Respondent's accounts remain titled as Respondent wishes; that L. Harry Zinn, Esq., remains Respondent's counsel for as long as Respondent wishes; that Respondent's independence and autonomy are protected from coercion or undue influence of the kind recently effected by Mr. Clayton Kohler as described herein; that Respondent receives assistance and supervision in the home only to the extent recommended by his treating physicians; that there is no further misappropriation from Respondent's financial accounts and assets; that Respondent has full and independent access to his residence and mailbox; that Respondent has full, undisrupted and independent access to phone calls and mail from friends and relatives to the extent he wishes; and that Respondent's assets are maintained and dedicated for his needs and best interests.

There was a "General Statement of Respondent's Property" in the body of the Petition. It showed two checking accounts, a savings account, U. S. Treasury Direct account and Bodie's account at Fidelity Investments. The estimated value totaled $287,000. The list did not include the value of his house. I don't know, but this is shaping up as the kind of battle that nobody should fight unless it's for a million dollars or more. Marisa didn't care if it was over a five dollar bill.

Sure enough, Harry had attached that double-weird typewritten note from Clayton to Bodie about assigning the house to him as Exhibit "A." Bodie's Living Will was an exhibit. The General Power of Attorney to Clayton was an exhibit as well as the Medical Power of Attorney to Marisa. The last exhibit was the doctor evaluation letter of Bodie which was already out of date since he had awakened since this was filed.

Angela came out of Bodie's room. Good. I've read enough legal paperwork for this day.

"What did Bodie tell you?" I asked Angela. Marisa stood too, wanting to hear about Bodie.

"Nice to see you too, Jerry. How are Lola and Lily?" Angela replied looking annoyed with me. I'm used to it.

"Hey, they're good. Lola got released, but she sits in the same hospital room with Lily all day anyway. Lily is better but they say she'll be here awhile longer. Oh, thanks for the officer outside. That was great."

"No problem. We don't have the manpower to put an officer on both Lily and Dr. Kohler right now. Intensive Care has more people watching all the time, so the officer is spending more time down near Lily. They'll be spending time in both places, though, until we get more of this thing figured out," said Angela and she looked at both Marisa and me. "Dr. Kohler does not remember the attack at his house. Maybe his memory will clear up as he improves. We'll see."

"How about the van," I remembered to ask, "Any luck with that?"

"Actually, yes. We have two blue vans with AB25 on the plates that we are watching. A bakery owns one van. Some Limited Liability Corporation, an L.L.C., owns the other one. Both are in Ft. Worth. Neither seems to have an obvious tie-in to our accident and neither has apparent body damage consistent with such an accident. But they could have gotten it fixed over a couple of nights if the damage wasn't too bad. I'll let you know how that goes." She started to leave.

"Wait! Angela!" I said roughly. Angela can be unbelievably irritating. She always wants the information flowing in to her, never out. "How about Duchtin?"

Angela sighed. She finds me as annoying as I find her. "He came in for questioning just as he promised. He's lawyered up, though. He claims to have been at Ridglea Country Club when Joanne was killed. He furnished names of witnesses. We'll check it out. If his Denver story checks out, he was there during the attacks on Dr. Kohler and on Lola and Lily. We'll check that too. He claims no knowledge of any of these events. He knows we are looking hard."

Angela just looked at me. I looked back and forth from Marisa to Angela. "That's it? Nothing about the girlfriend, the multiple girlfriends, the photos I gave to Joanne? C'mon, Angela."

"Ease off, Jerry. I'll tell you what I can. It's an ongoing investigation. See you later." Angela looked right at Marisa. "I'm so pleased about Dr. Kohler. So is my husband, David. I will check back on him." Angela walked away.

"That SUCKS so bad and so much!" I wanted to say something loud enough for Angela to know how irritating she is. I probably couldn't have said anything much stupid-er. Well, on second thought, maybe I could have. Watching her walk away, she probably thought the same thing. She did not flinch.

"Come on, Jerry," Marisa said, trying to change my focus. "Take my turn to go see Papa. Be nice. Talk to him about like sports or something that doesn't require thought."

I sat down and waited to see Bodie. Marisa handed me a *Highlights* magazine for children and said, "Here's something you will find really interesting." When I looked back up at her she was laughing. I had to join in.

"C'mon, Bodie. We need to know this. There is a lot of work to be done. Was Duchtin there?"

Bodie was way better than yesterday.

I had just finished telling him about Lola and Lily and their accident. Bodie got tears in his eyes. I felt terrible for even telling him in his condition, but it's time to go after Duchtin. So I pulled the conversation back to whether or not Warren Duchtin had beaten Bodie. So much for Marisa's request to talk sports. But I only have five minutes with Bodie. We had to get right to business.

"Jerrah? In the masterful work of *Gulliver's Travels* by Jonathan Swift, after Gulliver left the Lilliputians and after he left the land of Glubbdubdribb, Gulliver sailed on to Luggnagg where he hears about the Struldbrugs, who are Luggnaggians that have eternal life. They will live...forevah."

Bodie was smiling. I was not. Not much brain damage going on here, I thought. I've got more brain damage than Bodie does. On my best day, I wouldn't remember this junk. I rolled my eyes in disgust specifically so Bodie could see me do it. I was hoping he would then stop his silly, obtusely aimed lesson that I knew was coming.

He continued, undeterred by my theatrics, "Gulliver imagines what he would do if he were immortal. He might amass enormous wealth, obtain all knowledge and wisdom, teach the young, support fellow immortals or maybe fight against the corruption of mankind. As the story goes on, Gulliver discovers that although the Struldbrugs don't die, they do grow old, senile and envious of the young. They lacked the human attributes of honesty, kindness and hope, which are characteristics that Gulliver expected to find accompanyin' immortality."

"Bodie! What *is* the point?" I said with my usual impatience.

"The point is, mah friend, that livin' forevah ain't what it's cracked up to be."

I gave him my best and most annoyed comeback, "Good gravy! What has that got to do with the price of tea in China? Duchtin is a booger that I just can't flick off the end of my finger! He will not go away! If he is responsible for your situation, for murdering Joanne and for what happened to Lola and Lily, I want him and I want him now!"

I stared at Bodie, like that would make him remember better. Where did *'good gravy'* come from? I was a little excited. Bodie wasn't.

"Jerrah, ah simply do not recall and as frustratin' as that is to me, ah can see it is even more frustratin' to you. For that, ah am truly sorry. Ah presume you have made contact with Mr. Raymond Johnson of Boston, Massachusetts?" asked Bodie, yanking the conversation elsewhere.

"Well, uh, I've been a little busy with hospital business this week," I was back to trail-off talking. Bodie had an unwavering and demanding professorial look, even through the bandages. This was a look perfected by fifty years of teaching. Bodie had not lost his touch.

"Let us take a little inventory, shall we, Jerrah? You have just told me how well Miss Lola and Miss Lily are doin' with their respective recoveries. Then there is mah case. Clearly ah have not expired yet. Although ah am still feelin' significant discomfort from time to time, my medical care is more than adequate. Ah am fairly certain that you have not obtained an advanced medical degree this week, but ah *have* been rendered unconscious for a good bit of the week. So, ah could be wrong about that."

I hung my head, chin down towards my chest.

Bodie continued, "It certainly appears as if many of the most recent crises have been, well, averted. Just exactly how is it that you are still needed at this institution of healin'?" Bodie made me feel like I had failed to turn in my homework—again.

"Well, I was gonna…," I started, but trailed off.

"Jerrah, in the words of the great, immortal Rudyard Kipling, in his poem, 'If',

'If you can meet with Triumph and Disaster
And treat those two imposters just the same;
If you can bear to hear the truth you've spoken
Twisted by knaves to make a trap for fools,
Or watch the things you gave your life to, broken,
And stoop and build 'em up with worn-out tools'

Let's see, there's some more ah can't quite remember just now, and then it goes;

'Yours is the Earth and everything that's in it
And-which is more—you'll be a Man, my son!'

Quite appropriate, Jerrah, wouldn't you say? Ah have paid you good money and I now expect you to get to work."

What could I say to that? I got up to leave and go to work. As I got to the door, I turned back to see the grinning Bodie, obviously proud of himself.

"Hey, Bodie. Did you ever hear this one?" I asked.

'I know it's wet
And the sun is not sunny.
But we can have
Lots of good fun that is funny.'

"Them's the immortal words of *The Cat in the Hat* written by the great Dr. Seuss."

Bodie laughed too hard because it was followed quickly by an agonizing face scrunch of pain.

14. Lollipop Dreams

"Hello, Keystone Partners, may I help you?"

"Hello, is Raymond Johnson in today?" I asked. It is Friday. I hoped Ray was a hard worker.

"Yes, may I say who is calling?"

"This is Jerry Wilson in Ft. Worth, Texas. I am calling on behalf of our mutual friend, Dr. Bodie Kohler. Thanks."

'Click', and there was music playing over the phone on hold. Organ music. There is nothing like the Stones' "Get Off of My Cloud" being played by an organ while you are on hold. Oh, I take it back. Only to be surpassed by "The Baby Elephant Walk." Now that's a song that was written to be played on the organ….

"This is Raymond Johnson. May I help you?"

"Mr. Johnson. This is Jerry Wilson in Ft. Worth, Texas. I am calling on behalf of my friend, our mutual friend actually, Dr. Bodie Kohler. Dr. Kohler is in the hospital right now."

"Oh. Nothing serious I hope."

"Well, it was, but things are looking up about now. I have just come from the hospital and I spoke with him today. We believe he is on his way back to being himself. Uh, Mr. Johnson, Dr. Kohler has asked me to pursue information on how his oldest son James lived out his life in Vietnam all the way up until the time he was killed. This is something he has wanted to have more details on for many years. His recent brush with his own death has made him more intent on obtaining all the information he can. I have to tell you that I am an investigator. But my stakes in this are greater than that. I have been Bodie's friend for over twenty years. I am not much younger than James would be today had he survived the war. Bodie asked me to call you and discuss any and all facts you would be willing to disclose so we might put together a clearer picture of the final period of James's life."

I paused for Raymond to speak an approval or slam down the phone, but there was no response.

"Mr. Johnson, are you still there?"

"Yes I am." He had a really deep, intimidating bass voice, very James Earl Jones-ish. He said nothing else. There was nothing but silence.

I started again, "Well, apparently this was somewhat of a dying wish of Patsy Kohler to know more about their son's story. Knowing that he didn't do more to find out James's story while his wife was alive is now causing Dr. Kohler some distress. I hope to help him because of that." I took a breath and waited.

Finally, Ray Johnson spoke, "Look. That entire part of my life is hard to remember because I have made every effort to erase it from my memory and to go ahead and make a good life for myself and my family. You are not a reporter are you?"

"Hey, uh, no. I can't even imagine a reporter calling you to ask these questions. I'm just Bodie's friend who happens to be an investigator," I said.

Silence.

"I have no interest in the story of my Vietnam experience being told anywhere."

Silence.

"Whatever I learn, Mr. Johnson, will only be told to Dr. Kohler."

Silence.

"Well, I have told Dr. Kohler pretty much everything I know, already," he said.

More silence.

Finally RayJ began to talk, "You know, it took a lot of effort and tears to live through it and to forget any of it. I gave my own blood in Vietnam. I was lucky to come out alive. Once I got back, I studied the part of the war in which I participated. I spent a good bit of the decade of the 1970s reading about exactly what was going on that led up to me even having to be in Vietnam."

He paused again. Then he kept talking, "I can't say I have full understanding. When you take a step back and try to understand all the political factors and 'whys' to the story, it is just impossible to reconcile this with the fact that many guys I cared about died. I lose it, man. I lose how it might have otherwise made sense because I was there. I saw the result of the 'whys'. And now I have to live with the guilt of not having died. There's no reason 'why' for that. That's just the way it is."

There was another long pause, but I said nothing and he went ahead, "I loved James. He was family to me. He died in the battle for the town of Hue' in the Tet Offensive of 1968. He was a brave man, an amazing soldier and an even better person. We lost one of our best in him. Even after I had studied the background of Vietnam, the 'whys' do not justify such a loss. They never could. I was there and I don't even know how to start that story, much else draw the strength to finish it. What good will it do? Who is it to benefit if I can remember any of it? How will it help me to try to remember the most painful period of my life? Any answers spring to mind, Wilson?"

His questions were good ones.

I knew there were no answers that would satisfy him, but I spoke anyway, "James's father is almost seventy five years old. He asked me to do this. It is very important to him. He and I both want to know what happened to James. It will do some good. I know it will," I said.

Raymond would stop talking for a couple of minutes at a time. A couple of minutes of silence is a lot of silence. I just let the silence sit there with us. Neither of us gave up.

It wasn't as if he was thinking about whether or not he would tell the story, although that's what he kept saying. It was more like he was thinking, '*how do I best tell this story*?' He was going to tell it. He wanted to tell it. I could feel it. James was the reason he would tell it.

"Combat in Vietnam was utter chaos," RayJ said. "In the jungle, especially, you only heard the guns and mortars fire. You didn't see who fired them or where they were. You just fired back. They shot at us. We shot at them. Sometimes we hit the bad guys and sometimes we didn't. Going into Hue', it all changed. Everybody was a bad guy. We were in the city now. Everybody shot at everything that moved or made sound. Whether it was friend or foe, you might check it out after the battle. Maybe you would check. Sometimes, the good guys shot at the good guys and sometimes...those shots might have been...."

RayJ slowed to a stop. I had no idea how to help or what to ask that might help.

"I'm sure Dr. Kohler told you that we never went to Khe Sanh like he and his wife thought," Raymond continued. "We were in Hue'. Both were hell. Drop you into the middle of either and you would only be able to identify your surroundings as 'hell'. James and I both got shot in the hell of Hue'. I'll never forget it and James will never have to remember it. Hard to say who got the raw deal."

Silence.

Then RayJ said, "Have you spoken to any of the other guys, Wilson?"

"No, sir, I haven't. It was Bodie's recommendation that I begin with you. "

More silence.

I tried to fill some of it, "Just the other day, Bodie and I were talking about the Tet Offensive of 1968. I know that the North had promised a cease-fire for the lunar new-year, Tet. Then they broke that promise with a well planned attack on the U.S. Embassy in Saigon. Bodie said it was just a handful of V.C. commandos that launched that one. Then the North Vietnamese followed up by hitting a bunch of cities and towns previously thought impenetrable." I paused to see if any conversation was coming.

RayJ said, "Have you ever seen the film footage of the U.S. Embassy attack, Wilson?"

"No, never," I replied.

"I'll tell you a story, since you're looking for a story. Get the news reel of that attack. I don't know where. You'll have to figure that out. It's all in black and white. It took way too long for the news services to ship news film out of Vietnam. There was no 'Internet' and there were no communications satellites then. They had to wait for military flights out to physically ship their news films. It cut down the processing time from shipping to broadcast for them to only use black and white. Anyway, in one scene of the attack on our Embassy, you'll see a big Marine race by the camera on foot. Shots are fired at him and he's running in a zigzag trying to keep from getting killed. You can see the bullets hit the ground near him. It's really dramatic when you realize what you are watching. He runs back to a building on the Embassy grounds and tosses a pistol up to a second floor window to another soldier before he dives behind a retaining wall with bullets flying. Neither is ID'd by a reporter, but I'll tell you who and what you're looking at. The soldier catching the pistol is Captain Arthur Gray, a Marine who worked in the Embassy. When the attack began, he was unarmed. He usually worked while carrying a firearm, but it was before dawn and he wasn't even supposed to be at work yet. He caught that pistol and moments later shot the last two or maybe it was three enemy commandos dead as they crept into the Embassy to try and kill him. The U.S. Marine who risked his life to run across that compound with the gun to help save Captain Gray was a man who had just killed five of the other 17 or 18 V.C. commandos himself. Master Sergeant Billy Tyrell was that man. He was and probably still is a hard-nosed, hard-core U.S. Marine. This man was a piece of work and straight out of a comic book. It was less than a month later when Sgt. Tyrell came to take command of our unit and lead us into Hue'."

RayJ paused again.

"Alright then, here's what we're going to do. You need to see Tyrell, if he is still alive and my bet is that pure meanness has kept him going. The man was the champion of the entire U.S. Marine Corps with pistols in his day. He could handle automatic weapons and explosives at the same high level of ability. I'd wager he would still be willing and able to blow up anything his country needed him to if he's still breathing. I just don't know if he'll tell you much. As hard as this is to believe, I heard he runs a sailboat charter business either in San Juan, Puerto Rico or St. Thomas or St. John in the U.S. Virgin Islands. Name of his company is 'Starfish' and he goes by 'Captain Billy' now, not 'Sarge'. You need to build your story around him. If I can, I'll help fill in the gaps, but only if I can, you got it, Wilson? I got no promises for you. You're not Dr. Bodie Kohler, so don't expect me to be as straight-up decent to you as I would be to him. This is the way it has to be. Any questions, Wilson?"

"None. Thank you."

Well, I never suspected this would be easy.

"Hello, this is Starfish Charters—St. John."

A very sexy sounding Hispanic-accented female voice, in English, answered the phone on a recorder. "We can't get to the phone right now because sailing is too good and we are out on the boat. You should join us as soon as you can. Leave your name and number at the beep and as soon as we get off the water, we will call you back. Bueno." Beep.

"Hello, this is Jerry Wilson in Ft. Worth, Texas. I'm going to be in St. John in a week or so and need to check your schedule to charter a sail. I would like to sail with you as long as Captain Billy is at the helm because he was recommended to me so highly." I left my phone number and asked that she call me back. I had gone home to make my telephone calls. Later, I went back down to the hospital. Lily was asleep by then, so Lola and I ate dinner in the hospital cafeteria.

I told Lola all about my conversation with Raymond Johnson. Neither of us knows what to make of the possibility of Americans killing Americans in Vietnam. I think Raymond wanted to tell more about what he knew but he chose not to. Both Lola and I find it unfathomable that it could have been our guys that killed James and wounded RayJ. That made it too personal to even contemplate. How about friendly fire? Maybe it was accidental in the confusion of battle. How do you confirm such a suspicion? I had no idea. Lola helped me to worry about it. She had no idea either. We talked for awhile about understanding Vietnam and the war so many years later. Neither of us having been there, we both doubted having the ability of achieving total understanding. Each and every Vietnam vet Lola and I have known over the years seemed to retain the attitude that we could not possibly understand what they saw and did there. That attitude has kept our veteran friends that know what it was like from telling it to those of us who don't know what it was like. I don't know. Maybe they have kept us from understanding on purpose. I'm willing to put out the effort. It is surely important enough to try and explain properly. It is certainly important enough to try and understand properly.

"Jerry. I need to talk to you," said Lola.

Uh-oh, I thought, but without reason. It just sounded like I should think 'uh-oh'.

"When you went home today to make your telephone call to Mr. Johnson, Angela and David came to the hospital to see Bodie. Marisa let David go in to see Bodie for one of the five-minute visits and Angela came and talked to me."

I screwed up my face at that news. It's a dangerous combo for those two women to talk.

"Angela does not believe that Bodie cannot remember the attack. Let me say that differently. Angela believes Bodie does remember, he just won't say. It is a little odd that he can remember Marisa was about to bring dinner but can't remember the attack itself. Even the doctors think so. She asked David to quiz him gently on it hoping to find out more," said Lola. "David didn't have any luck with Bodie either. Medically, the doctors tell Angela that it is very possible that Bodie can't remember. But Angela thinks Bodie knows that Duchtin did it, or had it done, but he won't say so. Would you like to hear why she believes he won't say so?"

Uh-oh. I told you.

"Because Bodie is afraid of what you will do if you find out the truth about Duchtin. She believes Bodie thinks he is keeping you out of trouble by not telling the truth. Jerry! You threaten Duchtin all the time without regard to who is present. You punch Bodie's son in the face. Why wouldn't he think you might go nuts? What have you said to Bodie?"

"Nothing. Honest. We talked about him getting beaten up, but Bodie says he doesn't remember. I believe him but I am hoping he starts remembering soon. We talked about James and about me getting back to work. We talked about the *Cat in the Hat*. Jeez, I didn't do anything."

"No! Not yet. But it's what you might do that has your friend keeping the truth buried. And now you're driving around town packing heat? I swear, there is something seriously wrong with you. Somehow you have to convince Bodie that you are a reasonable man. Good luck with all that! But you have to try anyway. It's *your* sparkling personality keeping this investigation from getting anywhere. Angela has zero evidence against Duchtin. Zero. Every one of his lying stories is checking out. The police know it's just a little too convenient for him. So, until Bodie finds his memory and implicates Duchtin, they are stuck with nothing. Lily and I have to have armed guards everywhere we go. Fix it so the Police can do their jobs, Jerry. Fix it!" There was significant fire in Lola's eyes.

"Okay! Jeez," I replied.

Good comeback. That'll teach her.

I was swimming through the ocean with seals all around me. There were kayaks with Eskimos around too. Of course there were. All the Eskimos had lollipops in one mitten-covered hand and their paddle in the other. A submarine rose up out of the water suddenly and there on the frothy-water deck of the giant freshly surfaced nuclear submarine were about a hundred flopping seals, a dozen kayaks with parka covered, lollipop-licking Eskimos, and me in a tank top, running shorts and swim fins. Warren Duchtin, that stump of a human, stepped out of the submarine hatch wearing a hockey mask and yelled, "Gotcha."

I awoke and sat straight up. I was in my own bed.

Lola was there in the bed with me. The cast on her left arm was draped over me. She did not wake when I sat up. The clock radio showed 4:21 a.m. What is it with 4:00 a.m. and me lately? Am I doomed to wake up about this time every stinkin' day? I got up and tried hard not to wake Lola. Sometimes when I wake up too early, I can just tell that my night is over. No more sleep is available for me. There is no explainable reason. This was one of those times. I trudged out to make coffee wearing my Homer Simpson slippers that Lily got me. You put your feet right into Homer's mouth. Once on, your toes are about where Homer's brain would be and his mouth seems to be wrapped around your ankle. It's symbolic. Makes me laugh every single time I put them on. I sat at our kitchen counter in my boxers, T-shirt and Homer shoes holding the hot coffee and wishing Lily was here to make fun of my morning hairdo on a Saturday morning. As is my nature, pre-dawn is a great time for a thinking worry-fest.

The Pink Ponies have soccer practice today for the first time since Lily's accident. This would be a new test of my dedication. We had to practice though, because there is a game tomorrow. All the girls and their families had been down to the hospital to see Lily. They all came in to see her yesterday when I was home calling Raymond Johnson. One of the moms had bought little *Phantom of the Opera* hockey-type masks at the toy store for every one of them. Every girl wore one to the hospital to see Lily. Lily was the star of the party and it was a big party. Lola and Lily got hugs and kisses from every one of them. Lola said the parents all hung back in a rare display of good judgment on their part. Nurses just smiled and let it happen. It was a force bigger than medicine itself. Lily improved yesterday more than she had on any other day.

Maybe I have only liked little girl soccer because Lily is there. Maybe not. Those doubtful thoughts nearly evaporated when the girls all came to the hospital in those masks. I love them like I love Lily. I'm just not with them everyday like I am with her. That and they aren't really mine. I guess we'll find out now if I can do it as well without Lily. I'll give it a go.

If Bodie has continued his improvement by late this morning, they are going to move him out of Intensive Care and into a regular room. They're putting him in a room near Lily at the request of the Police. It will be much simpler for their duty officer. Bodie still can't move much because of his broken pelvis. He says nothing will heal in Intensive Care because they wake him up every twenty minutes checking to 'see if he's died yet', as he puts it. He's hoping that in a regular room they won't wake him up as often. He can't even roll over to pee in a pan yet, so I don't see much of a break coming for him anytime soon.

I've got to convince Bodie that I won't commit murder or torture Warren Duchtin if Bodie tells the police the truth about the beating. I have not come up with an intelligent way to accomplish this yet. If that Captain Billy ever calls me back, maybe I'll just go to St. John, U.S.V.I. to see if I can get *him* to talk. If I'm gone for awhile, maybe Bodie will talk to Angela about the truth and feel okay about it. I can't kill or maim Duchtin if I'm not here.

Maybe I could get the evidence on Duchtin myself through a side door. Maybe I could find out about Miss Blondielegs. I think she's got more going on upstairs than anybody might suspect. No, I don't mean there. I mean further upstairs. I don't have a plan for that either.

If Bodie goes to a regular room, Harry Zinn says he will come down to see him today and talk about the case. Even on a Saturday. Not bad for an attorney. Marisa wants me to be there for that. Bodie doesn't even know about any of it yet. It's Marisa's call, but I'll be there if she's ready. She's done everything right so far. Clayton and Ned Pearl filed their objections to the Petition yesterday. I looked at a copy with Marisa last night. It looked flat-out silly to me. Everything they said was obvious.

"Marisa Kohler filed a Petition for Appointment of Conservator. Clayton Kohler is the Respondent's son and oldest living child. (I would have liked to listen to Clayton argue with his own attorney that it should be worded 'oldest living biological son'.) Clayton Kohler objects to the appointment of Ms. Marisa

Kohler as Conservator. Clayton Kohler has statutory priority to be appointed the Conservator. Clayton Kohler denies all the allegations in Ms. Marisa Kohler's petition."

That was it. What a system! Everybody has to hire separate $250 per hour professionals to state the most obvious things for the judge to review. The only important thing in the whole process should be what is best for Bodie. Even my addled brain can figure that out. They could hire me for a lot less to declare that Bodie's asshole son is stealing money from his own elderly father. He wants to steal some more by putting Bodie in a home so it's easier to steal the money and so Bodie can't keep it from happening. Oh, and the son is a stinkin' lying, cheating thief. The thief's own daughter, who is also the victim's granddaughter, is trying to keep it from happening.

Here's my ruling.

Bad guys must stop being bad or you're going straight to jail. Good guys get to keep living their own lives apart from the bad guys as much as the good guys want.

Now everybody calm down.

Good guys get to go home and watch *SportsCenter*. Bad guys will be forced to watch *Oprah* and nothing else for a solid year, over and over again. Now, shut up and get out. This whole deal just makes me want to ralph.

How in the hot unholy Hades is Clayton Kohler paying an attorney anyway? The only way I see is if he stole some money from Bodie or from somebody else that we had not yet discovered.

Into the kitchen strolled the sleepy-eyed but truly stunning Mrs. Wilson. Once again her mere presence saved me from myself. The kitchen clock showed 6:26 a.m. The only light source was the little one in the hood over the stove plus the glimmering promise of a coming sunrise. Lola looks good in direct sunlight or by the shine of the stovetop hood forty-watt.

"Here she comes barefoot and groggy and in a very short nightgown with nothin' on underneath. Life is good. That little short purple satin nightie is a good-un, hon, but I prefer the all-access pass granted by those little hospital numbers."

I gently grabbed and sweetly mauled the nearly incoherent, very warm, extremely soft Lola and felt her in all the best places. Lola even smells good at six in the morning. She smiled a sorta-awake grin and half-heartedly tried to shoo me away with her good arm.

No such luck for her.

Later in the morning, just as we were about to leave for the hospital, the phone rang.

"Hello. Is Jerry Wilson in, por favor?" Ah, the very sexy Hispanic voice from the sailboat company phone recorder.

"This is Jerry Wilson."

"Yes, Señor Wilson. This eez Francesca por los Starfish Charters in St. John. You left us a message about sailing with us. Si'?"

"Yes, Francesca, thanks for calling me back. I am wondering if Captain Billy has any times open next week for a day sail," I inquired. I might as well see if it is even possible to meet him. Once I'm on the boat and I'm a paying customer, where's he going to go?

"Oh, the days are always booking fast here, Señor Wilson, but we can probably fit you in. Do you have a day that is best for you?"

"Sure. Today is Saturday. Tuesday, Wednesday or Thursday this next week would be great for me. How are any of those days? Oh and how much is the charter for a day sail? But I want to go with Captain Billy, if that matters."

"Si', Señor Wilson. Captain Billy and I will both be on each sail. The cost is $300. Cash only, por favor, plus any drinks are cash bar cost. Tuesday would be best and the weather projection are good all week. Can I confirm your reservation with deposit of one-half?"

"Sure Francesca, but I have to check one more agenda item for my meetings down there. I don't want to have a business conflict after I arrive, so may I call you this afternoon to give you my credit card for the deposit?" I had better check with Bodie on this little expense item.

"Si'. I will pencil you in, but you must call me back this afternoon and leave a message with your credit card and expiration to book our boat. Bueno y adios, Señor."

Let's see, short notice plane fare, food, hotel and a $300 sail plus no assurance of any information at all. I'll let Bodie decide if it might be worth all this.

15. Revocation

Lily was crying when we got to the hospital. Any improvement from yesterday has left and gone away. Everything hurts. She misses school? I told you girls were complicated. She wanted to go home and sleep in her own bed. I'm with her on that one. Now in the face of her pain, I have to try to convince Bodie that it doesn't really make me angry enough to smash Duchtin flat as a pancake underneath a steamroller on Hulen Street. Oh sure, I'll be really effective. After awhile I told Lola I was going to check on Bodie.

When I got up to Intensive Care, there was nobody in the waiting area. I asked the nurse and she said they had moved Bodie to a regular room about half and hour before. She looked up the room number and it was two doors away from Lily. So I headed back down there, but not before I thanked both the nurses on duty for their help and dedication to helping Bodie get better. They liked that I had even thought about it. They are amazing people, just amazing. I must have left Lily's room just before Bodie's entourage arrived. When I got back to Lily's room, there were Harry Zinn, Laura, Marisa and Lola all talking.

"Good," said Marisa. "Jerry, we were just waiting on you before we all go in and see Papa. I asked Lola to come in as well. We can use like all the help we can get on this thing. Mr. Zinn wants to show him the P.O.A. revocation today and see what he thinks. Are you ready?"

"Sure," I said, then looking at Lola, "How's Lily?" I noticed that Harry had brought a videotape movie camera and tripod probably to record this little meeting.

"Better, I think," said Lola. "She's snoozing now anyway."

No more Intensive Care. No more five-minute limits to visit.

It is time to tell Bodie the story about Clayton.

Harry Zinn was masterful. After talking with Bodie a few minutes even I could see he was satisfying himself that Bodie had his reasoning power and was himself. He did it in such a way that if you weren't watching for his method, you would swear he was just exchanging pleasantries with Bodie. The rest of us who had been seeing Bodie on visits already knew he was mentally better than the rest of us.

All of us, including Bodie, knew why the camera was whirring away on a tripod pointed at Bodie—to preserve the proceedings no matter what happened to Bodie afterwards. The presence of the camera didn't seem to have any noticeable impact on the discussion. I haven't seen the tape, but it probably only shows Bodie. You can probably hear the rest of us occasionally. Harry laid out the whole story, including making Bodie aware of the things from the past that Marisa and Laura had told us that Bodie didn't know that we knew. He didn't paint Clayton as bad and as nutty as I would have. But I realized that he was going to ask Bodie if he wanted to revoke Clayton's P.O.A. and he was trying not to influence Bodie. Bodie handled it all routinely, or so it seemed, until he spoke.

"It is unclear to me where ah have gone wrong with Clayton. He has become quite purposeful in his efforts to unseat me from what little money Patsy and ah managed to accumulate over time. Ah simply do not understand why. He seems to harbor quite a lot of resentment over James. That baffles me as well. James was killed when Clayton was only thirteen years old. That was over thirty seven years ago. It is senseless. Some of his resentment showed up shortly after James was killed. He demanded to be given the car that had belonged to James. Patsy and I nevah reached any understandin' of why Clayton was the way he was. Then he holds resentment towards me and ah have nevah been unable to determine the source of that anger. His idiosyncracies have nevah manifested themselves before in such a deliberate and purposeful manner."

Then Bodie shifted gears as he does so well.

"Marisa and Laura? Ah could not ask anyone to protect me and care for me any bettah than the two of you. Ah am very, very proud that each of you is mine. Thank you to mah good friends, Jerry and Lola. Lola, ah am so sorry that you had your unfortunate accident and all mah wishes are for you and Miss Lily to heal quickly and completely. Jerry, you are magnificent, as always. No mattah what happens, you must keep your anger in check. Do not stoop to the level of mah son or even lower, to the depth of that moral-less scoundrel, Warren Duchtin. You are bettah than that."

I wondered if Bodie was speaking to his beating or just Warren in general. Lola shot me a look that could smelt lead. I shrugged at her like I have no idea why she would do that. Nice one.

"Jerrah? Ah ask that you accompany Marisa to mah house. Marisa, if you will look behind the dresser in mah bedroom, there is what appears to be a grill coverin' an air conditionin' duct. You must move the dresser to get to it. Jerrah will help you with that. That grill is not a duct at all. It is simply a place in the wall to hide whatevah you desire. Remove the grill and beneath it should be a manila envelope. In the envelope should be a substantial sum of cash, $8,000 in fifties, twenties, tens and ones. Patsy and ah kept it in the house so it would be handy, just in case. You are all too young to remember the Great Depression in the 1930s. In fact, ah was but a child, but its impact on our lives and both of our families was significant for many years. Patsy and ah did not want to be without anything if there was a run on the banks as there was in the Depression. If the money is there, we shall use it to pay the fees of Mr. Zinn to take care of all these mattahs. If that money is not there, we know where Clayton has obtained funds sufficient to pay his own attorney. Ah suspect he has no other source of funds for such a purpose, unless he has somehow tapped mah savings. From what you have told me, Harry, that is unlikely thanks to your diligent efforts. In any event, ah will assume responsibility for all legal bills, past and present, presented by Mr. Harry Zinn in all these mattahs. Marisa? As soon as you have completed that task, ah request that you immediately return to the University and get caught up with your studies. There are more important mattahs demandin' your attention than Clayton's shenanigans and ah expect you to attend to them with your utmost efforts."

Marisa was crying again. Good crying. And now, Lola was wiping away tears. At least she wasn't shooting me any looks. I was thinking that Bodie was pretty smart to get that money information on the tape. Others would see it eventually.

"Harry?" said Bodie. "If you would be so kind as to present me with the propuh papers," Bodie then, unprompted, looked straight into the camera and finished, "I would like to revoke mah Power of Attorney previously granted to Clayton Kohler as soon as possible."

Harry brought over the papers and read the instrument to Bodie. He asked him if he understood what he was signing and its effect. There was no doubt in Bodie's mind and now there were five witnesses to that fact plus a film record. Bodie signed the revocation of P.O.A. Then he looked straight at the camera and said, "Ah believe it would be best if Clayton were not to come see me in here. I would prefer it that way if that can be done." Bodie looked at Harry Zinn.

"Sure," said Harry. "I'll pass that on to Ned Pearl, Clayton's attorney, right away."

"I'll tell the police officer outside so he can be sure to watch," I said to Harry and Bodie.

Bodie then said, "Harry? Ah believe it would be appropriate for you to draw up a new Power of Attorney, considerin' the current fragility of mah medical condition and the varied possibilities from this point in time. Laura, would you be willin' to serve your ol' Dad in that capacity? I would be proud if you would, darlin', along with Marisa and her Medical Power."

Laura nodded and hugged her Dad. Laura couldn't see Bodie's face at the time, but as glad as Bodie was to receive the hug, it pained his body to do so.

"Harry?" asked Bodie. "Ah cannot thank you enough for your excellent professional attention and personal kindness with this entire messy event. We'd best *legally* kick Clayton's ass." Bodie winked right at me.

"My pleasure," said Harry.

I waited until Harry had ended his taping session by hitting the 'Stop' button on the camera. "Bodie, if you are up to it, I need to speak to you about Raymond Johnson," I said. Bodie nodded.

"I've spoken with him. He was reluctant to tell me much. He claimed to have already told you what he knows years ago. He has referred me to Sergeant Billy Tyrell, the commander of RayJ and James's unit in Vietnam when they went into Hue'. Tyrell now runs a sailboat charter in St. John, U.S.V.I. RayJ has agreed only to fill in the blanks after I have spoken to Tyrell, provided Tyrell will tell me anything. RayJ leads me to believe that Tyrell will be very reluctant to speak to me about events in Vietnam. We will see, but I have made a reservation for him to take me on a day sail next week. Once he and I are isolated, my hope is to convince him to tell me the story. Before sailing off I wanted to run this by you. This trip could be expensive and it is unclear whether or not it will yield results. Do you have any better ideas?"

Bodie did not even hesitate, "Jerrah, ah trust your judgment completely on these mattahs and will pay the expense of your little sailin' boondoggle. It is simply incomprehensible that this Tyrell didn't move to Ft. Worth, Texas, and open a dry cleaner nearby in order to save me a little coin some forty years later. Those are the breaks. Ah undahstand that it is possible we won't know anymore after your trip than now. Hopefully you will enjoy the trip anyway. Lola? Any chance you might accompany Jerrah and make it a sailin' honeymoon of sorts? At least then we'd have some certain benefit of it all."

"I need to stay close to Lily right now, especially if Jerry is out of town, but thank you so much for offering, Bodie," said Lola.

I said, "I'll need to clear it with Detective Delano. I am remembering she imposed some travel limitations on me the other day, but I'll see if they are lifted yet before making a plane reservation."

"Uh, Jerrah?" said Bodie. "I have one little tip for you. If at all possible, try not to punch Mr. Tyrell in the nose. You'll get better results from him that way." Bodie smiled.

No brain damage there at all.

Marisa and I went to Bodie's house to look for the money. The house was stuffy with no one living there. It smelled like cleaning chemicals and disinfectant left over from the cleaning crew that had been there. Marisa and I moved the dresser and I removed the fake air duct cover. Bodie's description was exact. There was no manila envelope.

Behind the air grate where Bodie said his money had been, the only thing I found was a stack of white letter envelopes bound together. They were fastened together sort of like the letters from James to his parents, but not with a yellow ribbon. They had a rubber band around them. No care had been taken to protect these documents, no care at all. I pulled them out, looked at the dusty stack briefly and handed them to Marisa. She looked at me confused. I shrugged and said, "Let's see if there's any money in them before we call Bodie." Marisa and I headed to Bodie's kitchen table to see what we had.

We sat down and Marisa took the rubber band off the stack. There were three envelopes. The first one had only the letters "DAD" written on the outside. It had been torn open along the top. There were no other markings at all and the envelope was empty. Marisa picked up the second envelope. It was addressed to Laura and Clayton Kohler and addressed to Bodie's house where we currently sat. Marisa did not open it. She handed it to me.

"We better look at it," said Marisa. "Who knows what this really is. Either Papa knows this stuff is here and didn't say or he has no idea that these were here. We should check on what it is before saddling Papa with more heartache right now."

Marisa took back the envelope from me, opened it carefully and pulled out the contents. It was the same type one-page letter that I had seen from James to his parents. Marisa read it aloud:

November, 1967
Dear Laura and Clayton:
Hope you are good and not giving Mom and Dad too much trouble with me gone. I am fine but would rather be in Ft. Worth than in Vietnam. We've been on patrol in the jungle all night long. When we got back this morning, I had to laugh because Dad would kill me if I stayed out all night back home. Here we stay out all night long a lot, but not for parties. Ha. While I'm over here, I expect you both to be good and hold down the fort there. You two have to take care of each other for awhile. Don't get into fights with each other. When I'm not there, you are the oldest and the responsible ones. Take care of yourselves and take care of Mom and Dad.
Love, James

"That is really sweet," said Marisa as she handed me the letter.

"What's in that last one?" I asked. Marisa pulled out the contents and unfolded several pieces of paper folded like letters. She read aloud: ·

January, 1970
Dad,
It has been two years since James died. Since I will be learning to drive this year it is important that I have my own car. I cannot get a job since I must still go to school. James would have had his car back if he were alive and here. James did tell me and Laura that we were in charge since he is gone now. Since I am your oldest living biological son now, I believe that I should have James' car as my own. We should uncover James' car and it should be mine because that is what James would want. Please let me know of your feelings on this.
Your son, Clayton

"Like, how creepy is that?" said Marisa. "Dad had that 'oldest living biological son' thing going with Papa since he was fifteen years old? That doesn't make any logical sense at all. So creepy." She handed me that letter and began to read the next one.

October 22, 1998
Mom and Dad,
With Victoria dead now, I can assume my rightful place as the least important human still alive. You should take care of Marisa now. She would be better off with you. If James had a wife with cancer, I promise she would still be alive. This could never happen to him. You would have kept it from happening if it was James' wife. You would have gotten here a better doctor. You would have paid for a better hospital. You never gave me that car anyway. It should have been mine. I should be able to leave that car to my daughter.

"It isn't signed," Marisa said as she handed me the last letter with big tears in her eyes. She said, "Jerry? Dad is really nuts, isn't he?"

I just looked at her. I am such a help.

"Do you think Dad left these when he took Papa's money?" asked Marisa.

"Maybe so," I replied. "I'm not sure if I'm capable of thinking like

Clayton. But it is almost as if he took Bodie's money from its hiding place and left these behind for Bodie. It's almost like he is just thumbing his nose at his own dad. I'm wondering if what was in this empty envelope was that other 'oldest living biological son' note to Bodie from Clayton. You know, from 2003 where he was demanding Bodie sign over his house to him?"

"There is one more," said Marisa and she read it out loud.

January, 2005
Dad,
You owed me.
Your son,
Clayton

Marisa was upset and got up from the table heading for the bathroom. She said as she walked away, "You maybe should call Mr. Zinn." Her voice trembled with emotion. I couldn't exactly have denied that Clayton was crazy. I sure couldn't think of anything to tell Marisa that might make her feel better. I called Harry Zinn. Harry was equally interested in the missing money and the letters we found. He said the letters will add to our claim of undue influence and coercion, not to mention the near admission of taking the money. Harry said that a good attorney would deny that note as an admission, but we all knew what had happened.

"Well, that explains that. I've given it some thought. Those funds are very near exhaustion on Ned Pearl's legal bills alone. It could not hurt us for me to let Ned know that we know his client's source of funds and that it is almost out. At least Ned will think about it as the process continues. There is a very real possibility that Ned will not get paid unless Clayton can steal some more money. Let me talk to Marisa so she will speak to Bodie about it."

Harry and Marisa spoke for a short while. Marisa promised to let her grandfather know. We both headed back to the hospital. By the time we returned to the hospital, it was after lunch. Lola was napping in the chair next to Lily, who was also asleep. So, I called Angela on her cell.

"Hello Angela, it's Jerry Wilson."

"Yeah, Jerry. What's up?"

"I need to go out of town for a few days. Just checking in to get an okay after what you told me the other day."

"Where are you headed?" asked Angela.

"Well Angela, without a subpoena, frankly, it is none of your business." I paused for impact. There was none. She didn't even make a sound.

"I'm headed to the Virgin Islands on a case. I'll be gone three or four days, maybe a couple more if I have to go from there to Boston. Can I get dispensation for three or four days or not?" Now I put a little annoyance in my voice. That's all she's hoping for anyway. I might as well give it to her so I can get off the phone.

"Yeah. No problem. Are Lola and Lily doing alright?" Angela asked.

"Lily's still hurting. Lola's on the road to recovery. Anything new on Duchtin or the van?" I need to annoy her back a little now. She's counting on that too.

"Nothing. Our guys got close enough to both vans to determine there has been body work to both. It's hard to say if it was recent. We questioned the people attached to each van, but got nothing. We're still watching them both. I'm still hoping Bodie's memory improves. I hear he's a lot better," said Angela.

"He is. Maybe his memory will improve if I'm out of town," I said. I wanted her to know Lola had told me about their conversation, but she was just counting on that as well, so I probably ended up making her happy.

"Hope so. Virgin Islands, huh? Wish I could get some business trips like that," Angela said.

"You've got different benefits," I said, "like a paycheck. If you can, would you have your guys watch my family while I'm gone? You've obviously already convinced Lola that you will or she wouldn't be letting me go. I guess I have you to thank for me going on this trip. Don't let me down. Lily may or may not get out of the hospital while I'm gone. I'm more than a little jumpy about leaving town with Duchtin's ass still not in jail."

"We'll stay on it, Jerry. Don't worry," replied Angela.

Yeah, it's not like I ever worry.

16. John Woo Movie

Lola dropped me off at D.F.W. Airport on Monday morning at 6:00 a.m. I was awake at 4:00 anyway. She held my face for longer than usual with her good right hand and kissed me for a long time in the car at the airport. I think she might miss me.

It is painful to leave my girls right now. I cannot believe that I am leaving town at a time like this. Lola won't be staying at home while I'm gone. She'll stay at the hospital in the room with Lily. It just feels like everything is up in the air and dangerous.

I am headed for San Juan, Puerto Rico. Five hours of my own thoughts. Yikes. Lola got me a spy novel because she is all too familiar with my worrying ways when I am by myself and she knows I like spy novels. I'm not sure how I could have survived to age fifty without her.

I've got a two-hour layover in Puerto Rico. A two-hour layover anywhere is only long enough to sit and people watch. My only tour of Puerto Rico on this trip will be from the air on approach to landing and on take-off of the exiting flight two hours later on a smaller plane that takes me to St. Thomas.

St. Thomas is a big sister island to St. John in the U.S. Virgin Islands. From the map in the airline magazine, it looks like it's about a driver and a seven iron over to the British Virgin Islands. Hey, I'm talking golf here. I have no idea if you can see other islands from any of them. We'll see.

What a death march of a butt-whippin' this trip could be.

First the five hour flight from D.F.W. to San Juan. Then it's a two hour wait for the little plane. When I finally finish the forty minute flight from San Juan to St. Thomas, I have to catch a taxi to either Charlotte-Amalie or across the island to Red Hook to catch a ferryboat. I am told it is a fifteen minute taxi and then forty five minute boat ride from Charlotte-Amalie to Cruz Bay on St. John. The alternative is a forty minute taxi across St. Thomas and a twenty minute boat ride from Red Hook to Cruz Bay. Having never been there, I have no idea, which of those choices might be better. The price seems to add up to be the same either way you go. It's fifteen dollars either way. Probably government regulated or they'd each be undercutting the other until nobody made any money. I think I'll take the longer boat ride. I've already been on too many car rides in my life.

Once I finally get to the island of St. John, it is another fifteen-minute taxi ride from the dock to the Westin Resort Hotel where I will be staying. All the hotels we priced on the Internet were expensive — $300 to $500 per night, so I stayed at the Westin where Tyrell's boat is located. Tyrell's sailboat is picking me up Tuesday morning at 9:00 for a five hour sail. When I called back to reserve the sailboat, Francesca answered with her great voice and told me to have my party at the dock at 9:00 a.m. I asked her the maximum number of people I could bring. She said a total of eight, including me. Well, that'll be interesting when they realize I'm the only one. Any chance we could get seven stunning beauties to come along and sun themselves topless on my chartered sailboat for a few hours? I'd rate the possibilities at just below doubtful. My guess is that as long as Tyrell and Francesca get paid, why would they care?

It's such a fine beginning for the plane to be late leaving D.F.W.

Yesterday at our noon game, the orneriest Pink Ponies I have ever seen kicked the collective butts of some unsuspecting suburban girls' team. The other team had nice fingernails and their hair looked sweet, when we started the game. My girls hammered them six to nothing. "Six-Nil" as they like to say in Europe. At my insistence, my team purposely let up most of the second half.

My girls had no mercy in their hearts at all in the first half. Not any of them.

Everybody was charged up about Lily not being there. It came out in the girls as serious and quiet determination. I usually don't see such traits in the twelve year old girls that I know. I missed Lily so much it hurt. The other girls missed her too.

After all six goals, three of them within the first four minutes, they sprinted straight to the sideline in a line, ran past and high-fived me. I mean after every single one of them. They didn't seem particularly happy about the goals, just fired up and serious. That has never happened. I'm not sure it means anything except they were thinking of me and of Lily. They were *Bloody Mud Mamas* for sure. No wimpy *Pink Ponies* were on that field yesterday.

Our opponents and their parents were not amused. There was a lot of yelling at the referees in the second half. The Ponies took a game ball to take to Lily in the hospital today. She will be pleased. Lily is one of our best players, but we didn't need her yesterday. After a game like that, none of them were happy about no practice this week. But I will be out of town. No game until next weekend anyway.

There was nothing left to do in the afternoon, so I followed up on the only lead I had left on Duchtin. That would be Miss Blondielegs. This took me back to twenty years ago, before I spent so much working time with Bodie. It went fine, but there is no question that working with Bodie is a ton more fun than without him. He would have pulled off this act with so much more flair, more class, more joy and more pure colorfulness than I will ever be capable of feeling or projecting.

I thought about this plan for awhile first but I did not tell Lola about it. She would have squelched the whole thing and batted me silly for even thinking it might work. I had dropped her off at the hospital after church and before the soccer game, so I had our only car. After the game, I put back on my suit from church. I looked presentable enough to be a salesman. I headed straight over to the townhouse where Blondielegs lived.

Here's the plan: find the mailboxes and hope for a name on it. Even if there isn't a name, I will knock on the door and award her with a free three-month gym membership to a new gym. The gym is real and newly opened in the area. The actual owners will soon be shocked to find that somebody has given away a new membership. If they get a look at Blondielegs, they just may honor the fake membership to get the opportunity of looking at her working out. I had no doubt they would thank me if they caught me. They won't catch me.

My only fear was that Duchtin would show up while I was there. Sunday afternoon? I hoped that it wasn't likely, but I would look around carefully before going ahead. I decided I would take the chance. I wanted to nail that guy in the worst way.

What I had not noticed the other night when Bodie and I were there was that the mailboxes were outside the complex on the street. I knew Blondielegs' unit number—2020. I drove up to the mailboxes like I owned the joint and got out to pretend to retrieve my mail. Sure enough, the mailboxes have the same numbers as the unit numbers. Written on a plastic label on the front of box 2020 was the name "Loving, Brandi." Yes, there were little hearts as the dots over the two "i"s. I had no doubt there would be. I pulled up to the guard shack. Fortunately, it was a different guard than when I was here the other night.

"Hi. I'm here to make a delivery to Brandi Loving in Unit 2020. She's expecting me." The guard wrote down my license number. I didn't like it, but there was nothing I could do. After he wrote down the number I feared he would call her. He didn't right away and I watched him in my mirror after he opened the gate and let me in. I don't think he called anyone. I drove back to her building. The red Porsche was parked just where it had been last week. I suspected it was hers, but didn't know that. There was no sign of Duchtin's Mercedes. I parked next to the Porsche where Duchtin had been parked. After looking around from my parking place and seeing nothing to scare me off, I headed up the stairs to Brandi's door.

She answered my knock pretty quickly.

I was nervous.

Up close, I was stunned at how young she looked. But those legs just keep getting better the closer you get. When she smiled upon opening the door, I was rendered extra stupid. Wow. I did my best to be subtle about looking her over, but it was not easy. She must be 5' 10" and most of that height is legs. I'm 6' 2." With her in those heels, we were eye to eye. Oh, yes, she had on the heels.

"Good afternoon, Ms. Loving. I am here on behalf of Max Curves Gym, conveniently located in the Hulen Crossing Shopping Center right up the road here. Have you visited our gym yet?"

"No, I haven't, but I noticed it had opened last month," she said enthusiastically. She had the voice of a child.

"Well, I wasn't sure if you had entered our drawing or someone had entered for you, but your name has been drawn out of our Grand Opening drawing for a free three-month membership to Max Curves. Congratulations to you!"

"Oh my God! I have never won anything in my life!" Her life may have only been barely twenty years so far, from what I could tell.

"Well, you have now. If I may come in for only a few minutes, I have a form to fill out and then I will leave you with a congratulatory letter. The first time you visit, you may present the letter and receive your new membership card," I said.

"Sure. C'mon in. This is so exciting!" said Brandi.

I had prepared a form and a congratulatory letter on the computer last night. Thanks, Lily, for all the computer lessons.

Brandi's Sunday afternoon ensemble for a cool, maybe not cold, winter day consisted of a flame red cotton shirt, with no buttons fastened whatsoever. The shirttail and that portion of the shirt which, if worn correctly, would cover all the velvety-ish looking skin below her ginormous breasts, was tied up underneath them. Yes, I am talking underneath said breasts and knotted in front. If I were her Dad (and I am willing to bet her Dad is younger than me) and she was wearing this, my advice would be for her to not make any—repeat—*any* sudden moves, else anyone in front of her would get quite a show. Clearly she had not received such advice from anyone as she proceeded to jump up and down in those heels.

I wasn't looking at the heels, though.

Those breasts had separate minds of their own. They went everywhere while she was jumping, including out of the shirt, such as it was. She was not the least bit embarrassed or concerned about her breasts being out of their cover. She was just plain excited about winning the gym membership.

"Do you think my friend, Charla, entered me? I know she started going to your gym. She loves it," and Brandi squealed with delight again.

Below the waist, situated way, way below the actual waist, and maybe closer to her crotch than her waist, Brandi wore a pair of what I only know to be "hot pants." Now this is a ridiculous name for unbelted short-shorts from the 1970s, but these stark white hot pants would fit tightly on most twelve year old girls. These hot pants might qualify as a belt to some girls. Any twelve year old girl would be embarrassed to wear them due to their lack of sufficient fabric. Up close it is easy to see that Brandi has the hips of a twelve year old girl, so why not? She reassembled her breastage under the red top and sat down a little too close to me on the couch, ready to fill out any form I wanted.

"Let's get started and I will get out of your way quickly, Ms. Loving."

"Oh, it's Miss. I'm not married."

"Ah. We were hoping you might be so your husband would join as well."

"Well, I have a boyfriend. Maybe I can get him to join."

"Excellent. We will be happy to offer him a fifty percent discount on the membership fees if he joins with you." *(They won't be quite as happy at the gym if Warren shows up.)* "Now, your name is Brandi Loving, we know from the entry card and we have the address. May I have your phone number?"

"Here," she said, and she took my clipboard and pen right out of my hands. "I'll fill it out. It will be a lot easier. Oh, this is so fun!" she squealed with pleasure and began writing furiously as if it were an essay exam and she already knew all the answers. "You know, my boyfriend just refuses to live with me for right now. He used to be like married and says he needs to live alone for awhile. He was separated and his soon to be ex-wife died recently."

She whispered 'died recently' like that would make it less painful for me. She was talking about a hundred miles an hour and writing on the form at the same time and with the same pace.

"I guess it's okay, because he rents this like, really nice place for me, but it gets *sooo* lonely when he isn't around. You know his ex-wife was sooo mean. I mean, I'm not glad she died or anything, but she was sooo mean to Warren. Warren Duchtin is my boyfriend. Do you know him?"

I shook my head 'no'.

"Her divorce attorney sent somebody over here to take pictures of me with him and the whole time she's got Wesley as her boyfriend on the side. Warren didn't send anybody to take pictures of her and Wesley! Can you believe that? She had other boyfriends before Wesley too. Warren told me. I didn't know her or anything. I'll just never understand why Warren married her in the first place. Warren is *such* a smart man. He is a very, very, very successful businessman. Maybe she was nice at one time, I don't know. Warren's a little bit older than I am but we get along like sooo great! He bought me a car last month. Did you see that little red Porsche downstairs? It is just so cute and sooo sexy! A couple of months before that, he bought me these." Brandi, still holding my pen, put her hands under the red top and onto her breasts with her arms crossed across her body. Right hand with pen on left boob, left hand without pen on right boob.

I thought she might bring them out to greet me again, but no such luck. She looked at my face while holding her own boobs and laughed right out loud. "I think I love them like maybe more than Warren does." Then she returned to writing on my fake form with total delight in her voice. She had not stopped talking, not even a pause. I did not even see her inhale.

"Warren says maybe after his wife's estate is settled, I can move over with him and maybe we'll even like get married. Oh, but we could still belong to your gym. What's your name, anyway?" Brandi stopped writing and talking and just stared at me smiling, waiting for a response as if it was my turn now. She cocked her head to one side like a cocker spaniel hearing a high-pitched squeak and waited for my turn to speak.

"Uh, it's Phil. Phil Cousteau." I had rehearsed myself to be Paul Drake, from the *Perry Mason* show, but Phil came out. Bodie would be so much better at this. "The gym is not mine. It belongs to my nephew, John Philip. I am retired, but I work for JP part-time now because I enjoy getting out and meeting people. You know." Brandi was totally enthralled by this riveting drivel. I had no idea where the story was going.

"Well," she started back writing on the form the instant that she started talking. It was as if one or the other wasn't an option. It had to be both at the same time. I don't remember that many blanks on the form, but Brandi was writing multiple chapters on it. "It *is* good to get out and meet people. I need to do something like that. I used to work in

130

Arlington at the Hooters restaurant, but that was before I got these."

Yes, she grabbed her own breasts again, this time on the outside of her shirt. This from a woman/girl who believes Hooters is actually a restaurant.

"Isn't that funny?" She scrunched up her nose and smiled at the same time, cocked and uncocked her head again. She was so much like a young kid that it was not funny. I smiled anyway and nodded. Then back to writing and talking went Brandi. "I met Warren at Hooters. Our friend Wesley introduced us, Wesley Drake. Do you know him?"

I'm sure I just sat there slack-jawed with my mouth open and no sound coming out. My silence didn't hamper her story at all.

"I met him at Hooters, too. I really think both of them just came in to talk to the girls, but lots of guys do."

Ya think? I thought.

"Before that I was a student at T.C.U. for a semester, but my grades weren't so good. I partied like way too much. I thought Wesley wanted to ask me out, but Warren did. Turned out that Wesley already had a girlfriend but I didn't know that then. Isn't that funny?" More nose scrunching. She stopped writing and I prayed that her breasts would be left alone for this explanation. She looked right at me. I steeled myself for more boob grabbing.

"Turns out Wesley's girlfriend was Warren's wife! How about that? Can you like believe it? Wesley works for Warren anyway. Now I'm thinking Wesley maybe just introduced us so maybe Warren wouldn't be so upset to lose his own wife to Wesley. I don't know. There. All done."

I took the clipboard from Brandi. I quickly looked over the form, which was completely full of narrative with little hearts dotting every "i" that she had written on the page. I didn't know where on the page to look first. I did notice that she was born November 16, 1983. Good God, she's just turned twenty-one! I cannot imagine this could be Lily in less than 10 years, but maybe that's what Brandi's dad thought too, some ten years ago.

"This looks great Miss Loving. Here is your congratulatory letter. Now please present it to the desk on your first visit and they will get your card right away."

Wear that outfit and they will race to get you a card, I thought.

"I'm off, Miss Loving. Thank you so much and congratulations."

I looked back once more from the bottom of the stairs and Brandi Loving was dancing. There was no music. But she was dancing like crazy just inside her own doorway. She had danced before, that was clear. She had danced before at this level of clothes wearing or even less, maybe with a pole. She let out a whoop and closed her door.

That's it.

The only question I had asked was her phone number. Got it and a little more. I scrunched my nose and cocked my head to one side in celebration. It was a stunning afternoon. There isn't a human alive that would believe this story. Maybe Bodie will because he's seen her, but meeting her in person adds a new dimension. Before, she was like a photograph on a page. Now she had life.

I felt sorry for Brandi Loving. She is another victim of that snake, Warren Duchtin. I pulled up to the gate to leave the complex and it started its automatic slow open. I rolled down my window and waved at the guard, then turned right to head out to Hulen and on home to call Lola. I was laughing out loud.

Glancing in the rear view mirror I saw a blue van following me closely.

It was *the* blue van.

There wasn't a doubt in my mind the instant I saw it. He had pulled behind me from a position parked on the street outside Brandi's complex. Even with the backwards letters and numbers in the mirror, I could read the plate—Texas AB2558. It was a dark blue Chevy van with blackout tint.

I floored the accelerator of the Jetta.

A hundred yards later, I was at fifty miles per hour. While accelerating, I reached over the center console down between the seat and the console of the Jetta. My window was still open completely. With one hand, I flipped the safety off my .38. I've got five shots. It always seems like it's enough until you need it. Maybe I need some James Bond pistol with 9 or 10 shot clips. Nah, then shell casings fly around. They'd probably hit me right in the eye.

I held the steering wheel with my left hand and my thigh preparing to aim out my window.

My sudden acceleration had put a little space between the van and me. But they were coming hard.

I spun the steering wheel hard left and the rear end squealed protest as the Jetta spun around. I hit the brakes hard and the rear of the car spun around harder.

The van was coming straight at me with full power and speed.

As my driver's side window turned from the spin to face the oncoming van, I held the gun out the driver's side window with both hands, steadying with my elbow resting on the door frame of the stilled Jetta. I squeezed off three rounds as fast as my finger would pull.

The echo of the shots within my car was deafening.

Squealing tires and smoking rubber imbedded the scene in my memory.

The driver's side window of the van exploded into a shattering mess as they drew even with me and then went by. The speeding van passed so close to my car that pieces of glass from their shattered window fell into the open driver's side window of the Jetta and on me.

It was like a John Woo movie, but it was me. It was real. I was wishing I was Tom Cruise balancing on one wheel of his super power motorcycle in unbelievably slow motion while firing deadly accurate bullets at the decisively bad guys. But this was my own impossible mission. I did not choose to accept it. It chose me.

They did not hit Lola's spinning Jetta. They missed by maybe a foot.

I popped open the driver door and jumped up, pistol and hands on top of the Jetta pointed at the rear of the blue van. Pieces of window glass tumbled off me as I got out.

The van weaved like they would lose control. Their brake lights did not come on. They were still accelerating. Tires squealed.

I held fire. Two left in the gun. I had no additional ammo. Not even a Barney Fife bullet. I might need those last two if they come back at me.

The van regained control. They nearly spun out turning onto Hulen and away they went.

I was dialing the cell phone before they had it under control on Hulen. I looked up and down the street. No one was out. No cars and no people. I could see all the way back down to the guard shack at Brandi's complex several hundred yards away. Nobody was around.

Nobody saw the exchange that I could see.

"9-1-1, what is your emergency?"

"Shots fired from one car at another."

"Sir...sir, what is your location?"

"Shut up and listen!" I shouted and she did.

"My name is Jerry Wilson. I am a licensed P.I. Shots fired by me at a late model blue Chevy van, Texas license plate AB 2558. Intersection of Hulen Drive and just south of Vickery between Colonial Country Club and the railroad tracks. They tried to run me over and kill me. I shot at them. Unknown injuries in the van. I can confirm that the van was hit by some of my shots. I am not hurt. They ran my wife and child off the road four days ago and nearly killed them. Contact Detective Angela Delano as soon as possible. She is working the case. I will not stay on scene for fear they are still nearby. They are northbound on Hulen Drive two minutes ago and driving way too fast. Two minutes! Get somebody looking for them now! Tell Detective Delano I went to my home if she needs me. She knows where it is."

I hung up on 9-1-1.

I was shaking pretty badly and not just because I was going to have to tell Lola I had fired my gun. I started heading the Jetta towards my home. Thirty seconds to a minute later, Angela called my cell. "What's your twenty, Jerry?"

"I'm not following them, Angela! They got away from me. I'm headed home to my house. Lola is at the hospital, so if they come after me, I'm the only one home. Is your guy still at the hospital?"

"Yes. I will advise him. Are you hurt and did you see the guy driving?"

"No, I am not hurt and I did not see anyone in detail. A Caucasian male with stringy brown hair, mustache and sunglasses was driving. Blackout tinted windows on the van. The driver's window was busted by one of my shots. Texas plate AB 2558, blue Chevy. Don't know how many of them there were. But there are at least three bullet holes in the van put there by me. I hope when you find the van, the interior is full of blood and dead bodies. They tried to ram me from behind, just like Lola. They did not hit me."

"Jerry, there will be an officer at your house when you get there. He will have to ask you questions to file the report. He is on your side.

Do not, and I mean it—DO NOT try to piss him off like you do me. Cooperate so we can get these guys. We've got units in your area now and we are looking for the van. It is the L.L.C. van of the two we were watching, but that doesn't mean much right now."

"Track 'em down, Angela!"

Just like she told me, the officer was at my house and standing on my porch looking up and down the street when I pulled up. I did as Angela asked and he took down all the information I had. If I pissed him off, he didn't show it. I did not try to.

Finally, I told him I had to go to the hospital. He said he would be out front for awhile anyway. They would have extra patrols by my house all night. Before I left for the hospital, I reloaded my gun. For me to have to fire that gun—it will be serious to Lola. She will be uneasy about this case now, as if being run off the road wouldn't do it for her.

Lola handled this story better than I anticipated. We, uh, "discussed" whether or not I should still go out of town tomorrow. My position was that the trip was off and there was nothing else to say. I needed to be in Ft. Worth and protect my family from these idiots that are trying to kill us all. Lola's position was that the police would be with her and Lily whether or not I was in Ft. Worth. The risk then becomes how much trouble Jerry can get into if something else happens.

Lola asked, "Would you shoot again if in a similar spot, Jerry?"

"Yes I would."

Lola asked, "Would you like to kill first and ask questions later, Jerry?"

"Yes I would. What is your point?" I asked her without a hint of a smile.

"Hmmm...I wonder what my point is," replied Lola, but she didn't smile either.

Lola said, "The only question that should be in your mind, Jerry, is whether or not the police can do a good job of defending us in this hospital."

Here is the clincher—Lola had been talking some more to Angela. Uh-oh.

Detective Delano felt, before the new incident with the blue van, that the only way she would get a new angle at Warren Duchtin is if Bodie started remembering his beating. Will Bodie speak about it with Jerry around? Angela said "no."

Lola said, "Look, Jerry. As much as I don't want you to leave right now, we may not get out of this mess for awhile unless you go ahead and go on this trip. I am not interested in having bodyguards all the way until the *someday* that Lily gets married."

"That is not funny, Lola. How can I leave town now? No way!" I said to her.

Then she smiled at me. I so wish I could put that smile in my pocket.

"Way," she said.

I told her I thought it would be best if she stayed either at the hospital or at a hotel while I was gone. I said if she wanted to argue with me that I would not leave town at all. She let me think that I got my way, but that's what she would have done anyway.

Angela came to the hospital to try to reassure us both. It was clear that Angela had already talked to Lola while the officer asked me questions at the house.

I was being ushered out of town. I was done for.

They did not locate the van yet. I told Angela and Lola the story of Miss Brandi Loving, but in light of the afternoon's excitement, it wasn't nearly as funny as I thought it would have been. I think the problem was in the telling. Maybe it will be funnier later. Angela took notes. Sure, now she takes some notes. She would never laugh anyway. I just wanted to make Lola laugh.

Joanne having a boyfriend, Wesley Drake, and Joanne already having a divorce attorney were the two significant new pieces of the story. Plus the fact that Joanne's boyfriend worked for Warren Duchtin. This was a new chance to nail him. If Duchtin knew about the boyfriend and/or the divorce attorney, there was a link to Duchtin having been the one who killed Joanne. That pig didn't need a motive. I believe he'd kill Joanne just for sport.

It was just another typical Sunday afternoon in Ft. Worth, Texas.

17. Layover

It was planes, boats and trucks to get to U.S.V.I. No trains.

To get to St. John, you generally have to go through Miami or San Juan, Puerto Rico from almost anywhere, including the known center of the universe, Ft. Worth, Texas. My ace travel agent, Lola Wilson, booked me through San Juan because the layover was a little shorter but it didn't matter to me a whit where I was stuck for two hours.

Welcome to San Juan International Airport. Wait until we call you. Our call may or may not be in your mother tongue.

In any airport, people-watching reveals the immense world we live in and enormous number of people in it. I'll tell you that if you spend most of your life in the sweet bubble of Ft. Worth, Texas, which is a good thing, it gets easier over time to forget how big this world really is.

Occasionally in this mass of humanity on the move, you too might spot *Long Stride Guy*. Most striking about *Long Stride Guy* is the generous distance between the top of his head vertically down to the top of his belt. Not his waist—his belt. Waist location on the body is not relevant here.

Conventional length shirttails are completely inadequate for *Long Stride Guy* to tuck in. Sizes vary, but average size pants for *Long Stride*

Guy would be a 48 waist, 26 inseam. Now, I'm a 38 waist and 33 inseam. I can still remember being a 32 waist, 34 inseam, but those memories are fading fast. It is unclear why my inseam has shrunk. Weight gained over the years must have compressed my spine. I'm gettin' shorter, I guess.

I defy you to locate a consumer who has actually seen size 48/26 pants available at any retail location. Maybe you have, but only at 'Hiram's Lo Waist/Long Stride Shop for the Obtusely Short Legged'.

What bold designer decided to make men's pants with an eighteen-inch zipper? When *Long Stride Guy* walks down an airport concourse, the top of the inseam on his pants strikes leg just above the knee forcing shorter than natural steps. The short legs of the pants prevent steps of normal length. *Long Stride Guy* takes twice as many steps as you and me to cover a given distance. To get to gate E-29 in the airport concourse, it is one-half mile for us and a full mile hike for *Long Stride Guy* because he has to take shorter steps. The hip-hop culture has adopted the *Long Stride Guy* look as its own and made every effort known to man to make it seem cool. But it there isn't any doubt in my mind that it originated with extremely heavy, mildly retarded Caucasian guys. But hey, that's just my opinion. No doubt it looks good on you.

Shopping at the same stores and buying the same pants, but wearing them in a jaunty, stylish manner, is *High Waisted Bulging Package Guy*. This method of wearing the long-stride pants is to present the belt on that portion of the torso that yields the smallest circumference for the pants to fasten around and to pretend that this is the actual waist. Generally this location is a significant distance above the belly button and accompanying love handles and a comfortable distance below the bulging man-breasts. Hip-hop culture has yet to adapt this variation, to my knowledge. Yo, man, keepin' it real.

Older variations on such presentations include the *Slant Waisted Middle Age Guy*. As the belly has grown, the belt must be continuously pulled up, but *only* in the back, so that the backside of the hem is well above the shoe top and the front side hem completely covers the front of the shoes. Sometimes it's sandals with black, nylon socks if headed for a beach vacation. To set off the ensemble, backside pant hiking is a full time hobby for this guy. Belt buckles on this model can actually appear to face the ground in front. Note to self: Design and market a big belt buckle with a flashlight built-in. With a big belly and the buckle facing the ground, it would be like having a headlight to see where you are walking.

"Ladies and Gentlemen, we are now ready to board our Platinum Club passengers on Flight 2449 from San Juan to St. Thomas. We will continue general boarding by row number in just a few minutes."

Thank you God, I thought.

The little plane was cool. You get a better view from a little plane that flies at a lower altitude. That part of the world was really beautiful. A full thirteen hours after waking—over eight hours from Dallas/Ft. Worth takeoff, two cab rides, a one mile hike through a construction ravaged San Juan airport; being blessed with one great new get-rich-quick marketing idea ('The Belt Headlight'), one ferry boat, another ride in the back of a pick up truck from an enormous but friendly and smiling black man who seems to understand English (what he spoke in return was positively unidentifiable), I stood before a desk clerk in the open-air lobby of the Westin Hotel & Resort on the island of St. John in U.S.V.I., Caribbean Sea, planet Earth.

"Reservation for Wilson, Jerry," I said.

I spoke to Lola on the phone after I checked in. Lily is better. Bodie is better. Everybody is better since I left town. Fabulous.

The police have taken Wesley Drake into custody. He sought treatment for a gunshot wound to his left side from a doctor in Hurst, a suburb of Ft. Worth/Dallas. The doctor called police as he is legally bound to do with any gunshot wound. Ft. Worth Police also have the blue van now. They have *the* blue van. They have confirmed upon close inspection that this is the van that ran Lola and Lily off the road.

Wesley had not admitted anything yet and he had not implicated anybody else. His only claim, made with his attorney present, was that he had been watching his boss' girlfriend for his boss, Warren Duchtin, when some guy started shooting at him randomly. Angela told Lola not to worry about it. They made it clear to Wesley that he was being held for the investigation of the murder of Joanne Duchtin and on charges of attempted murder on Lola, Lily and Jerry Wilson. I felt big relief that he was in custody and was absolutely thrilled I had shot him. My only regret was that he survived.

Ned Pearl notified Harry Zinn that Clayton intends to continue on the hearing in his absurd attempt to declare Bodie incompetent. If Clayton wins, the revocation of Clayton's P.O.A. would be rendered null and void. Through his attorney, Clayton agreed to stay away from the hospital and Bodie. Lola and I agreed that if the judge sees the tape of when Bodie revoked the P.O.A., it would instantly be game over. That hearing is in a couple of days.

Bodie still hasn't remembered the beating or so he tells Angela. When she pressed him he did manage to recall that he was beaten with a metal baseball bat, but that's all he remembers.

I told Lola in my best imitation of generic rich guy, Thurston Howell III, "Lovey, I am just too tired for words and I simply must go sailing in the morning."

Made her laugh.

18. Puppies in the Pound

There were only a few guests scattered around by the pool as I made my way down the hill to the bay to look for Tyrell, Francesca and their boat the next morning at about ten minutes to nine. It must have been a little early for resort living.

It felt strange to not have crispy, cold air on a February morning. It was, uh, tropical.

The pool was huge and wound around down near the bay with a beautiful beach between the pool and the bay. There must have been a hundred boats of all kinds moored out in the bay. There was a permanent *Activities* hut built on the beach near the only visible dock. Sailboards and other water toys were lined up and ready for the day.

On the beach next to the dock was a dishy young brunette, maybe in her mid-twenties. She wore a teal colored, torn, sleeveless T-shirt that covered some of her shoulders down to not quite below her not-insignificant breasts. There it was torn off all the way around. The bottom portions of her breasts were the same mocha tan color as her taut midriff. There has not yet been a childbearing event included in this girl's life. The neck of the shirt was also torn down in the front. I suppose this would allow sufficient breathing room for the tops of her breasts. Her torn top covered more of her than a bikini top would, but it's a much more startling look.

The rest of her body was very athletic and lean like one of my young soccer players, but very much grown up. Something was scripted across the chest of her shirt in gold, but it I could not quite read it. I might like to study the script for a bit, but not because I give a care about what her shirt says.

Besides flip-flop sandals, the only other items of clothing worn by this woman were banana yellow bikini bottoms that were big enough to cover critical body parts only. I was looking forward to the rear view when I walked by. She sported stylish, athletic looking sunglasses and a faded red baseball cap with a small flag. As I closed in, I could read the embroidered name 'Puerto Rico' sewn into the flag patch on the hat. Dark hair cascaded everywhere from beneath the back of that cap.

She was surely Hispanic in heritage, based solely on her looks. It was clearly worth hoping that this might be Francesca. As I walked nearer to her at the start of the pier I could see that her skin was the color of lightly creamed coffee and was the exact same tone of darkness everywhere on her you could see. I could see almost all of her. There were no visible tan lines.

This girl stood in a manner that was more than confident. It was cocky arrogant. Her hands were on her hips and one leg out to the side a little as if she didn't want to wait, but she must. This girl had way more important things to be doing than to be waiting for some idiot sailing passenger. She was adorned by at least a half dozen gold bracelets on each arm of varying widths. The bracelets rattled together when she moved any part of her body and she continuously moved in her fixed position with severe restlessness. People would look toward that sound if they heard it. She had cornered both the sight and sound senses. No one, male or female, could keep from looking if they heard or saw her.

The gold looked great against her skin.

Anything would look great against that skin.

There has been no sign of any other person since I walked past the pool. Please be Francesca. She broke out a grin as wide as the bay. Flawless teeth appeared to be bright white because of how tan she was. She said, "Señor Wilson, yes?"

"Si', Francesca?"

It is already such a good day.

"Si'. I am Francesca. Nice to meet you. How many are we waiting for, eh?

"We are waiting for no one. I am the only passenger today, Francesca. My partners all wish to stay on land today, so I will sail alone with you and, I hope, Captain Billy." I lied. I didn't really hope.

Francesca shrugged and said, "But you will still go sailing, yes?"

"Si'," was my only reply, as I was now suddenly stricken fluent in Spanish.

"Okay, is bueno," said Francesca and she smiled like that would be even better than she could have imagined. I wish. "We go to the boat by tender. Right this way, please, Señor Wilson."

She gently removed her flip flops and gracefully waded into the water a few feet from the beach to a tiny pontoon boat with a small outboard motor fixed to the back. Once she reached the boat, she stood in the knee deep water and waved me out. I took off my big, clunky sandals and plodded after her with the coordination and exact same weight and dimension of a walrus. She waved me into the boat and I stumbled aboard onto the front bench facing the prow, uh bow. I faced the front. Whatever. Francesca untied the little boat, spun it around and hopped from the water into the back, all in one motion. She pushed us off and away from the beach. I turned and watched her pull the cord on the outboard. Off into the bay we went. The morning water was mirror smooth in the bay.

The hills on both sides of the bay were fairly steep and tall protecting the bay from the wind. Each side was covered with expensive looking homes. I could see a handful of them that were either under construction or under renovation. In either case those houses looked like an absolute mess. No one was visibly working at any of them at 9:00 a.m. on a Tuesday.

Looking back at Francesca was difficult if not impossible to resist. Behind her, the hotel looked like a country club from the water view. We weaved between several moored boats and came up on a huge catamaran, all white with blue accents and a mast that must extend up sixty or seventy feet. A very tan old man was sitting on the deck smoking a cigar.

This guy looked like an extra large version of Popeye the sailor man with a cigar instead of a pipe. Francesca swung the pontoon boat around the back and up to the ladder where she motioned me up the ladder. As I climbed up, the old man was suddenly standing at the top. He offered me a ham-hock of an arm without changing his scowling facial expression. I took his help to climb the last part and heard the little motor rev. Francesca moved the tender up the center of the big catamaran underneath the deck to the buoy up front where she tied it off and climbed on board the cat up front.

Popeye looked me up and down through squinty eyes and finally spoke in a deep, gravely tone and a hint of Southern U.S.A. to his accent, "Hope you got some sunscreen. If not, you'll be lobster boy by noon. You the only one today?"

There wasn't a cloud in sight. He was probably right.

"Yes sir. You Captain Billy?" said lobster boy.

"I am," he replied. "Same price, eight of you or one of you. Any problem with that, lobster boy?" But he grinned a little.

"Nope."

"Great!" said Billy, "More to drink for the rest of us!"

Billy kept watching me but hollered, "Francesca! Looks like a great day for sailin'. Let's get her underway." Francesca was already moving ropes or sails or something when Billy yelled. She seemed to just ignore him and kept doing whatever she had been doing. I thought it must be a script. Soon I would discover that nothing about Captain Billy is scripted.

"You Wilson?" Billy asked.

"Yes sir. Jerry Wilson." Billy harumphed when I said my name, as if he was thinking, 'we'll see about that'. I sat on one of the benches along the sides of the deck. There was a cabin up front and down some stairs. Inside the cabin were a big bed and another room, maybe a bathroom, with a curtain over the little doorway. Opposite the bed were a counter and some shelves with doors over them. Maybe it was a makeshift kitchen. Everything looked clean and well kept. The cat was huge. There was a big wooden ship's wheel at the back that looked like it might have come off the HMS Bounty or some such. Captain Billy sat down back by the wheel and smoked his cigar, looking around the bay. Francesca slaved away all over the catamaran making ready. It was a pleasure to watch her. If you looked at all, you saw pretty much all of her.

A few minutes later from the front of the boat Francesca shouted, "Bueno. Casting off, Captain Billy." She had untied us from the buoy and immediately scrambled up onto the deck above the cabin and began raising the mainsail. It looked like maybe she could have used a couple of linebackers to help her, but Captain Billy was the only one in sight and he was interested only in his cigar and something mesmerizing on the side of the hill along the bay.

I noticed she had removed all her bracelets which rendered her into stealth mode. Also barefoot, there was little chance of hearing Francesca now. But it was nearly impossible for me to look away from her. As the sail went up, the big cat began to move. Billy spun the giant wheel left and the boat responded immediately. Francesca was a busy girl for the next five minutes. I have no idea what she was doing. She was tying and untying ropes. She was moving ropes through pulleys. Who knows, but the big boat was already moving and we weren't yet out of the bay.

"I've never been sailing before. First time," I said to Captain Billy. He did not respond to me at all, even with a glance. I get that a lot.

A couple of minutes later we were leaving the protected bay into the open ocean, I presumed. The boat began to pick up speed as we got the full effect of unimpeded wind. Captain Billy was standing at the ship wheel looking straight out over the front of the boat, the bow, and he said, "Well, you'd never know it."

When he spoke, I turned and looked at Billy. I realized he had already tossed me a cold beer. It was airborne and on target. Not at all prepared, I fumbled it. The can of beer dropped to the deck. I pounced on it quickly. I looked up at Billy from my knees on the deck as he popped himself one and pretended not to notice my fumble recovery. The beautiful Francesca looked down at me from the forward deck and grinned big.

Even in what I thought was the open ocean I could see islands all around me. "What are all these islands?" I asked Billy.

"This one we just left is St. John. We just left Fish Bay and then passed Rendezvous and Chocolate Hole. That there is Cruz Bay where the ferryboat comes in from St. Thomas that I guess you rode over. We'll go around the corner and see Honeymoon Beach and Caneel Bay that has a big resort hotel. On down the way, we'll see one of the prettiest around, Cinnamon Bay, lined with some expensive homes. But they're all expensive, even the shacks. Back over there is St. Thomas. That's probably where you caught the ferryboat over to

St. John. On down the way there through all those little cays is Jost Van Dyke. It belongs to the British. It's got a few people on it and *Foxy's Bar* is there, but that's about it. It's pretty famous. When we swing around the other side of St. John, you'll be able to see some more of the British islands, but they look just like all the others that aren't British. This little one over here is a private island and it's for sale for about seven million dollars. Bring your checkbook?"

I just smiled, glad he would finally talk a little. Captain Billy never seemed to smile completely.

"Hey, Wilson." Billy said. I squinted a look back at him. "Francesca wants to know if you'd take offense if she took her top off."

What a great day.

"No problem-o as long as I can take mine off too," I replied. I am relatively certain there must be a local ordinance against someone in my weight division taking off his shirt. Not only by weight, but my skin was as white as Francesca's teeth. People from miles around would have to strap on sunglasses from the glare.

Billy gave me thumbs up. God, he looks just like a giant Popeye, wrinkled, sour face, sailor hat and all. I smiled at the thought just looking at him. I looked up front. Francesca wasn't even wearing her shirt anymore and was moving ropes or something but dressed only in the red cap, sunglasses and the yellow bikini bottoms. Told you there were no tan lines. She wasn't the least bit concerned about offending me or anybody else. By all indicators, she never wore a top while in the sun.

We sailed on for a ways and things calmed down a little bit onboard. Billy and Francesca tacked the boat back and forth through the wind. The water seemed pretty calm to me, but I've got no basis to judge. I got to go on a twelve foot Sunfish sailboard on Eagle Mt. Lake once for about half an hour. That water was rougher than the ocean.

There were times when Francesca sat on the upper deck facing the front. She leaned back supported by her own arms, stiff behind her, palms down on the deck. She seemed—happy. I know I was. Billy smoked his cigar, drank beer and steered. I witnessed little to no communication between Billy and Francesca. Billy is probably in his mid-seventies, maybe near eighty. He looks at least eighty-five. I guess Francesca is about twenty five. They were such different people that the whole scene was surreal. Who knows what their relationship entails? I didn't ever sense anything stronger than mere familiarity between them.

"Buy you another beer?" I asked Billy.

"Anytime," he replied and he tossed me another. I caught this one. He also got himself one and I wondered what the beer was costing me, uh, costing Bodie. I noticed the beer cooler stayed in the back near Captain Billy.

"How about Francesca?" I asked him.

"Nah. She don't drink. But she can sail the shit out of any boat you want."

"You guys married?" I pried.

"Neither of us is married," Billy answered. I have no idea what that means and that is exactly how he meant it. "You?"

"Oh, yeah. For fifteen years. One daughter, twelve."

"I've been married three times. Never took," said Billy. "Never had kids, myself. I traveled a lot," Billy was suddenly a wellspring of information.

"I hear you were a U.S. Marine in Vietnam," I had sneaked up on him.

Captain Billy shot me a scowling look of curiosity. "Francesca don't even know that, so must've been somebody else told you. Somebody stateside, huh?" quizzed Billy.

"People talk," I said. "Were you a Marine in Vietnam?"

I waited an uncomfortable length of time for any answer, but didn't get one. I started again, "I have studied a little about Vietnam. I was a little bit young to have gone, so it didn't happen. College. Studied accounting. But I read a lot about it even recently. I looked over the history of the Tet offensive in 1968. Were you there then?"

Captain Billy Tyrell did not react in any way to the question. He just steered the boat.

"Hey, I don't mean anything by it. Just interested," I said.

In a normal calendar year, I drink maybe four beers spread way out over the entire year. Never two of them back to back. It's just shy of 10:00 a.m. on a Tuesday and I'd already had two. I'd guess two or three beers would be a regular breakfast for Billy. It made me feel bold and a little fearless.

"I'd be interested in hearing about your Vietnam duty if you'd be willing to talk to me about it. During your service in Vietnam, you ever hear about American soldiers killing other American soldiers?"

Uh, really bold and a lot fearless.

Billy's eyes narrowed with a look that could bore a hole through a brick wall. He pointed a very tan, thick, experienced index finger hard in the air towards me and spoke in his smoky, gravely, worn voice, "Boy, you got some diarrhea of the mouth there, son." Captain Billy paused to snarf smoke out of his large cigar. "I'll tell you right now. I blame them stinkin' E.D.C.s for me not being able to get laid. That why you're here? *Economically Develop* us with another *Corporation* built to evade U.S.A. taxes by moving down to U.S.V.I.? Or are you some member of that Economic Development Commission our Congress set up to generate business down here? And, Jerry, huh? Is that some kinda stinkin' '*kraut*' name? Gerry was the name we called them Germans in W.W.II. Ahhhhh, it just meant that when you turned that stupid lookin' Gerry helmet upside down, it looked like something you ought to take a piss in. I guess Gerry was some word for pisser. You a pisser, Wilson?"

There was immediate, emphatic head shaking by me, "No. I— uh—was just, was asking…"

Captain Billy started again, without regard to whatever my response would have been. "Who knew when them evil E.D.C.s was created by our industrious congress we got that they'd be a thousand rich white guys movin' to the island every six months for a bunch of years. No income taxes? Let's move to the islands, *mon*. Jesus H.! Pretty soon, all these rich white guys are biddin' on the same properties to buy on the island. They build some and buy some more. Guess what happened to them real estate prices? Think I'll ever be able to buy something here now? Shacks in the hills are half a million dollars!"

I didn't respond since I didn't know what to say. I looked up for Francesca, but she was sitting way up front and not listening at all. What a bronze goddess she was on the front of the boat.

Billy took a deep draw on the cigar as if the only oxygen he needed must be heavily mixed with smoke. I envisioned his lungs the same leathery brown as his skin on the outside. The smoke seemed to ease Billy off a bit and he continued, "So I pick up this lady down at the Beach Bar. It is on the beach, but the name of it's the Beach Bar. It's down there next to Joe's Rumhut. Anyway, I bring her back to my boat one night. See, I have to live on the boat 'cause them rich white guys in the E.D.C.s done drove real estate prices so high that I'll never be able to buy a place on St. Thomas or St. John. So I got to live on the boat. One thing leads to another. Pretty soon, nature calls. I point out the bathroom behind the curtain over there. Turns out if she's got to pee in the can, it's a deal breaker. She headed straight outa here and back to the Beach Bar. So, I can't get laid 'cause ah guys like you and them stinkin' E.D.C.s."

At this absurdity, I did my best to stifle a laugh that was threatening to erupt. Beer passed through my nose and onto the deck. Captain Billy kind of smiled at that. He kept on going, "Just got our first white senator down here. Him or somebody like him has been runnin' for that office for fifteen years. Finally got enough white guys here to elect one and it ain't sittin' too good with the mob. And theys the ones created this mess. That's all it is, the mob and one white guy runnin' these islands. A little envelope full of cash still gets more done than a dozen guys could, white or black. Least that's still the same. Or so I hear. Not that I'd know. Don't have enough cash to need an envelope, myself. Ahhh…this sailin' business is okay, I guess. Like to look at the scenery, like Francesca," Billy said nodding her way. Francesca was busy out of earshot. "I'm thinkin' of becomin' a day trader. You know, stocks, options, maybe some commodities. I hear guys talk on this here boat. Beans in the teens, huh? Seems like everybody's makin' a bunch of money but me."

I had no idea what he was talking about, but I smiled and nodded knowingly. I looked at Francesca. Truthfully, at that point, that's all I wanted to do anyway.

Billy said, "I was gonna buy me one of them laptop computers and learn the software for tradin'. But I ran into some health issues. Had to get a colonoscopy. Turns out it was the same price as a laptop. They rammed a garden hose up my ass and had a little look-see. Took two polyps out. Benign, both of 'em. So instead of a laptop I got a hose up my butt. Some say that's what I'll get if I start day tradin'." Billy smirked a half smile again.

Despite receiving way too much information, I could not keep from laughing. Now I'm unsure of the risks involved so I ask again, "What about Vietnam, Captain Billy?"

Billy didn't even acknowledge that my words were spoken, much less that anyone else but he was present. I figured he was still stewing about not being able to get laid and how else that could be my fault. I sipped my beer hoping to cover my nervousness. If I sipped, maybe when I laughed it wouldn't bless the deck again through my nose.

Then all tension left Captain Billy's manner entirely. "Yeah, you cravin' them sea stories, ain't you? You know down in St. Barts them Germans brung subs over to the Caribbean during W.W.II in the 1940s. They came over and got stuck here because there ain't any *German* diesel available anywhere in the Caribbean. Hear they finally talked some Puerto Ricans into stealing them some fuel. The Gerries bought it from 'em for a hell of a lot of German marks, even more stolen American dollars and gold jewelry. Hope them peckerhead krauts all drowned on the way back to the mother country. But while they was stuck, it was a hell of a war, right down there in St. Barts. Them and our very own U.S. Marines. I know because, well, I was there."

After a big inhaling draw, cigar smoke swirled Captain Billy's head and away with the wind while he decided whether to tell more. "You know, I love Puerto Rico. It is so beautimus. I'm wantin' to move there. And hey, them Puerto Ricans are okay," he argued to no one's comment but just in case someone was thinking ill of Puerto Ricans, then another downshift in Billy's tone, " as long as they don't kill ya."

Having just taken a big swig, I unsuccessfully snuffed another laugh blessing the deck with more beer snot. This story was better than any answers to my questions might be.

"They don't like gringos much, but I'll be okay. Yeah, I'd like to buy a couple of acres up in them hills on that north side of Puerto Rico. Land is still pretty cheap over there. Every afternoon a big cloud rolls over and it rains. They say it's so humid that it's hard to grow great dope, so that's a drawback, but the women—Gawd." Billy squinted a long look at the lovely Francesca, who did her best to stretch for ropes or whatever. She was very aware of being nearly naked and being admired. She smiled back at Billy and at me, but there's no way she could hear what was being said. "Francesca is Puerto Rican, ya know."

I gave up and laughed out loud. Drunk as I've been in fifteen years—on two beers. What a wussy.

There was no uneasiness in Billy's voice, only pondering consideration. "Every stinkin' turn in the road there are more beautimus women. They're young girls really, not even twenty-one yet. They got skin like caramel. They walk away from you in them sarong skirts and nothin' on underneath. It looks like two bobcats in a tow sack leavin' town." Captain Billy was talking faster now. Hard to say if it was to get further away from things he'd just as soon not remember or just on more quickly to more preferable subjects. "Them beautimus P.R. girls with all that beautimus skin, they get all cleavaged-up in their push-up bras."

The seventy some year old, linebacker-esque Captain Billy raised his huge arms straight up in the air waving them back in forth and prancing like a pony in his best teenage girl voice, "It's like—pick me, pick me, pick me. Oh baby! It's like puppies in the pound! Puppies in the pound! Gawd, I love Puerto Rico."

I was laughing so hard I forgot why I came to the Virgin Islands.

Even Captain Billy was chuckling, mostly at the sight of me laughing. Billy handed me another beer and helped himself to another. How many more hours of sailing and drinkin' to go, I wondered? "Captain?" I started, "It's hard for me to ask these questions about Vietnam and I appreciate that..."

Billy interrupted with a calming tone, "Yeah, you just cravin' them sea stories and I got 'em, baby. We'll see. We'll see. Francesca! Take this goddamn boat back to the dock, pronto," said Billy.

"Si'," she responded, but she looked as puzzled as you could, while nearly naked. We had not been gone an hour yet.

"Wait!" I said to the Billy. "Please. I've only been reading about Vietnam because my friend wants to know about his son. My friend is Dr. Bodie Kohler from Ft. Worth, Texas. His son was Corporal James Kohler who was in your unit when you went into Hue' in 1968. He was killed there and his friend, Ray Johnson, was wounded. Johnson won't tell me anything. He told me I had to talk to you first. I don't want to trap you or sue you or do anything else to you. I just want to know what you know. That's all," I pleaded.

Billy let all that just sit there like a giant smelly pile on the boat. "Listen, Jerry, was it?" Captain Billy made a face worse than his normal tan, wrinkled grimace. "I'm gonna call you—'Joe'. 'Jerry' is the guys we was shootin' at in 1945. Yeah—Joe. That's a good American name."

"Here comes Joe, cravin' them sea stories. I got 'em, Joe. I got 'em. Listen, Joe, we was killin' Germans and they were killin' us, all over St. Barts. Yeah…St. Barts! Most people don't know that. Well, we couldn't figure where they came from, but then that old barkeep on the beach, Freddy. He told us that some German sub came and let 'em off by boat from the sub offshore. Pretty soon there was bullets a whizzin' by in all directions, 24/7. We were shootin' to kill and so were they. Took us a good long time just to figure out who they was. This was jungle fightin'—not like any other places of that war. You couldn't see 'em but you knew they were there from the bullets flyin' by your head. This was Vietnam, only twenty five years earlier."

Joe, also known as lobster boy, also known as Jerr…, I perked up at the first reference to a subject in my original question. Hope jumped up and then fell back quickly. But it was the first acknowledgment by Captain Billy that the subject had been brought up at all.

Captain Billy forged ahead on his own uninfluenced agenda, "It was a couple of weeks after the shootin' all started. Nobody on the island had been out of their hiding places. A few of them Germans came to visit Freddy at his bar down on the beach one late Saturday afternoon. Oh, hell yeah. Freddy's is famous. At gunpoint, Freddy served them up some bottles of beer. He said he don't know if that's what they was asking for, but that's what Freddy knows to do and it seemed to keep 'em from shootin' him. Freddy said they were confused that the beer was cold but they didn't shoot him over that neither. Never have understood that one. Guess them heathens drink warm beer at home. Good Gawd! "

It was clear that Captain Billy would tell me only what Billy wanted to tell. I decided to just listen and look for an opening. That is all I could do.

"Wadn't long 'fore them Gerries was drunk, or pretty drunk. Nothing like a bunch of drunks with loaded heavy weapons to liven up a evenin'. Them dumbasses even started singin'! Nothing we'd ever heard before. Sounded like friggin' Oktoberfest out there. About twenty of us marines had got wind of this hoe-down. We made our way to a stand of trees within about seventy-five to eighty yards of open beach of the Germans. After observin' this mess, Sarge got really pissed that they was drinkin' beer while we were watchin'. But he didn't think that was all of them guys out drinkin' in the open and it coulda been a trap for us to get wiped out by the rest of 'em hidin' nearby. We just didn't know, but we did know Sarge was pissed."

I had stopped looking down at my beer or off in the distance or at Francesca and had actually become attentive.

"Listen, Joe," said Billy, "Except for Sarge, we was kids. Aww, most of was eighteen or nineteen. Sarge was a superhero to all of us. This combat in the Caribbean was totally unexpected. It was supposed to be a few weeks at the beach for us. All of a sudden our buddies was dyin' right beside us. Well, Sarge picked up his rifle, stepped out from the trees and started walking up towards the Germans. He didn't say nothin' to the rest of us. Just started walkin'. He looked like John Wayne! What a scene. A couple of us followed him right away and after a little hesitation, the rest followed. No shootin', just walkin' right into the face of the enemy. Still gives me shivers to remember it. I don't know what them drunk Germans must've thought to see us headed up the beach toward 'em in the half-light of sunset, but the singin' stopped right off and none of 'em hardly moved. A couple of 'em put their hands down on top of their guns on the table, but movement was real slow and thoughtful. They all looked real sober, but the beer musta' kept 'em from overreactin' and start shootin' at us. About thirty yards from 'em, Sarge came to a full stop and cradled his weapon in front of him. Not threatenin' them right off, but he'd a-been scary lookin' to any sober man on the planet. We all came up behind him and stopped as well, but we were kinda spread out a little. No guns was pointed. Nobody said a word. Joe, you look up the word "tension" in the dictionary, baby, there's a picture of that beach scene right there. Every day and every night for nearly two months these guys was busy tryin' to kill each other. Both bunches had some success."

Tyrell was genuinely interested in telling this story. It didn't matter who wanted or didn't want to hear it.

"Then Sarge, holding his stare at the Germans, hollered out for Freddy. Freddy poked his head out of the bar on the beachside of this group of tables where we were. Sarge didn't look at him but seemed to know Freddy could hear him with just his head showing out the doorway. Sarge barked, 'Beers for my guys, pronto.' Holy crap. Were we gonna' drink with these guys? Well, not with 'em, but near 'em. Freddy hustled out with bottles of cold beer, set 'em on the tables nearest us and ran back to the bar at lightnin' speed. All of us sat down real slow. Movements was extra slow. We were always facing the Germans who were statues, watchin' us close."

Waving that cigar around made Billy's story more dramatic. Francesca was putting her flimsy, torn top back on as we neared the harbor where the hotel was located. What a sinking feeling to see that.

Billy said, "Sarge stood up, set down his weapon, picked up a beer and took four giant steps toward the enemy armed only with a death look and a fist full of Falstaff bottle. Helmet less and weaponless. I'm tellin' ya, Joe, I have seen some shit! After a full two-minute stare-down from the Sarge to them Germans, the biggest, blondest, youngest lookin' German stood and copied Sarge's moves. That guy looked like he'd been lifting weights all day and eatin' 'em for lunch when he was through liftin' 'em. Sarge and the weight lifter hoisted their beers in the air and the cheerin' erupted from both groups of soldiers at the same time. Them guys yellin' in German and us in English and everybody knew exactly what was being said. We was slammin' brewskis with the enemy. Anybody got too unhappy and people was gonna die. Sarge counted in English, 'One'. On 'two', the big German matched Sarge's count in German. Every solder joined in on 'three'. After that there was upside down beers for the two of 'em, an unbelievable angry yellin' from both sides. Both soldiers drained 'em and slammed the bottles into the sand simultaneously. Tie! Back slappin' and congrats from both sides to their man came next and while everybody was cussin' and yellin'. A skinny American kid-soldier stepped up front with his beer in hand."

Captain Billy worked his cigar a bit and considered what would come out and what would stay where it was. He yielded his position at the wheel to Francesca without saying a word to her. He hadn't even looked at her but they both knew what to do. He sat on the bench opposite me, leaned back on the bench and kept on talking.

"I don't know. Okay, Joe, I was only sixteen, but the Marines thought I was my cousin who was eighteen. Nobody ever told 'em different, I guess. But I could slam a beer even then. It was one of the few times in my short life that I was really confident about something. I was thinkin', 'Send that weight-eatin' Gerrie back up here. I'll kick his muscle-bound ass back to Berlin.' I could be a cocky punk."

Yeah, but you clearly outgrew that, I thought.

154

"Amongst all that cussin' and yellin', the groups of soldiers were less than a first down apart now. It still felt like it wouldn't take much for bayonets to get pulled and everybody have a go. The countin' started. On three, the beers got hoisted. I slammed the beer, threw the bottle down in the sand and jumped into the arms of my hollerin' buddies before that stinkin' Gerrie had drained his. There was yellin' so loud that if shots had been fired nobody could've heard it. As the celebrating went on, it started rainin'. We ain't talkin' 'bout no shower. It was a turd floater and a rock mover. The Marines and the Germans never even thought of leavin' that beach. We kept up the one on ones right through the storm, like the outcome of the whole war depended on the results of that drinkin' contest. The front line of the war was moved to Freddy's Bar. Freddy kept bringin' the beer. Never saw any money change hands for the beer. I'm tellin' you Joe, stick with me 'cause I got the sea stories."

I was at a loss, and I was amazed. Wondering if it was even possible to exert any guidance to what might be said next, I told Billy, "I'm stickin' with you."

Captain Billy held his look on me as if there *needed* to be a hole through my body. Billy sucked another hit off the cigar and plunged ahead. "The smartest guy there was Freddy. By about 8:00 or 9:00 p.m., everybody was colossally shit-faced. But even drunk, the Germans stayed at their tables and we stayed at ours. The longer we all stayed there without shooting each other, the closer Freddy got to feeling okay that we were all at his bar and that he might not die because of it. Freddy brought out a coin and explained in his island-English-German that he was gonna call heads or tails and he was gonna flip the coin. He knew that none of the soldiers was currently capable of making the call or the flip. If the call was "heads," the Germans leave first. "Tails," the Americans leave first. When the Germans "won" the flip and had to leave first, Freddy told us all to come back next Saturday and we'd do it all again. As drunk as we were, nobody really took him seriously, I didn't think. Spreckin' ze drunk, huh?"

Billy actually smirked. It was the happiest smile I saw out of him.

"Them Gerries backed away carefully from the beach, stumblin' and helpin' each other. Guns didn't go off, so except for hangovers, there were no casualties to this little episode. By Monday at dawn, we were all tryin' as hard as we could to kill each other again. This wadn't no *McHales' Navy*. Kids died and it was bad. Most of us were sick the whole time. Conditions were terrible. Weather was terrible. That next Saturday, all the talk was whether or not it would happen again. It did, but with a little less tension this time. If possible, we was all drunker that second time. Later, Freddie flipped his coin and off we went. Man, Joe, by Monday, it was to the death again. After that it was every single Saturday night. You could always tell when there was new guys on the island, 'cause they would come up to Saturday night at Freddy's with their finger on the trigger. No matter how much the new guys might've been told by their own guys, it was not quite believable that we would be having drinkin' contests with the enemy once a week. It ended real quick a month or so later. Some say all them Gerries was dead. Some say a sub came and picked 'em all up. We'll never know."

Billy paused to ponder, and then said, "You know, Joe, back then, things was different. More innocent. Pure. We fought for our country without question. Doubts or hesitation never entered the picture. You fought. It was right. They were the bad guys and it was clear. Freedom was important and we played a role in it. No doubts. Simple. Right."

Captain Billy considered where he would go next with the story as more cigar smoke surrounded him. Francesca had guided the big catamaran all the way into the dock that leads up to the beach. She scrambled all over the boat and was busy tying it off to the dock.

"Twenty some years later, that skinny kid from Tupelo was a full-growed Master Sergeant in the jungles of Vietnam. There was no drinkin' with the enemy there. Hell, we never saw the enemy, hardly. We felt their bullets though and their mines and their rockets and their hate. Different war. Different time. I wasn't the hero to my men that Sarge was when I was the kid. It was a different deal altogether. Half the kids didn't want to be there and didn't mind saying so. To my marines in 1968, it wasn't as clear that we were in the same boat together and everybody had to row or the boat would run aground. Yeah, I was there. I was in Vietnam. I had men in my charge that I had to take care of. Some died. Some lived. Not much of it ended up feelin' right. Maybe it was leadership that was lackin'."

Billy raised one eyebrow through a smoky exhale. He adopted a stern tone of finality, pointing his inflamed eyes straight through me.

"That'd be *my* leadership, Joe. Maybe it was the times. Lots of killin'. Even more dyin'. I mean some of 'em that lived—they died a little. Hippies all over the place back home protesting the war. You seen what I seen? You wouldn't have much to say either. I don't wanna talk about it. And I don't care who wants or needs to hear it. I don't *have* to talk about it, Joe. You need to have a beer and be glad you can feel the sun on your face. A lot of good men, better'n you or me, can't do that, Joe."

Billy just stared at me. Then, without losing his stare at me, he shouted, "Half price sail today, Francesca. No charge for the beer, Joe. Have a nice life."

Captain Billy turned immediately away and walked, well, limped down the pier away from his own boat. He didn't look back at Francesca or me at all. I thanked Francesca, paid her $200 and went back up to the Westin. I went straight to the bar and ordered a beer.

I wanted and needed to talk to Lola that night. I got some good news I was hoping for. Lily got released from the hospital. They said that Lily had far outpaced the normal recovery timetable for her injuries. They suggested that she should take it a little easier. Lola said Lily got way better once it was clear that they got to leave the hospital. My girls got a room at a fancy hotel in downtown Ft. Worth. Angela got them the official police business discount they get when they have to guard witnesses. So Lola and Lily were holed-up watching DVDs and movies-on-command and ordering room service. Right then, Lily and three other members of the Pink Ponies soccer team were bundled into bed in their jammies and watching some teenage girl movie they probably shouldn't be allowed to watch, and giggling—a lot. I was on an island in paradise and I was jealous of them.

"She liked the ride in the squad car the best, until they got to the hotel. Then she liked the hotel the best. Angela had our Jetta put into the police impound lot for a couple of days, so if anyone was watching our car to get to us they'd just have to watch the cop's parking lot," said Lola. Lola seems to have a lot of confidence in Angela. I would too if she didn't go out of her way to piss me off all the time. Lola said there was at least one plainclothes guy in the hallway at all times. Angela told her that most of the day and night there would be a uniform in the lobby as well. Sounded extra double safe and I was glad of that. At least Angela was doing what she promised.

I told Lola about my day. Maybe I held back a little. It was a heavy day. I needed to think about home and not the obnoxious Captain Billy. As for Francesca, well, I might have described her as a "sort-of earthy, Birkenstock and tortoise shell glasses wearin', overly tanned, NPR listenin', sailboat living Hispanic chick who worked for Captain Billy and pretty much ran the sailboat herself." All pretty true. Kinda. Except maybe the bit about her being maybe a little heavy-set. None of the hard truth would bother Lola as much as it bothered me. Call me crazy, but I was embarrassed by the stunningly beautiful, nearly naked young woman who sailed the boat. I'm a sick man. Faced with the absolute truth, there's no doubt Lola would just laugh that I was embarrassed.

Bodie's competency hearing was scheduled for the next day. Harry Zinn convinced a judge that it was an emergency because his client's assets were being stolen while he recovered in the hospital. Lola said Marisa was confident because Harry Zinn was confident. Bodie still didn't remember anything about being attacked, even with me out of the picture.

Lola saved the best news for last. She said, "Wesley Drake is still insisting that he didn't attack anybody –Warren's wife Joanne, me, Lily, Bodie or you. Wes says he loved Joanne. To prove he didn't do anything, he gave up the two guys he says did all of it—guys named Rad Khanani and Will Dunton, both of who also work for Warren Duchtin. The Ft. Worth Police picked up both men. This guy Dunton was missing two fingers on his right hand. Well, it's a very recent injury. Dunton claims that his was an accident with a circular saw while doing some remodeling for his sister. Turns out he's right-handed. How do you cut two fingers off your main hand? By sawing boards with your least coordinated hand? They are pretty sure it is from a gunshot wound, probably from your gun and that they think he was in the front passenger seat in the van when you shot them."

This tidbit made me laugh. "So, I shot two of them with three shots? The only crummy part about that story is that they all lived and Khanani was unhurt in the shoot-em-up," I told Lola, knowing full well that comment would get back to Angela.

Lola had more, "Wesley Drake did a little more talking to the police. Seems Wes used to be richer than Warren Duchtin. Can you believe that? But Wes is a gambler and a loser, which is a deadly combo. He lost it all. So now he's not a gambler anymore, just a big stinkin' loser. So, one thing leads to another and Wes starts working for Warren Duchtin at *Perma Press Plaques*. What a pair, huh? So, Wes knows stuff, a lot of stuff, about Warren. Wes actually works for *Xanadu L.L.C.* which is the company that owns the blue van. *Xanadu* is owned by *PPP, Inc.* which is the corporate sole shareholder of — *Perma Press Plaques, Inc.* Turns out Warren Duchtin doesn't own *Perma Press Plaques*. He owns *PPP, Inc.*, so that's how he owns the blue van. Angela thinks maybe Warren was trying to hide assets from the impending divorce by burying ownership of his main company. So, the police have all the bad guys in custody, except Warren and if this keeps going, they'll have him soon. Isn't that great, sweetie?" Lola was pretty happy.

"It's awesome!" I said.

I just wish I'd been the one to turn this stupid case and corner these jerks. Angela got to do it while I sat here 3,000 miles away in exile talking to 100 year old Popeye the sailor man about drunken Germans in W.W.II and pretty Puerto Rican minor girls that the idiotic ancient mariner Popeye *fantasizes about.* Fortunately, I did not say this thought out loud like I do most of my thoughts.

"Please don't move back home until Warren's in shackles along with his henchmen. Do you promise?" I said.

"I promise," pledged Lola.

"Sounds like I won't have to twist Lily's arm to get the same promise, huh? I love you, Lola. Please tell Lily I love her too."

It was 10:00 p.m. in St. John, 9:00 p.m. in Ft. Worth. I hiked up to the lobby and caught one of those open air cabs, which is essentially a pick up truck with benches in the back and a canvas cover overhead. "Can you take me to the Beach Bar in town, please? I think it's next to Joe's Rumhut." I have no clue if the driver understood me or not, but off we went.

159

19. Billy and Hue'

"Here comes Joe, cravin' them sea stories. Come over here Joe and I'll let you buy me a beer. You're a fun guy. I'm gonna put you on my rounds and let you watch me operate," said Captain Billy.

Captain Billy was drunk.

There was no one near him at the bar. The bar was packed with people, locals and tourists alike. Billy was clearly too loud and obnoxious when drunk, even for a loud, obnoxious and drunk crowd.

I didn't really expect to ever see him again. I have a policy about not engaging drunken people in conversation. Lola says my policy is more encompassing and specifically anti-social. She says it is actually, 'Don't engage anyone in conversation, ever.' She also is a little quick to point out that 'complaining' is not 'conversation.' Guess I'm just trying to talk myself out of missing Lola. No chance of that.

"Tell me something, Joe," said Captain Billy, loud enough for almost anyone to hear him over the loud island beat of music. "What are you responsible for, Joe? What exactly have you ever been responsible for? Tell me that, son."

This whole trip has sucked, well, except for the sight of Francesca.

My case at home has sucked. My client was murdered, probably by her own husband. He especially sucks.

Bad guys are trying to kill me and my family and people I care about.

I have been shuttled out of town so others can solve problems that I am causing by just being there.

My friend's nutty son is trying to take all of my friend's money and hasten his death. I haven't been able to help him at all. Now this arrogant jerk just wants to take everybody else in the world down a notch so he can feel a little better. Billy's act has grown tiresome. This guy sucks. I told him so.

"Captain Billy, Sergeant Billy, whatever? I am not your 'son.' Now that I see you in your natural habitat, I think I see why it is you can't get laid. It has nothing to do with E.D.C.s, whatever the hell they are."

"Fuck you, Joe," snorted Popeye.

"I don't see how you'll have time for that! You're too busy screwing yourself, Sergeant Tyrell. For some unexplainable reason, you seem to think no one is capable of understanding what you think you understand. Or what you went through in Vietnam—if they weren't there. Maybe that's true. I don't pretend to be able... But could a father of one of those marines understand any of it? How about a father of a fallen marine who saw combat himself? Could *any* father understand any of it? Not that you would know. Just sit here and wallow in your self-pity, Tyrell. You are pretty damn ignorant for somebody three days older than dirt. I'll tell you one thing. I am certain you don't understand half of what you think you do! You think you've cornered the market on responsibility because you saw kids die that you cared about? I think the only market you've cornered is the belligerent sunburned asshole market, you sorry bastard," I said, working myself into it a little. I stood up as I finished chewing on him. I was hoping to hit something or somebody. Looks like I found a cooperative target.

Billy showed his extensive experience with invitations to brawl and attempted standing. Stumbling, he knocked over his stool and another to the moans and complaining reactions of others nearby who had been trying to stay away from him. Then Billy started to fall over like the stools. On his way down to the floor, he yelled a drunken version of "snot-nosed punk" in my direction.

"At fifty years old, maybe I am that, to a hundred year old drunk has-been like you, Tyrell," I answered. Billy was currently no match for my state of sobriety, in wit or in fight. Nobody, including me, made any effort to help him. Over he went taking another stool with him. His cigar was left smoking itself on the bar.

"When I sober up, Joe, I'm gonna clean yer clock," the old, drunk pirate mumbled from his position lying on one side beneath the bar. The bar's customers had pretty much stopped down for the show by now. Island reggae music thumped endlessly.

"Why don't you see if you can crawl out of bed by tomorrow at noon and meet me here, Tyrell? Think you can get sober by then? I doubt it, but I'll put you on *my* rounds and let you watch *me* operate, you dickhead. And my name is 'Jerry', not 'Joe'."

I walked away.

I didn't really want to spend time in a U.S.V.I. jail for beating up a 100 year old drunk local. That's the only place this was going to go. I got a taxi-truck and rode back to the hotel.

In the morning I took another taxi-truck over to the other side of the island to see Cinnamon Bay and Caneel Bay from the island side. This is a beautiful place. I vowed to come back with my girls to show it to them. Uh, maybe we'll come someday when we can afford it. Mostly I spent my time thinking about all the things that had happened recently. I was thinking about all the things that had been said, understood and not so understood. I spent no time thinking about what to do or say to anyone next. I think my little confrontation with Tyrell was freeing. For once I did not induce my own festival of worry.

I did notice when the morning was slipping away. I decided that it couldn't hurt to see if Tyrell had even remembered my lunch invitation from last night. I took the taxi back over the hill to the Beach Bar. I walked up to the bar and there was Captain Billy sitting on the same stool as last night, smoking a cigar and nursing a beer.

"Did you go home last night or just sleep here on that stool?" I asked Billy. There was nobody else in the bar but the bartender. Billy didn't even look up at me. He just snarfed his cigar. I sat down on the stool next to him.

"Beer," I said and the barkeep served one up. This would make six beers in two days for me. I had better check into rehab. "You definitely bring out the worst in me, Tyrell," I said. "You have that effect on a lot of people or just me?" I did not look at him when I said it.

Billy let the cigar smoke swirl around his head and said nothing for a minute. I wasn't sure how sober he was. "You know, Joe, in Vietnam," said Billy. "Didn't matter where you were, you were in danger. You couldn't tell a good-guy gook from a bad-guy gook and sometimes the gooks wasn't the problem."

I fidgeted at his uncomfortable ethnic slur. Like with most of what Billy says, he probably is just trying to piss me off. He and Angela are probably in cahoots on that goal. That term was used fairly commonly in the 1970s to refer to North Vietnamese enemies, but not now. It was painful to hear it out loud and used so matter-of-factly. My world doesn't really usually include all this aggressive cussing and macho posturing.

"If you wanted to survive, they were all bad guys. All of 'em," continued Billy. "There was no other way to see it. Units lost guys— sometimes everyday. Command would send new guys in like any of us were replaceable. We had to plug the new kids in where we might have had a solid marine before. Drugs was everywhere. Racial tension was everywhere. I mean black and white and Mexican races. I ain't even countin' the gook races. Sometimes our own guys were in as much danger from our other guys as they were from the gooks. There was lots of reasons a soldier might use poor judgment. When a soldier in war uses bad judgment—good people die. Sometimes the pure needlessness of death is stupid and just—painful. Real painful."

Just like all conversation I had gotten out of Billy so far on this trip, I had no clue where this would go.

"Kohler and Johnson? They were good corpsmen, good citizens and decent men. New guys came in and they'd be hard on 'em. I was hard on any new guys too. Had to be. Teach 'em quick or people die. All of our lives depended on it. Others' lives depended on it. It was important. I wasn't with that unit very long. I had been in Saigon at our Embassy when the V.C. launched Tet at the end of January."

"Yeah, I heard that story," I said. "I haven't seen the news footage of you running across the grounds with the pistol for Captain Gray, but I heard about it."

Now Billy looked at me hard. It was clear he did not like remembering any of it. I didn't blame him for that.

"Never saw that footage, myself," he said and he drew on the ever-present cigar. "Kohler and Johnson were the vets in that bunch when I arrived. I was sent to take 'em into Hue'. It was a big job to take that city back from the enemy. The V.C. had planned taking it for months. They had lists of the people they wanted eliminated when they took the city and that's just what they done. The V.C. took the city from several directions at once during the time I was in Saigon. There was complete surprise and little resistance. Them gooks ran up their stinkin' red and yellow star flag at the Citadel in the middle of town. Then they went house to house with their lists. They were just merciless. Over the next few years, bodies turned up in riverbeds, salt flats, jungle clearings, wherever. The V.C. killed thousands of people in their sweeps of the city. Women, kids, ministers, anybody on the lists died plus anybody close to 'em. Thousands of 'em. People weren't just shot. They were clubbed to death or tortured or they was buried alive. This was Vietnamese people killing other Vietnamese. We weren't even there yet. But you know what? Americans didn't even notice when the bodies started showing up later. The press in the U.S. was focused on *My Lai* by then. Our pissed-off and crazed guys massacred about a hundred peasants and kids there. That was the only story that got talked about in the U.S. Yeah, it was bad. No doubt. It was horrible. Look, there's no question about how terrible that was. But Tet was thousands of innocents tortured and murdered and the same press just ignored it.

"Man, we were used to fightin' in the jungle and the open rice fields. Now we had to go into the city. By the time we got there, any friendly gooks had been tortured and killed. This was a shitty operation. We took three battalions of U.S. Marines into Hue' near the middle of February a few weeks after the V.C. took over. The South took I don't know how many of their troops in, probably a similar number to us. The South Vietnamese were out for blood in this battle. They wanted to take the lead. They were bitter. Real pissed. It was a hell of a battle. Hell of a battle.

"Our unit had to cross a big river to get to town. The Perfume River I think was the name, but maybe we put that name on it. I don't know. It don't matter. We used landing craft to cross over. I'll never forget the dead bodies floating by in the river as we crossed. Seeing the floating bodies diverted our attention from the bullets landing near our heads. It was one of the only times I remember being cold while I was in Vietnam. It was cloudy and humid. Low clouds. Maybe it was cold. Felt cold, anyway. It only matters because tactical air support was impossible and that was our strength taken away right there. We started the whole thing with one arm tied behind our backs. Knowin' that there were no jets comin', the fear factor was high that day in our unit. We had way too many new guys for this fight. Command sent us a bunch of eighteen year old kids. Couldn't wipe their own ass, but they had heavy weapons. They were scared. Hell, probably half of them were hopped up on something that day. Everyday.

"I'm ashamed any U.S. Marines let their discipline go as bad as some units did in Vietnam. Kohler and Johnson had been with these guys longer than me. They'd pissed them newer guys off for quite some time, I guess, ridin' 'em, trying to teach 'em. Trying to teach a hophead anything was impossible." Billy paused for hits of beer and smoke. He would never comprehend the irony of his own behavior. I managed not to smile.

"V.C. peppered the boats with small arms fire from the moment we left our own shore. They knew we were comin'. They knew lots of people would die. We knew it too. Once in the city, we were winding through city streets taking fire the whole way. Shit. The city was a shambles. It was desolate and ruined. It looked like some of those pictures of the bombed cities in W.W.II in Europe. Burnt out tanks, trucks, houses, buildings, bodies everywhere—mostly civilians. All our units took heavy casualties coming into the city. Goddamn bodies were just everywhere. Some dead bodies just laying there smokin' in the cool, humid air. There was smoke from fires all over the place and the stench was somethin' I'll never forget. No one could forget. Tension was high. We all, even those of us with a lot of combat experience, expected the enemy to pop out from behind every corner, every building and blast away at us. It felt like a suicide mission the whole way. Emotions got away from some. Some of our guys wouldn't fight. It was only a few of 'em. Hell, they weren't sure where they were. Drugged up or stone sober, it was overwhelming.

"Understand, Joe, this battle went on for ten days. Ten days of hell and almost no sleep. We got to the Citadel. It was a really old ancient walled fortress in the middle of the city. It's where the V.C. operated from, once they took the city. It was where our side operated from before they took it from us. There was a complex of buildings and walls. There was a tower in the middle and another up on the east side. We weren't the first unit that got there. Had about two platoons and one tank all together once we were there. Our orders were to take that heavily fortified tower along the easternmost wall. We called in artillery. No jets in that weather. We shelled the shit out of 'em for most of a day with artillery and mortars. It didn't even dent 'em. Then we lost our radio operator and radio. We had no contact with our flank position. None. We lost our coordination. We couldn't be relieved of any orders. We started crawling toward that wall and tower. Most of us did. We cleared spider holes and tunnels one gook at a time. We killed one at a time drawing random fire from every building around us. Kohler killed one sniper less than ten feet away from us. It was ugly. It was caveman survival mode. Them goddamn Charley was vicious fighters. They were real soldiers in black pajamas. Johnson and Kohler saved the lives of our entire unit more than once.

"Some of our own guys, trained just like me, just like Kohler and Johnson—they wouldn't even fight. They couldn't defend themselves, much less their brothers! They'd give away our positions with their stupidity. It got so they thought me and Kohler and Johnson and some others were their enemies.

"Over several days, our artillery finally had an impact. We had to take that tower. Spotters gave whoever was in that tower a huge advantage. We wanted to direct artillery from there. As it was, our own shells were exploding within yards of us for days. We couldn't eat. It smelled like death. It felt like we were there so long, the smell would be permanent on us. We were too tired to eat anyway. We took the tower but lots of our guys died doing it. South Vietnamese troops tore down the V.C. flag at the Citadel. It was costly. The South Viets lost several hundred troops. They fought well. Damn brave men. Artillery probably got most of the V.C. that died. Finally we got air strikes in, but we killed our share of 'em in person. We lost over 150 Marines in the battle for Hue'."

Billy turned and looked at me, one of the few times during his telling of the story. "Not all died by the hand of the enemy and not every man I killed was an honorable man."

I did not know what that meant. I didn't know what to say. It just lay there.

"I did what had to be done to take care of the things that had to be dealt with. That's all you get to know," said Billy. The shittiest part of this little story?" said Billy; "We destroyed that town to save it. What little of it was left after the V.C. came in; we tore up fightin' 'em for it. And then, by the middle of '68, less than six months later, the Americans *abandoned* both Khe Sanh and Hue'. Make any fuckin' sense to you, Joe? Abandoned! Like it wasn't important after all. Like my guys died for nothin'. How can this story be told properly? How can it be told so you can see how good, decent soldiers felt and how well they did their jobs? I'll tell you this; it wasn't anything like the American public felt. We weren't babykillers. Men who died were honorable men. Not all of them, but most. Men who survived were never the same after Hue'. We thought our country sent us there to do an important job and we were doin' it. We did it with honor because they told us it was the right thing to do and we believed it. We believed it. And we did it. Then, after we completed our mission, they told us—they showed us, maybe it wasn't such an important job after all. How do you tell that to the families of the men who died doin' it? Where's the honor in having done a job that wasn't so important after all when you were killed doin' it? Was it worth it, Joe? Does that have value to Kohler's dad? He's got questions huh? How about my questions, Joe? Who answers them?"

Billy pointed that giant index finger at me again and his eyes narrowed. "Get out of my life, Joe, and don't ever come back into it. If you do or if you cause others to enter my life over what I have told you, the price to you will be very high."

Billy limped out of the bar.

"In one way, I think I should have asked more questions, Lola. I should have pressed him more," I told Lola on the phone, "but if you had been there you would have said 'Jerry, you got everything out of him that you were going to get. He wasn't going to give you more'. He wasn't, Lola. I don't know if he killed James or not. I haven't found any reason why he would have done such a thing. He'll never confess to it to me, I know that."

"Do you think you will be able to get anything more from Raymond Johnson in Boston?" Lola asked.

"I hope so. My plane leaves St. Thomas at 10:30 tomorrow morning, but that's two taxis and a ferryboat ride away, so I have to catch the 7:00 ferry. Did anything happen with Bodie today?"

"Quite a shock. Bodie's competent and Clayton's P.O.A. revocation stands valid," said Lola. "A good bit of the hearing was the premiere of the short, made-for-TV movie, *'Revoking the .P.O.A.'* starring Bodie Kohler and produced by Harry Zinn. It was really overwhelming evidence. You looked great in a supporting role, sweetie. Oh! You should have seen! It was major drama when Bodie went through the description of the money in his wall and the probability that Clayton stole it. Clayton about slid under the table. When Bodie looked at the camera and said it was best if Clayton didn't come see him, Clayton just put his head in his hands. Clayton went nuts when the judge gave his decision. He jumped up and yelled at his attorney, saying, 'You have screwed this up so bad! He has to pay me what he owes. This is my money. This is wrong. Wrong.' Then he stormed out in a huff. Jerry? That Clayton is nuts! He really thought the judge would find in his favor and would give him the right to operate all Bodie's accounts. Nobody seems to understand why Clayton thinks Bodie owes him anything. Clayton doesn't seem to be able to focus on anything except himself. He seems baffled as to why everyone else isn't looking at him and his problems. He's really bugs!"

"How's Marisa holding up?" I asked.

"Marisa is—sad," said Lola. "She talked to Bodie about those letters you found where the money was supposed to be. Bodie knew they existed, except for the one about "you owed me." But Bodie didn't know they were in the duct. Everyone feels that Clayton left them all there when he stole the money, you know, as a message to Bodie just like you thought. Clayton was just taunting Bodie about having taken his money. Bodie said Clayton had confronted him about signing over the house again. It's been going on for a long time. At some point, Clayton wadded up that note and threw it at his dad. Bodie was the one who smoothed it back out and put it in his desk with other papers. Bodie said he had not seen it in some time."

I said, "Any word from Angela?"

"No. I didn't talk to her today," said Lola. "I went to the hearing and then felt bad that I had left Lily alone so long, so I stayed at the hotel with her. She would have called if there was anything."

"I want to talk to Angela, so I'll call her and I'll let you know if there's anything new," I said. "I love you and Lily."

"Love you too. We're watching movies. Lily is still sleeping a lot, but she gets her walking in so I think she's doing well. Call me tomorrow night from Boston."

As soon as we hung up, I dialed up Angela.

"Hello, Angela? This is Jerry Wilson. Anything new from our boys who work for Duchtin?" I asked.

"Hey. Jerry. Where are you?" asked Angela."

"I'm still in U.S.V.I. I'm headed to Boston tomorrow and back to God's Country the next day. Anything new or not, Angela?"

"Yes, there is. About an hour ago, Wesley Drake gave up Duchtin in the murder of his wife. Wes says Warren Duchtin ordered him to kill her and Wes refused. He says Warren only wanted him to kill Joanne because he had found out about their affair. He says the actual killers were Rad Khanani and Will Dunton, Wes's co-workers. They're all warped. We're questioning Khanani and Dunton now. Wes tells us they are good for the attack on Lola and Lily. They'll talk eventually. It's all starting to cave in. We're getting the warrant for Warren Duchtin's arrest now. We should have him in jail tonight."

"What about the attack on me and on Bodie?" I asked.

"They'll roll on that too. Right now, no, but let us do our jobs," said Angela.

"No? What's that all about?" I asked.

"Well, right now Wes Drake says he doesn't know anything about Bodie. He says they were just watching Duchtin's girlfriend and you attacked them. They'll roll, Jerry. Don't even think about it," urged Angela.

"That's a pile of hooey I can smell all the way down here, Angela," I started.

"We know that, Jerry. Take it easy."

"When you button up Warren Duchtin, do you think Lola and Lily can go home?" I asked.

"Absolutely. Probably tomorrow. They seem really pretty good, Jerry. I think they like hotel living," said Angela.

"Yeah, I'm sure they do. But surely I don't have to remind you about me not having any salary? You hear about Bodie being declared competent?" I asked.

"Yes. David went to the hearing and then to see Dr. Kohler later. He seemed to be doing well today. Gotta run, Jerry."

"Okay. Thanks."

20. Boston

I ambushed Raymond Johnson. That is, he had not expected me at his office in downtown Boston. I had some fear that if he were forewarned, he would not be available at all. This was too important to me to chance that.

It was late afternoon by the time I got there from Logan Airport. Boston was cold and snowy. Not my natural environment, but then neither was the beach in U.S.V.I. I miss the bubble environment of Ft. Worth. In Ft. Worth, they only try to run my family and me over with blue vans. This emotional distress on the road is way worse. But the things I needed to know would not and could not be said into a telephone. This I knew.

Raymond's welcome was not warm, but he let me in. He is a big man to go with that big voice. Social greetings were bare minimum. We talked about Vietnam and war, and life—and death.

"By the end of '67 we, the U.S.A., had half a million kids in Vietnam. President Johnson and General Westmoreland had increased the head count during '67 alone by 100,000 soldiers. Westmoreland had requested over 200,000. But Johnson was already pissing off most of the nation by escalating support to the war. Me and James and 99,998 others joined the first 400,000. When we went over in the middle of '67, this country was already war weary. Really sick of it. Protests all over," said RayJ. "Seemed like people hated me for a new reason then. It wasn't just because I'm black. It was also because I was a soldier. It got so bad here at home that many of us tried to hide the fact that we were soldiers. It was all misplaced and screwed up, but when you're eighteen or nineteen years old, everything is personal. Kids like me weren't able to recognize when anger was misplaced. It was just anger. You react. It doesn't matter if your black or not, but because I am black, I was already well practiced reacting to anger."

I slipped in a question, "When you were on the ground in Vietnam, did you know about the big picture like the Communist troop build-up preparing for the Tet offensive?" For the most part, I needed to listen and keep quiet.

"No way. I know now only because I read about it in the '70s and '80s. That's when writers and reporters started filling us all in on what had really happened to make us be in Vietnam. By then we could finally learn about the decisions that were made at the war management level. But at the time, on the ground, in the jungle, we were just hoping to survive another day. If we did, we hoped the next patrol would be uneventful. That was all we knew. Don't trip a Betty. That's what we knew. That war had no front lines. It was impossible to feel safe anywhere. Clerks at H.Q., potato and carrot peelers in the mess, M.P.s in Saigon, infantrymen in the jungle—all were at risk at all times. The dangers weren't just with the V.C. in the jungle. I have read that only a small minority of American servicemen actually encountered and battled Vietcong regular army, mines, booby traps or were actually ambushed. But about all of us were on the receiving end of enemy mortars or rockets. Our unit saw it all. James and I saw it all. Like I said, we were in Hue'. They threw it all at us in Hue'."

I said, "Tyrell told me the story from his point of view. Just getting it from him met my tension quota for the year. I want to hear it from you, anything you are willing to tell me. But I have to say right up front—Tyrell says that not all the men he killed were honorable men, but he did what had to be done. That's pretty much a quote and I won't forget it. Then he wouldn't speak to me anymore. He threatened me if I pursued it further with him. So, I have to ask if you will fill in the gaps as you said you would do? Was it Tyrell that shot you and James?"

There it was. I asked. Now it's all up to RayJ whether or not the answer reaches the light of day.

RayJ stood and put his hands in the pockets of his very expensive looking dark suit pants. He walked across his enormous office on the 32nd floor to the window overlooking the rest of downtown Boston and the Atlantic Ocean. "Sergeant Billy Tyrell did not shoot me or James. He is a warrior and a hard and tough U.S. Marine and will die that. He would never have killed or even hurt James or me."

RayJ turned and faced me as he spoke, "He was and undoubtedly is a man of utmost honor. It is woven into the fabric of his soul, no matter how his life has gone since I saw him last in 1968. He lives the code. Hell, he's old enough, he may have written the code. Regardless of what you thought you saw in him, I am as sure of it as I have ever been of anything. Tyrell sits at the highest level of honor that exists for mortal men. Maybe it is requisite for such an evaluation to come from a man who has fought battles with him and faced death with him. Neither you nor anyone else could convince me otherwise. Tyrell killed the men who did shoot us. They would have killed me and Tyrell too if he had not. Sarge saved my life more times than just then. I would not be here today, would not have had a life at all without having known him."

RayJ turned back to the ocean view and said, "The men who shot James and me were Americans. They were American Marines. They were young kids not much younger than me and James, who were pissed we were their superiors, that we had trained them hard and driven them to the brink of insanity. They were scared they were about to die because we were forcing them to follow orders. They wanted to survive and in their drugged-up stupor they thought *we* were the obstacles to their survival."

RayJ turned back to face me, "They did not survive. James and Tyrell and I were fighting V.C. at Hue' and we were fighting a few of our own men too. I thought what happened would eventually destroy Tyrell because of what he did—what he had to do. It is a testimonial to him that he even had a life at all after that experience. Now you know, Wilson. You do what you have to do. I know Dr. Kohler is responsible for you being here. I submit to you that if he knew this detail of his son's death, it would not comfort him in any way just as me telling you has not given me any relief from its knowledge. At a bare minimum, you are now saddled with knowing. James was everything I have told you that he was and more. His death was a loss for his family and all of us who loved him. It was a tremendous loss for our country that he was fighting for, whether or not that has been acknowledged properly. Kind of gives new meaning to Nixon's statement about 'peace with honor' when we finally got out of Vietnam doesn't it? Well, the truth is the truth. Congratulations on your diligence. It's a pretty tough reward, in my opinion."

"Let me add some more to that," RayJ said, stepping closer to my seat in front of his desk, "I understand there is a probability that you will tell this story to Dr. Kohler. If I am contacted about what I have told you by anyone, including Dr. Kohler, I will deny anything you have said about this. Full denial! And I will brand you a 'liar' whether you are that or not. In fact, I will disavow any knowledge of your existence if necessary. If this information ever surfaces to public knowledge, I will get with that old warrior, Tyrell, and he and I will descend on you in the darkness of night when you least expect it. I have the money and the motivation to make it happen. You will pay for your actions from this point on and you had best keep it in the front of your mind. I barely know you, Wilson. But I have a recommendation for you. Let your future actions in this regard be guided by your own sense of honor. Better yet, be guided by Billy Tyrell's sense of honor."

I returned to Logan Airport to try for the 9:00 p.m. flight to D.F.W. I missed Lola and Lily.

While waiting for the flight, my cell phone rang. Caller ID says "Ft. Worth Police."

"This is Jerry."

"Jerry, this is Angela Delano. Do you have a minute?"

"Sure. Go ahead."

"Clayton Kohler is dead. He asphyxiated himself over in Forest Park last night. There is no doubt it was suicide. He left a note, but there's no sense to it."

"Damn. How's Marisa? How's Bodie?"

"Both are doing their best to make their way. It is clearly not easy."

21. Suicide Note

The dizzying pace to my life over the last few weeks came to a screeching halt. Lola picked me up at the airport. She missed me as much as I had missed her. The sadness of Clayton's actions overshadowed everything and would for a good long time. Angela showed me a copy of Clayton's suicide note the next day.

Dad,
It wasn't anything I wouldn't have gotten anyway if you had died.
I know you almost did. I am now sorry for my recent actions toward you
The judge is right. You are very competent.
Victoria had the better deal than me, but she suffered. It wasn't right.
Mom didn't suffer. That's how it should be.
I didn't suffer doing this. The suffering was being alive.
There's no peace here. I need to look elsewhere.
This was not casual. It is clear and decisive, and that is unlike me.
My life was casual until now.
Hope to be with Victoria and Mom and James.
I love you Laura.
I love you Marisa.

It was unsigned. The note was in Clayton's front shirt pocket. Ultimately, the contents of the note are impossible to understand. Clayton's choice was wrong for him and for the people in his life that he loved and those who loved him. It just all seemed so fixable until he did this. It was a selfish choice, a crazy choice. It was the ultimate confirmation of his insanity. At least he left some hope for Marisa to have a life. He loves her? I hope it keeps the guilt away from her in coming years. I have doubts.

Clayton had backed up off the road to a grove of trees with his car. He had bought a large, heavy bottle of helium that he put in his trunk. The helium is like what is used for welding. Anybody can buy it. He ran rubber tubing from the bottle rubber tubing into a plastic bag. Duct tape held it all together. He fastened the bag over his head and around his neck with a bungee cord, opened the valve on the helium in the trunk and sat down on the ground against his car. Pretty quickly, the helium replaced his oxygen.

The helium won't kill you. It's the lack of oxygen. Your body doesn't react like when you are underwater. The lungs accept the inert gas like they do oxygen, but the rest of the body shuts down from the oxygen shortage. Angela said that once oxygen levels are below 6%, the human body slips into coma within 40 seconds. Clayton probably passed out and then he died sitting on the ground behind his car.

I don't want to know such things.

I don't want to know such things are even possible, but there it is.

Clayton was a sorry bastard to do this.

In the back pocket of Clayton's pants was a policy summary on a life insurance policy covering the life of Clayton Kohler. It looked like a term policy in the amount of $100,000 that he bought six years ago not long after his wife, Victoria, died. Marisa was the sole beneficiary of the policy.

I checked so Marisa wouldn't have to. It had a two year exclusion of benefits in the event of suicide, but that had long passed. If Clayton's premium payments were made in a timely manner, Clayton left Marisa something besides the pain. If Clayton paid the premiums on time, he probably stole Bodie's money to do it.

I know her. She'd rather have her dad here than have the money. It's not even close. Clayton was an idiot.

Lola and I went with Laura, her husband Josh and Marisa to see a suicide survivor counselor in the afternoon. Marisa asked us to go with her. The counselor told us it was significant that Clayton chose to do it in a neutral place like the park. She told us that it showed he wasn't proud of what he was doing and didn't want to burden people he cared about with finding him dead. She told us people who do it in this manner expect a stranger or cop to find them and they prefer that. She told us that Clayton felt desperate and hopeless. The counselor started to explain exactly what a "narcissist" was, but she caught herself and ended up explaining that his personality would have him feeling that way regardless of his life circumstances. She told us that Clayton was incapable of thinking about anything but himself, right or wrong.

The main forces contributing to his death were internal within Clayton. They were unavoidable and unaffected by others around him. She said there was nothing that could be done to keep him from doing what he did and that applies to all his behavior when he was alive. I hope what she told us helps Marisa. Lola and I have doubts.

Marisa said she had taken the counselor to the hospital to see Bodie this morning. It went fine, but Bodie really wouldn't participate. He just treated the counselor like he was at a cocktail party by making small talk and talking about everything except Clayton and what Clayton had done. The counselor is afraid this will be the big elephant in the room with Bodie for a long time.

Maybe that's the explanation for why Clayton would do this. Maybe he wanted to burden his father by being the focus of his father's attention for the rest of his dad's life.

Angela says our van-driving pals from *Perma Press Plaques* and its corporate cousins are going down for the murder of Joanne Duchtin.

Will Dunton and Rad Khanani did the actual murder. They rolled on Warren Duchtin, who they say ordered them to do it after Wesley refused to kill her. Now these slugs will probably get out from under the death penalty for turning on Warren. Will Dunton and Rad Khanani also confessed to attacking Lola and Lily with the blue van on orders from Warren Duchtin.

At first, both Dunton and Khanani said they weren't sent by Warren Duchtin to kill me. They were only supposed to watch Brandi

Loving, Warren's girlfriend. Khanani and Dunton say Wesley Drake was acting on his own in attacking me with the van, but both those guys have an axe to grind for Drake because Drake fingered them for the murder of Joanne. Under pressure from questioning, they both finally admitted Warren had ordered my murder too. Wesley Drake, Will Dunton and Rad Khanani all attacked me with the blue van. Khanani confessed that he was in the back seat of the van. When they tried to run me over, I started shooting, hitting Drake in the side and Dunton in the hand.

Warren Duchtin is in jail and will be for a long time. Prosecutors have indicated that they will seek the death penalty against him for Joanne's murder. He will undoubtedly spend a good bit of his fortune on his defense, but this is not California. It is Texas. Murderers don't usually get away here. Usually, they don't live out their natural lives here either. Hopefully, Joanne can rest with a little peace now.

Nobody in this 'Three Stooges' crime team has blamed the other or admitted participation in Bodie's beating yet. Angela believes it is only a matter of time. But Angela did admit that they are a little confused why these guys would admit murder, but not a beating.

Saturday, February 12 is Clayton's funeral. Bodie will not be able to attend. His broken bones and other injuries still have him in a hospital bed. Without a doubt, he is feeling distress over not being able to attend. I dressed in my funeral/wedding/court/gym membership selling suit and went to the hospital a couple of hours beforehand. I had spent yesterday with Marisa and my family, so I had not seen Bodie since before leaving for U.S.V.I.

I hugged the old man right there in his bed when I saw him and he hugged me back as best he could. We were both teary when we finally let go.

"Jerrah, despite all the recent discord between me and mah son, this tragedy is so very painful to me. Clayton has always been troubled in so many ways, but ah nevah thought this to be a possibility. It is only intensified for me since ah have to lay here and visit with my own thoughts so much of each day and each night. Ah am so very glad to see you today."

I said, "I got back late Thursday night from Boston. Yesterday I was running around with Marisa and just hanging around with Lola and Lily. I missed them. One thing we all did was to see the counselor. I understand she was here to see you too. She had some good points about Clayton and I hope that Marisa was helped by her."

"Yes. She is a nice young woman. How was your trip? Did you meet with any success?" asked Bodie, diverting attention as he did so well.

"It was fine, Bodie. I did gather a significant amount of information that you will be interested to hear. But right now I want to talk about Clayton and what has happened here. I will not accept your stiff-arm on this. I want to see how you really are doing and what you are feeling. It's just you and me, Bodie. There is no one else here to deal with or guard yourself from. There is no one to protect from these horrible feelings. I can take whatever you dish out. Whatever you and I say here can stay here, between us."

Bodie's tears grew bigger. It was a very sad Santa in that bed. His white beard was now full and dominant of his bruised face and bandaged head.

"Did Clayton hint to you at all that he ever considered doing such a thing?" I probed gently at him.

"Not at all, Jerrah. Ah have not seen Clayton since the day ah incurred mah injuries, so he would not have had an opportunity to telegraph such intentions in mah direction. Oh, he has written me some distressin' notes ovah the years, but ah never could have forseen this. Clayton was certainly despondent when his wife died."

The pace of Bodie's speech has picked up while I was gone. It has moved back up in speed to just being slow, and still wordy, always wordy.

"Ah sure wish Gertie was here today..." Bodie said. "Jerrah, Clayton nevah was happy, even as a child. Overshadowed by his big brother in intellect and abilities, Clayton viewed his own position as the inferior little brother. Even after James's death, he continued to play the part he chose for himself. But with James gone, Clayton took on an inner sense of entitlement that bore no resemblance to the real world. It was as if Clayton felt that with James gone, Clayton should be first in line for everything. Forget that Laura was the next born. James' death had a terrible impact on him. It did on all of us, but particularly Clayton. After that Clayton always felt that the world owed him somethin'. He was always so self-centered. Patsy and ah thought that his marriage to the lovely Victoria had changed Clayton forevah.

"When Marisa was born, he was a new man. He was confident, proud and in control of his own life. But after Victoria died such a gruesome, painful death, all those quirky personality traits quickly converted to anger and resentment toward his life that he had always accepted until then. Ah suppose it was very natural for him to feel cheated under such circumstances. But it became like he could no longer live with being denied anything. It was like he would no longer accept being 'cheated', or at best, feeling cheated. He conveyed ovah and ovah again that he was owed somethin' from everyone, especially me."

"It all manifested itself in his focus on money. He did not make much so he felt ah should have to give him some on occasion to ease his financial situation. Ah have nevah had much money myself, Jerrah, and while ah wanted to ease his burdens and help him along—he is mah son, after all—after a long time of this, it became too much of an expectation. As ah began to feel taken advantage of, the arguments began more earnestly and took a nastier and nastier turn. Ah nevah expected this. Nevah."

'Since the day he incurred his injuries?' 'Nastier and nastier?' Lightning bolts of heartache struck me. While Bodie spoke about Clayton, all the clues tumbled from my brain onto my shoulders like bullets striking soft tissue, *my* soft tissue. Each clue hurt me as I added them up and realized what had happened. It was painful and especially painful that I hadn't added them all up before now.

"Bodie?"

Oh, God, how do I say this to my good friend?

"Clayton is the one who almost killed you last week, isn't he?"

The only expression difference on the old man's face was the tears that finally became too heavy for his eyes to hold anymore. They flowed down his leathery cheeks and disappeared into the new white beard.

What a poker player Bodie would be.

"Bodie?"

"Jerrah, ah don't know what—you have been smokin' down in the islands," Bodie said haltingly. But the tears told it all.

179

No one had noticed anyone coming or going at Bodie's house the evening Bodie was beaten. It was a good probability that only Marisa or Clayton or I would not be noticed because we are always coming or going at Bodie's house. If it had been the blue van or a different vehicle than was usually seen there, maybe it would have stood out to someone. I know that neither Marisa nor I had beaten Bodie.

Clayton had hung around the hospital, off and on, when he wasn't plotting with his attorney. Then when it was confirmed that Bodie had woken up, Clayton had stormed out. He did not to return. No one could understand why. I was beginning to understand why. With Bodie awake, Clayton was toast. He would be found out or so Clayton thought.

Immediately upon waking in the hospital, Bodie claimed he could not remember the attack. Doctors backed him up. So he stuck to the story. But Bodie could remember that Marisa was coming for dinner that night? I doubted Bodie all along, but for all the wrong reasons. I, along with everybody else, thought he was keeping me from smashing Duchtin for the beating by not remembering. When Bodie realized what people were thinking, he went with it. He enhanced that view at every opportunity. Bodie did want to keep me from smashing Duchtin—because Duchtin had nothing to do with it.

We've all been looking at clues for why Clayton did the things he did and why he killed himself. Now, the clues were all too clear that Clayton tried to kill his father over money. Clayton killed himself because he was a selfish moron. I suppose a trained counselor would call him a "narcissist." Clayton was not capable of thinking of anyone except himself. We were all too busy looking at other things.

Clayton never did complain to the police that I punched him in the nose. He didn't want any interaction with the police even as a complainant. I'm sure he thought that he would be found out any second and the police would want him instead of me.

In the hospital, Clayton never did go in to see Bodie. Bodie had mentioned several times that he didn't want Clayton to come in to see him. Or he had asked where Clayton was. Not particularly unusual, unless added to all the rest. Bodie was afraid Clayton would come in and finish the job.

Once Clayton realized his father hadn't given him up for trying to kill him, Clayton couldn't wait to have Bodie legally declared incompetent so he could take over the finances. He probably thought that getting control of Bodie's money while Bodie was in the hospital was his last hope. In fact, I imagine Clayton was more certain than ever that it could still happen if Bodie just wouldn't give him up. Bodie never did.

Bodie never said that Duchtin's guys did this to him. He only insinuated it to deflect attention from his son. I was remembering the day Bodie revoked the P.O.A. when he lectured me to keep my anger in check. 'Don't be like Duchtin,' Bodie had said to me. What a diversion. Then Bodie took the opportunity to tell the camera that Clayton shouldn't be allowed at the hospital to see him. So smart.

Whenever I brought up Clayton to Bodie, he successfully deflected the conversation to his preferred subjects. Bodie is the ultimate master at this deflection and misdirection with conversation.

Clayton's emotional outburst at the judge's decision suddenly made sense. It was his last hope and it was gone.

The suicide note! 'Sorry for my recent actions toward you' was no reference to his legal claims against Bodie. He was apologizing to Bodie for having nearly beaten him to death! Based on my experience with Clayton, the only thing he was really sorry for was not winning in court or not having been successful at killing Bodie. In fact, now I am certain that Clayton had tried to kill his father, but like everything else in Clayton's life, Clayton failed. Bodie could read my face. He could literally see the clues come together in my brain as my head shook gently from side to side. I was amazed at my own stupidity. I was some detective.

"Jerrah, regardless of what you believe you have discovered, ah will nevah, evah confirm such thoughts as facts. You'd best consider just exactly what good might come from you exposin' your outlandish theories on the matter. You are like a son to me, Jerrah. So much like the son I lost so long ago."

Bodie was rallying his own emotions under control now.

"Clayton is gone," Bodie continued, "The police have no evidence regardin' mah attackers. No one will be wrongly accused because the gentlemen they have in custody will not admit their complicity. Whether or not they are complicit will eventually simply disappear into their murder and attempted murder charges. The only result of your unfounded theories bein' expounded will be hurt for Laura and for Marisa, and frankly, ah will have none of it. You had best keep your grotesque thoughts to yourself. It would be the only honorable thing to do. ¿Sabe?"

Bodie must be getting well. He's back to splashing in some Spanglish.

The funeral was way nicer than it should have been for that slug, Clayton. He did not deserve this kind of attention from anyone. If they all knew what I am now certain of, who would be sad then?

I didn't tell Lola about my epiphany on Clayton. Nor did I tell her about Ray Johnson giving it up about James and exactly how he had died. Not yet.

I had to consider just exactly what is the right thing here? What is the honorable thing to do? Is Bodie correct and there is only one honorable thing to do? What is right? Is it okay if I reach a different conclusion to those questions than Bodie or someone else might or should the right answer be clear to everyone? Maybe it should be clear to me. Nothing was very clear to me, except that life was messy.

Epilogue—Two Months Later

Bodie got out of the hospital a few weeks ago. He hurts sometimes, but seems happy to be alive. He still has to use a walker, but he may eventually return to only a cane. I suspect he will use it now. He is back to teaching.

Bodie kept the white beard. He claims it makes him look very 'Hemingway-esque and gives him a little legitimacy that was always missing'. Dream on, Bodie. A few more pancakes and you *will* be Santa. He also has given up cigars. Bodie's time in the hospital apart from them gave him the perfect opportunity. Besides, he says his beard is a healthier hobby than cigars.

Marisa is wrapping up a very successful freshman year next month and she stops in and visits her grandfather often. The word 'thriving' comes to mind.

I have never told Marisa about what I know about her father and grandfather. It is my judgment that she carries enough baggage through life. That knowledge would not help her in any way. Not that she needs any help anyway. Marisa is better pasted together than most all the rest of us put together. Any fragility she has is smothered by her success. It is success she has earned on her own. There is no evident reason why she is so accomplished. She just is.

If there is ever any reason for her to hear the story of her father and grandfather, I will be there. I can't imagine such a scenario. My guess is that there will be no need. For Marisa, it is on to better things. I learned from Captain Billy and from RayJ and even from Bodie, about not having to tell everything you know just because you know it. Maybe it's okay to ask the question about what good could be done by it. If the answer is 'none', maybe it's okay to keep it to yourself. This is tough stuff, but true stuff.

I just finished another tax season and am looking forward to getting some sleep, maybe even with the beautiful green-eyed Lola.

I told Lola the whole story about Clayton having nearly murdered Bodie as well as the true story of Captain Billy, RayJ, Vietnam and James's death. I need an ally to help me carry this around. Lola is a great ally. Sometimes it is heavier than other times. Lola knows that I need her support on this. If she disagrees with my decision to keep it to myself, she doesn't say so. That means she doesn't disagree with me, because it would be impossible for her to not say so. Maybe that's not what she would do in my shoes, but she accepts that I'm the one who has to decide, not her. Once again, she has put what I need ahead of everything else—*everything* else. I'd marry that girl again in a heartbeat.

Oh yeah, I told Lola the actual story about Francesca too. She laughed at me, not with me.

With one more win, the Pink Ponies will finish their spring season with only one defeat. This Sunday is the last game of the spring season and Lily is back in action. She is spleen-less, but laden with talent and beauty. Thank God she looks like her mother.

Clayton doesn't come up in conversation much anymore that I know of. That man will never have peace, or honor. I am confident of that now. President Nixon was kidding himself if he believed his own famous speech about the U.S. having "peace with honor" when we left Vietnam. There was no peace when we were there and none after we left. The honor was on the battlefield with guys like James that died. The honor goes to the survivors who returned home after serving their country well. Honor for the decision makers of that war remains evasive in my view. I don't have to dwell on it. History will judge.

I told Bodie about most of the things I found out about James in U.S.V.I. and Boston. I told the truth, just not the whole truth.

James now has peace with honor and it was right. It is right. There are no doubts from me.

Bodie has some peace and he certainly has honor. He wrote letters to Raymond Johnson and to Billy Tyrell thanking them for their help in piecing together the story of his son in Vietnam. He told them how proud he was of James and of them. He meant it. Bodie can be so very eloquent. He let me read the letters before he sent them. I could not have added anything to make them any better. Both recipients of those letters will be proud when they read them. Maybe they'll each have a little peace now. That is my hope.

I have discovered a little bit about honor. It really helps to understand that most of us don't see honorable people very often. That makes it sometimes difficult to recognize clearly, even if it's right in front of us. It's especially difficult to recognize when you don't know the facts. Billy Tyrell and Richard Johnson would do well to learn such things.

Angela called me. She recommended a potential client to give me a call. T.C.U. has had some spring semester problems with furniture being stolen from dorm lobbies. T.C.U. police believe dorm students are involved, maybe dressed as 'Maintenance' men. But they are hesitant to conduct all-dorm searches. Something about student rights, or some such ridiculous nonsense.

Angela suggested someone undercover, but it would have to be a private hire. Ft. Worth police can't get to it until well after the spring semester is over and the students have all gone home, some with new furniture. In addition, T.C.U. Police want me to pursue what they believe to be a fake student I.D. ring. Students are obtaining free student benefits by using the fake I.D. cards—sports tickets, athletic building access. It's pretty small stuff and way more my speed.

This sounds like the perfect case for the extremely effective and heavily bearded Dr. Kildare or Dr. William Wallace or maybe even Colonel Sanders.

Printed in the United States
44526LVS00005B/292-435

9 781424 105380